A FIT MONTH

Other fiction by M.T. DOHANEY

The Corrigan Women
To Scatter Stones
A Marriage of Masks

A Fit Month
for Dying

M.T. DOHANEY

GOOSE LANE

Edited by Laurel Boone.
Cover photograph by Frank Scott, Spectrum Stock.
Author photograph by Noel Chenier.
Cover design by Julie Scriver.
Book design by Ryan Astle.
Printed in Canada by Transcontinental.
10 9 8 7 6 5 4 3 2 1

Canadian Cataloguing in Publication Data

Dohaney, M.T.
A fit month for dying

ISBN 0-86492-312-0

I. Title.

PS8557.O257F58 2000   C813'.54   C00-900992-2
PR9199.3.D535F58 2000

Published with the financial support of the Canada Council for the Arts, the Government of Canada through the Book Publishing Industry Development Program, and the New Brunswick Culture and Sports Secretariat.

Goose Lane Editions
469 King Street
Fredericton, New Brunswick
CANADA E3B 1E5

for Anke, my friend

Prologue

My GRANDMOTHER, who died long before this story took root, was fond of parcelling out prophecies, especially ones with calamitous endings. Because her credo was "forewarned is forearmed," forecasting the inevitable was probably her way of lessening the sting of destiny. She always told me that if you're born in Newfoundland, sooner or later life will break the heart of you.

"Yes, my dear," she would say ominously, rubbing her thumb and fingers together as if she were sprinkling turnip seed over freshly dampened soil, "if yer born upon this Rock, sooner or later life'll break the heart of ye. It'll break the heart of ye into pieces smaller than the putty mounds of a tinker's dam."

And if at the time of this foretelling she happened to be standing in the kitchen stoking the fire — a chore she spent a lot of her time doing, ramming in lengths of wood through the small damper openings of the cast iron stove — she would always add, "Yes, girl, it'll break the heart of ye into pieces even finer than the ashes from this junk of old wet spruce."

But not all of her prophecies were so dour, nor did they limit themselves to a vague and distant future. Indeed, many of her prophecies held more imminent and specific outcomes: *Laugh before dawn, weep before dark* was her most constant. I have no idea why she considered this prediction to be so apocalyptic and so worthy of frequent repetition, other than to teach me that happiness is both fleeting and capricious. She repeated this prophecy so often that after a while I heard only the words, not their message. Being young and invincible, I felt I had no need to listen to the maunders and mumbles of a prophecy-prone old woman.

However, when she predicted an upgrading in my physical attributes — I would come into my own in my early twenties — I was more than willing to listen to her maunders and mumbles. Coming into my own, I was certain, meant bigger eyes, thinner cheeks, longer legs and redder hair. Above all, redder hair. In short, just enough refashioning to make Dennis Walsh regret he had ever chosen the priesthood over me. Actually, the redder hair had nothing to do with Dennis Walsh or, for that matter, with my perception of upgraded beauty. I wanted the red hair because it was a strong Corrigan trait. My black hair was the legacy of my American progenitor, a *persona non grata* in the Corrigan household for as far back as my memory serves me.

Now, just because the story that unfolds on these pages contains reminiscences of my grandmother, it does not follow that it will be a story about her. No indeed. The story that is going to unfold has being dredged from the heart of a family and, therefore, it cannot be expected to move either forwards or backwards in a straight line; it will not follow the King's advice to Alice to begin at the beginning and go on from there until she came to the end, then stop. No. Not at all. The story I am going to tell will twist and turn. Bend and curve. Dart around corners. It will even fork without warning. Sometimes it will become so snarled and tangled it will double back upon itself, encircling some people from the past, one of whom will be Bertha Corrigan, my grandmother.

Chapter One

HUBERT SLADE IS DYING. Imminently dying. In all likelihood he won't see another daybreak. His family accepts this. Greg, his sober and serious-minded lawyer son, accepts it. Danny, his come day, go day, the devil take Sunday son, accepts it. Even Philomena, his wide-shouldered, indomitable wife of fifty years accepts it. Indeed, just this morning she admitted to me that for all the good her fervent and feverish praying has done Hubert, for all the good her rosaries and litanies have done him, she might as well have been beseeching the slop bucket beside his bed instead of the saints in heaven. If anything, Hubert's condition worsened during the course of her praying.

Yet despite her gloomy outlook and on the off-chance a miracle might still be pulled off, she has, in the face of ridiculous odds, continued throughout the day to intercede for his recovery. In fact, around noon, when Hubert's fitful sleeping turned into a peaceful slumber — the kind of slumber that eventually slides into death — she redoubled her efforts. More Hail Marys, more litanies, more rosaries.

However, now that evening is here and Hubert has begun drowning in his own breath, she has given up all hope of a miracle and has informed us that the strangling, watery noise coming from Hubert's throat is the death rattle. She says this rattle, which sounds like stones in a drainpipe and which is setting everyone's nerves on edge, is a sure sign of the beginning of the end. This rasping, nerve-tearing noise can be heard in every room in the house, but especially in the kitchen, directly below Hubert's bedroom. It is loud enough to be heard over the ferocious late spring storm that is scourging Hubert's wood-framed house, slamming gusts of wind up against the clapboards and threatening to pry the windowpanes loose from their puttied moorings.

The family is gathered in the kitchen because it is the warmest room in the house and because it is suppertime. The four of us, Greg, Danny, Philomena and myself, along with Paddy Flynn, a neighbour who came over to keep the death watch with us, sit around the table to eat the fish chowder I have cobbled together in between making a dozen or more trips up to my father-in-law's room to tend to his needs. By now, though, Hubert has no needs. At least, he has no earthly needs, and as far as spiritual ones are concerned, Philomena considers these to be solely her domain. The strain of Hubert's sickness can be seen in her face. She looks as weather-beaten as the clapboards on the house.

"You're worn out, Mom," Greg coaxes. "Why don't you take one of the sleeping pills the doctor left for you and go to bed?"

"Let me alone!" she snaps. "I'm not closing an eye until yer father reaches the other side. Even if I have to use matchsticks to keep the lids open." She bores her eyes into Greg and lets her soup spoon drop heavily into her almost untouched bowl of chowder. "I'm staying up until the bitter end because I wants to make sure he gets a Catholic death, and that's not something I can depend upon any of ye people to do for him. I knows that as well as . . ."

"Hell, Mom, Dad's not even Catholic," Danny interjects. "You're the Catholic in this house. And besides, what in the hell do you mean by a Catholic death? As far as I'm concerned, death is death, whether you're Catholic, Hutterite or Doukhobor." He tempers his voice. "But if you'll go to bed I'll see to it that he gets whatever kind of death you want."

"He's right, Missus Phil," Paddy says, placing a compassionate hand on her arm. "Ye needs yer sleep. Ye needs yer sleep to give you strength for the funeral and the wake that's coming right up."

Paddy's hair is still dripping from the rainstorm savaging the Cove. Although his house is close to Philomena's — in fact, they share the same lane — he was drenched when he came in, so drenched he had to shake the rain from his jacket before hanging it up on a nail in the porch. And he had to brush off the frothy patches of foam that blew over the beach and pelted him as he took the short cut across his meadow.

Although he addresses only Philomena, he lets his eyes roam the table to include the rest of us. "Like I jest finished telling Brendan, jest before I came over here," he says, referring to Greg's and my almost-eleven-year-old son, whom Bridey, his wife, had earlier taken home with her to get him away from a house that is filling up with death, "if he wants to get up early in the morning to help Bridey milk the cow, he better go to bed early and get some sleep. And yer no different from him, Missus. Ye needs yer sleep."

Philomena makes no response. She absently finger-combs her hair, which is straggling around her face. She usually keeps her hair tightly curled in parallel rows, like hay raked into windrows, but for the past several days she has barely combed it, much less curled it. Danny picks up one of the drooping curls, stretches it out full length and then lets it spring back against her head. It sags around her ear like a misshapen corkscrew.

"Look, Mom," he says, picking the curl back up and surveying it. "It's coming unsprung, like my bedspring back in the bunk-house. It's time it went back to the factory for a recoiling job."

Philomena swats his hand impatiently. "Is that all ye have to say, me son? With yer father at death's door? With him ready to meet his Maker? It's that kind of foolishness that forces me to stay up."

"Aw, come on, Mom," Danny cajoles as only Danny can. "Just trying to cheer you up."

"Tormenting me isn't cheering me up. Is it now? Telling me I haven't the sense to know when to go to bed isn't cheering me up. And when I asked ye to come home, I thought ye'd be a help to me. Not a nuisance."

"I have been a help to you," he replies, holding his voice even, refusing to take offence. "You haven't had to bring in a stick of wood or a bucket of coal since I got here. Have you?" He refrains from reminding her that Greg has been pestering her to go to bed, not him.

However, seeing the weariness on his mother's face, he, too, tries to coax her. "You're so worn out you look like a fugitive from the undertaker. And if the only thing that's keeping you up is that you're worried about Dad not getting a Catholic death, don't give it another thought. I'll do that for you. I promise you. But like I said, first you'll have to tell me whatever in the hell a Catholic death is."

"That's jest what I means," Philomena retorts, vindicated in her long-held belief that her backslider of a son is non-redeemable. "You spends yer life in the lumber woods in British Columbia and then comes home here to make smart remarks while your poor father is at death's door. No respect for the dead and dying."

Danny lets the subject drop. He lights up a cigarette and begins blowing perfectly round smoke rings. He allows a ring to soar almost all the way across the table before he reaches up and pokes his finger through it, breaking it open. In the draft from the leaky window casings, the smoke quickly disappears.

Greg finishes his chowder and then reaches across the table and helps himself to a piece of partridgeberry pie. Before taking a bite of it, however, he makes another attempt to get his mother to go to bed, repeating Paddy's warning that she'll be needing her strength in the morning for the wake and still later for the funeral.

"Lay out what you want done, Mom," he promises, "and I'll do it. Rosaries, litanies whatever it is you want. I've never been around a dying Catholic before, or a dying anyone for that matter, so I've no idea what you have in mind."

Philomena acts as if she doesn't hear him. After a few minutes of silence, she says to the room at large, "I have me reasons for staying awake. I can't expect ye people to understand why I can't go to bed — why I can't be grogged on sleeping pills when Hubert is trying to die."

She absently moves the spoon around in her chowder, as if contemplating whether it is worth her effort to try to make us understand. After a few seconds, she tests the waters. "If I was to go to sleep, I couldn't depend upon any of ye to wake me up for Hubert's last breath. Could I? Ye'd say, 'Let her sleep.' Wouldn't ye? Ye'd say, 'There's nothing she can do.' I know ye fellows well enough for that. And I have to be there for his last breath. I wants to make certain he has a lighted candle placed in his hand during his last few seconds of life." Her eyes sweep the table, indicting us out of hand. "Ye thinks a lighted candle is just a bunch of foolishness. Like I said, I knows ye well enough for that. Too well, perhaps."

Greg forgets that if he wants her to go to bed he has to cater to her perverseness and irascibility. "What in the name of God are you talking about, Mom? You're so tired you're raving. Surely you don't intend to place a lighted candle in Dad's dying hand!"

"See! I knew it! But that's exactly what I intends to do! And that's why I have to stay awake. And that's jest what I expected ye fellows to say."

"But Mom," Danny begins, "what in the hell . . ."

"Enough!" Philomena holds up her hand like a traffic cop. She has already dug out the candle. And the candleholder as well. "Five or ten minutes before it is needed," she explains, "the candle has to be lit so there will be no scurrying around at the last moment. And 'tis no good putting it in his hand after his last breath. That's why I have to do it meself. To know fer sure. When I got that candle on Candlemas Day, I said to meself that it would be kept fer Hubert because I knew he was done fer even back then. I promised myself that even if the lights went out, I would stay in the dark rather than use it."

She wearily pushes herself away from the table and walks to the centre of the kitchen. She stands there surveying us, once again deciding whether to ignore our ignorance or to waste her breath in an effort to educate us. Again she decides to waste her breath. "I knew it all along," she says, stuffing wayward strands of hair behind her ear. "I said to meself that it would just be a waste of time to tell ye about the candle. But now at least ye can see why I can't go to bed even though I'm dead on me feet. If I goes to sleep and he dies, none of ye will place the lighted candle in his hand. I knows that as well as I'm standing here before ye."

Danny's mouth drops open. He looks from me to Paddy to Greg. "What bloody foolishness is she going on with — ramming a flaming candle in Dad's hand!" He points to the kitchen ceiling, to Hubert lying in his room. "For the love of God, that man is so weak he couldn't hold a fart in his hand, much less a flaming candle. What's she trying to do, cremate him?" He darts each of us a challenging look. "Tell me I'm not hearing right. Tell me she hasn't turned into a lunatic."

"Yer hearing right," Philomena hotly confirms. "And I can tell ye meself that I'm no lunatic. And ye don't need to ask them whether I am one or not. I can speak fer meself. A lighted candle in yer father's hand. That's exactly what I said. And I'll make sure he gets one even if it takes the last breath out of me to do it."

Greg cuts in quickly, partly to diffuse Danny's words. "Mom, that only disturbs the dying person. Besides that custom went out with Prince Albert tobacco. Hardly anyone does that anymore."

"And you're getting as bad as that other fellow there. The Church's rituals are nothing but a bunch of foolishness to him. But I expected more of you."

"I don't know what gives you . . . you've no right . . . you're dead wrong" Greg blusters, trying to navigate his way through a rebuttal that will contradict her comparison without affronting Danny.

Philomena tosses up her hands. She crosses the kitchen and pulls up a chair beside the stove and hauls her sweater tighter around her as another gust of wind rocks the house. "I'm goin' to sit here and warm me poor feet for a few minutes," she announces, forestalling any more discussion. "And then I've got to get right back up there in case he goes faster than I think fer."

She takes a look at the half-empty wood box beside her and

closes the subject of the candle. "I swear to the Almighty we burnt a cord of wood today. I thinks the wood whips up the chimney whole, with jest a few sparks on it. I bet the roof is covered with junks of half-burnt spruce."

Greg goes to the stove to wrestle another piece of wood into the fire and adds a shovel full of coal from a blackened bucket beside the wood box. When he sits back down, he reopens the subject of the candle.

"Like Danny said, Mom, Dad's not even Catholic." His tone is calm, appeasing. "Besides, you must know it's not considered proper anymore to shove candles in a dying person's hand. Surely you must know that. Everyone knows that."

Philomena, exhausted, wipes her hand across her forehead, wishing she could let Greg's remarks go by unchallenged. But she can't. "Don't take that high and mighty tone with me, me son. Don't tell me what I should know and shouldn't know and what is proper and what ent proper. Yer father's getting a blessed candle in his hand. And that's the end of that. Me mother got one. Me father got one. Even little Bridget got one. And the three of ye'll get one, too, if I'm still around when ye goes." In the full awareness of his ignorance, her tone softens. "Don't ye know, me son, it brings peace to the dying person, that's why 'tis done. Surely ye knows that. 'Tis the last thing ye sees on this earth, a light pointing yer way to heaven. Ye must know that. You just *must!*"

She reads his answer in his blank stare. "Of course ye don't know. If it was something about a court case ye'd know. About getting some rowdy off the hook. Some Duckworth Street souse out of jail. Then ye'd have all the ins and outs at yer fingertips."

Greg does not respond. Paddy and I, as outsiders, carefully avoid exchanging glances. Danny butts his cigarette in his saucer. A line of smoke quickly drifts toward the leaky window casings like a jet stream streaking across the sky. Danny's eyes follow the smoke, looking out through the window at the spruce trees in the yard heaving in the gale. After a few minutes, he says, "Light your way to heaven, eh. A hell of a lot of good a candle will do on a night like tonight. The thing would gutter out in less than a half second. A smudge pot would be more like it. Even a northeast wind couldn't put one of those damn things out. Dad would be better off with one of them."

Philomena pounds her fist on her knee and barks, "That's enough disrespect out of you, young man! Ye don't know *that* much about the religion you were baptized into. Not *that* much!" With her right thumb she measures off a sliver of nail on her left thumb to show the skimpiness of Danny's knowledge.

Knowing Danny will be quick to make a smart remark about Philomena's thumbnail, Greg gives him a cautioning look, and Danny quickly changes his tack. He lights another cigarette and cups it in his hand as he usually does, confining the smoke to the fleshy part of his thumb that is already yellow from nicotine. He goes over beside the stove and squats at Philomena's knees.

"'Pon my soul, Mom," he says, crossing his heart with the hand that cups the cigarette. "I give you my word I'll do it for you. I'll make sure that candle will be in his hand at the last minute. Like you said, I won't even wait until the last minute. I'll light the bloody thing up at least ten minutes beforehand. I'll hold it in his hand myself. With a death grip, you might say. So you go on to bed. And leave everything to me. 'Pon my soul, I won't let you down."

Philomena pulls herself up in her chair, squares her shoulders as if readying for battle. "'Pon *your* soul! My Jesus, Mary and Holy St. Joseph, b'y. Me depend upon *your* soul! *Your* word! Where in the name of the Blessed Mother of God would that leave *me*? Let alone your poor father."

Yet the childish sincerity of his pledge upon his neglected soul reawakens some warm memory in Philomena. "Yer right, me son," she says, abruptly getting up out of her chair. "I thinks I'll go to bed after all. And I'll take a pill before I goes. Tess, you'll place the candle in Dad's hand!" I am a conscript, not a volunteer. As an extra precaution she threatens, "Remember now, Tess, I'll hold you accountable for Dad having a proper death. I'm putting my trust in you."

In my eagerness to get her to go to bed, I almost cross my heart and say 'pon my soul, like Danny did. Instead, I say with all the assurance I can muster, "You can count on me, Mrs. Phil. I won't leave Mr. Hube alone for a minute. I'll be right beside him the whole night."

"I wants ye to remember that if Hube's condition worsens, ye'll rout me right away. At the slightest change for the worst, I want ye to rout me. Even if I've jest fallen asleep."

I promise her I will remember to do just that. So does Greg. So does Paddy. As she is leaving the kitchen, Danny reaffirms, "'Pon my soul, Mom, I'll remember to call you even if the others don't. And I'll ride herd on Tess to get that candle underway. Trust me on this!"

"That's good," she says over her shoulder as she opens the door and steps into the unheated hallway that leads to the cold upstairs. "Because I've got enough to account fer already without letting yer father die and not doing all in my power to get him safely to the other side."

Each word holds a lifetime of self-chastisement, a lifetime of unpurged guilt.

Philomena is a stout Catholic, all the more stout because she unhitched herself at the age of twenty-eight from the Church's centre when she mix-married Hubert, a Church of England Protestant. Even though she had gotten married in the Catholic Church — and that was no easy feat at the time — she believed then, and continues to believe, that her mixed marriage constituted a form of disloyalty. In the intervening years, as a way of making amends for her betrayal, she has always adhered strictly to form and format, rite and ritual in all things Catholic. In fact, once in the confessional a priest told her in a way that wasn't complimentary that she was trying to be more Catholic than the Church itself. When she called him on his remark, he explained that she was being overly scrupulous and that she should ease up on herself.

But she tossed away his advice the minute she stepped out of the confessional. As she explained to me years afterwards, she felt she had no right to ease up on herself. She had failed with both of her sons. Failed miserably. Despite all of her efforts to bring them up solid Catholics, they had thrown off the Church. One son threw it off when he was little more than a child, and he had grown to manhood without hanging on to as much as a shred of her religion. The other son shut himself off from receiving full benefits of the Church by marrying a "grass widow" — a woman whose husband was still very much above the sod.

Philomena takes her sons' straying from their religion as her just punishment for having watered down her religion by marrying outside it. She also takes it as her just punishment that Danny has never been able to grab life by the neck and hang on to it. She believes that because he has had no religion to ground him, he became a lackadaisy, a piece of flotsam cast adrift without direction, a man without stability, a crow on a pole ready to fly off at the sight of any shining object.

One thing that has always amazed Philomena about her sons is that the two of them are so startling unalike. Other than that they both eschewed the religion she loves so dearly, they have little in common. For all they resemble each other, either in temperament or in physical makeup, or, for that matter, for all they resemble either herself or Hubert, they might just as well be strangers. In fact, there were times when she could easily have persuaded herself there had been some switch at birth if that had not been impossible. They were both born in her home down the bay in her big four-poster bed that Hubert had built out of white spruce — spruce which had warped and twisted as it dried so that the mattress never fit properly. Her mother and mother-in-law and a midwife were the only people in attendance at the births. Even Hubert had made himself scarce.

Danny is slight of build, and he is careless about his appearance. He always looks a bit scuffed in a haphazard, unreined-in way. He saunters along as if he has all day to get wherever it is he is going, thumbs hooked over his back pockets, dragging them down. His unruly hair tosses this way and that way even if there isn't any wind. Philomena hates his unkempt hair, and whenever he comes home, he is barely in the house before she is asking him whether the barbers in British Columbia are on strike.

Greg is a solid man, a muscular man, and he makes sure he keeps his muscles toned by doing regular exercises and by walking several miles each day on a trail close to his house, the Rennies River Trail. Although Greg buys his clothes off the rack, he always looks tailor-made. In temperament Greg and his lawyer profession go hand in glove. He is sober minded, moderate in all things and fond of saying "the devil is in the details."

Philomena loves Greg for his wholeness. She loves Danny for his brokenness. She can see this brokenness is his eyes, which she says are as blue as the Virgin Mary's gown and as sorrow-filled as the Virgin's own eyes when she crouched at the foot of the Cross. Mother-of-Dolours eyes, Philomena calls them. Having lost a child herself, she can understand the Virgin Mary's eyes being sorrow-filled. What she can't understand is why Danny's eyes should be sorrow-filled. She has noticed that even when he laughs that mischievous laugh of his, his eyes never laugh along with him.

Danny is the cinder in her eye, the cross on her shoulders, the hitch in her heart. Countless times over the years she has wondered out loud why this child of hers, who was born on a Tuesday, born with the fair face of a Monday's child, the woe-filled eyes of a Wednesday's child and the blithe and bonnie spirit of a Sabbath Day child had not been given one whit of the peace and holy grace of a Tuesday's child. And it wasn't as if he had been born on just any Tuesday. He had been born on Shrove Tuesday. This, she feels, should have entitled him to an extra helping of grace instead of a lesser amount. But then there has always been so much about Danny she has never been able to fathom that she has given up looking for answers and has chosen instead to take comfort from aphorisms: No cross no crown. No thorn no rose. If you don't have him to make you cry, you won't have him to make you laugh.

And Danny, she is convinced, can make a cat laugh. This was the main reason she wanted him home from British Columbia. She knew he would be able to bring a smile to Hubert's pain-streaked face.

And true to her belief, Danny's presence did have a good effect upon Hubert. In fact, he improved so much during those first few days after Danny's arrival that everyone began to hope the doctors had been wrong in their assessment of how much time he had left to him. He rallied enough to laugh at Danny's bunkhouse stories. He even told a few stories of his own from his days working in the lead and zinc mines in Buchans. Sometimes he even summoned up enough strength to chastise Philomena for always needling Danny about one thing or another.

"Philly, leave the boy alone," he would say whenever she came into his room to minister to him in some way, shape or form. "I heard you badgering him jest now. Get off his back. He was good enough to come home."

Of course, what Hubert called badgering, Philomena called concern. And her concern was usually couched in rhetorical questions. Many times she asked Danny, not expecting an answer, or at least not expecting a sensible answer, "Is there any reason, me son, why ye can't go more than a few hours without a half-empty bottle of Black Horse in yer hand?" Or "Do you always have to go around looking like an unmade bed?" Since Hubert's sickness, her most frequent question has been about Danny's smoking. "Me son," she says, whisking smoke trails away as if warding off fumes from an open sewer, "must you always have a cigarette dangling from yer mouth? Yer lungs will end up looking like yer father's. He can say all he likes that it was working in the lead dust in Buchans that did it. I sez it was that bloody pipe of his. It was that plug of tobacco that he couldn't go without."

Unfortunately, Hubert's rallying only lasted about a week. One afternoon while he was sleeping, Philomena and I tiptoed into his room to tidy it up. He sat bolt upright when we came in and shouted, "Mother! Mother!" Terrified, he reached out both arms. "Mother! Mother!" he called again and then pressed back against the pillows, as if he were being pulled against his will across a great chasm and he wanted his mother to yank him back, out of harm's way, as she must have done many times during his childhood.

"Oh my God!" Philomena said, hurrying out of his room and making the sign of the cross over herself as she ran down the stairs to tell Danny and Greg.

"He saw his poor mother," she gasped. "He must be going soon. I've seen the same thing happen before. Especially with men. They always calls fer their poor mothers jest before the end. He'll be gone within the day." She then launched into an account of the time she saw her own mother ten years after her death. It happened the day she placed a water heating coil in a tub of wash water and then reached down to pull it out without unplugging it. While she was pressed up against the wash tub, paralysed as stiff as a poker, electric currents gushing through her body, she saw, not only her dead mother but the Virgin Mary and Saint Joseph as well. But Hubert's vision was different from her own. Hers had only been a momentary thing, brought on by the electrical shock. Hubert's was definitely a forerunner of his death, no more than a day away, maybe even within the hour.

But Hubert made a liar out of her. It took him over a week to begin to die in earnest. In fact, it wasn't until this very afternoon and the onset of the death rattle that everyone took his dying as imminent, and Philomena finally gave up praying for his recovery and began to make plans to help him cross over to the other side.

The instant Danny hears the thud of Philomena's swollen bedroom door, he begins clearing the supper dishes out of the way. He scrapes the leavings of the fish chowder into a dish that he puts in the porch for the cat and then draws the kettle to the front damper of the stove so there will be plenty of hot water for washing and rinsing the dishes. He knows he can't depend upon the small water tank behind the stove because it has to labour just to keep a couple of gallons heated. Paddy chips in, stacking the plates and bowls, helping Danny to get the job done. The sooner the dishes are out of the way, the sooner the deathwatch can begin and the sooner they can start drinking beer.

Just before the four of us leave the kitchen to go upstairs, Paddy goes to the porch and brings in a case of Black Horse that he had stashed out there on his way in, out of Philomena's sight. Danny goes into the pantry and comes back out lugging his own case of Black Horse. A bottle opener is stuck in his shirt pocket.

When Hubert became bedridden, Philomena had relegated him to the guest room, the nicest but the smallest bedroom in the house. She considered this room to be the most suitable one for a sickroom, the most suitable one for doctor's and priest's visits, although whenever these people would come to see Hubert, a straight-backed chair had to be borrowed from the kitchen and squeezed in between Hubert's bed, a night stand, a free-standing electric heater and a white enamel pail in case Hubert took a spell of vomiting.

As soon as the kitchen has been put to rights, Paddy and Danny, each hugging his case of beer, and Greg and I go upstairs to begin the deathwatch. When the four of us begin to settle ourselves on the floor beside Hubert's bed, we realize that the cramped space is far too small, especially with having to accommodate the beer. With little fanfare we break camp and move into the hall just outside Hubert's door. I take pillows from the other bedrooms so we can squat on them and keep the linoleum floor from freezing our kidneys.

Upstairs the storm sounds even worse than it did when we were in the kitchen. It seems to have gathered strength. Rain pelts hard on the flat, tarred roof, and the house sways with each raging surge of wind that rams against the clapboards. Although we all wear heavy sweaters, the damp coldness immediately penetrates our flesh. It even seeps up through the duck feather pillows. We shuffle ourselves around in an effort to block out the cold.

A naked forty-watt bulb hangs by a long cord from the hall ceiling, and in this dim, yellow light, Greg tries to read material for an upcoming court case. Danny and Paddy smoke cigarettes and drink beer until the air around us is fog-coloured and the wall that separates the hall from Hubert's bedroom is lined bumper to bumper with empty bottles. As fast as one cigarette burns down another is lit, and as fast as one bottle of beer is emptied, another is uncapped. The two of them take turns sharing their Black Horse, two bottles out of this case, two bottles out of that one. Knowing that neither Greg nor I smoke or drink beer, they never bother offering to share with us. In between their smoking and drinking they swap jokes, their voices growing louder and louder as the beer disappears. Over their raised voices, I keep an ear cocked towards Hubert's bedroom, vigilant for some sound that will send me scurrying to hold the lighted candle in his hand.

The strangling, watery noises escape from Hubert's throat as loud as ever, so loud the raging wind can't muffle them, sending shivers through all of us Even Danny's raised voice as he tells Paddy still another raucous joke can't drown them out. When Hubert emits a particularly harsh rattle, Danny shouts, "Paddy, me son! Did I ever tell you about the time I was in St. John's, walking down Duckworth Street with Mick O'Brien?" He doesn't wait for Paddy's reply in case he says he has already heard this story, which will force him to dig around for another one.

"Well sir," he begins, "it was winter, and the wet snow was as slippery as chicken shit on damp grass. Mick had just bought a flask of cheap red wine with his last couple of dollars, and the minute he came out of the liquor store he fell down on the ground, right on his arse pocket, right where he had stuffed the flask." He pats the back of his hip to demonstrate. "Well sir, in seconds that snow around him turned blood red, and when Mick saw the red snow he didn't know whether he had smashed the flask to pieces or cut his arse wide open, so he grabbed up a fistful of the soaking red snow and licked it. After a few licks, a big smile spread over his face, and he said, as relieved as all hell, 'Thanks be to God. 'Tis just blood.'"

Paddy laughs uproariously and then launches into his own Mick O'Brien story.

"Don't you fellows know that hearing is the last faculty to go?" Greg chastises them. "How would you like to be lying in that bed dying and the rest of us out here laughing and joking?"

In their eagerness to apologize, their words tumble over each other.

"Sorry!"

"Sorry!"

"'Tis the beer," Paddy whispers, holding up an empty bottle. "The last thing we want to do is hurt Mr. Hube."

"Or wake up Mom," Danny adds. "She's grogged, not dead. If she gets up she'll scalp the both of us. It won't matter to her, Paddy my boy, that you're not her son."

Paddy nods. Philomena has been his neighbour for more than twenty years. Danny and Paddy fall silent. The silence magnifies the rattle coming from Hubert's throat so unmercifully that, after only a few minutes, Danny, who has been hugging his arms around himself and rocking back and forth on his haunches as if this will deaden the sounds, can't stand it a moment longer. He reaches out and plucks at Greg's arm.

"Talk to us, Greg," he pleads. "Put those damn papers away and say something. Tell us court stories. Crooked lawyer stories. Come on! Anything as long as it'll smother that noise. I can't stand to listen to that poor devil strangling himself to death."

Greg looks up from his reading. "At least he's not suffering now. He's beyond that. Not like last night." He returns to his work, not offering to take part in their conversation.

Danny scoots his empty beer bottle across the linoleum floor as if it were a bowling ball. As he intended, it hits Paddy in the leg, jerking him out of a doze.

"For the love of God, Paddy my son," Danny charges, "look alive! We're not here to death-watch you. Dance a jig! Screech! Sing! Sing 'Jack Was Every Inch a Sailor.' I'll join in." He begins to sing softly.

> *Jack was every inch a sailor,*
> *Four and twenty years a whaler.*

He breaks off, beckons with both hands. "Come on! Come on! Up! Up! Do something. I'm about to jump out of my skin."

Not waiting for Paddy to shake himself alert, he turns his attention to me. I am squeezed in between Greg and Paddy, my knees bunched up to my chin, my arms tightly circling my knees, my nerves as threadbare as Danny's own.

"For God's sake, Greg," he says, "take a look at Tess. She's all scrunched up like a cat in a passion and breathing jerkier than Dad."

Then, as if he can't keep the tension in his body boxed in any longer, he jumps up and begins singing again, just above a whisper.

> *'Twas on the Labrador, me boys, 'twas on the Labrador.*
> *'Twas on the Labrador, me boys, 'twas on the Labrador.*

He scuffs around the floor, doing a makeshift step-dance.

"Shut up, Danny!" Greg orders. "Sit down! No more singing! No more dancing! No more loud talking!"

"Then *you* throw those damn papers down and *you* do something to keep us from getting the heebie jeebies," Danny shoots back. "Come on, for the love of God, Greg, talk to us. You seem to know something about that custom of putting the candle in a dying person's hand. I never heard of it before. Tell me it's not some sort of Ouija board that she's got all ready and waiting in there. I took a look when I first came up. Starched white cloth on the table. Fancy glass candle holder. Like getting ready for a séance."

"I don't know much more about it than you do." Greg, annoyed by being pestered, rests his papers on his knee. "An old Druid custom, I think. And the Irish kept it up. Like she said, something about lighting your way to heaven. But it's been done away with for ages now. At least for the most part, it's been done away with. Some people may still keep it up."

"Then why? Why is she doing it?"

"She doesn't believe it's been done away with, that's why." Greg remains edgy. "People mostly die in hospitals now. So she doesn't know the custom's dying out. And it's been years since she sat at a deathbed." Greg picks his papers back up. "Just go along with her about the candle. It might help her. And it can't hurt him."

Without answering, Danny rummages around in the carton of Black Horse for two more bottles. Clutching both of them with one hand, he uncaps one for Paddy and the other for himself. "A bunch of horseshit. That's what it is," he pronounces. He takes a mouthful of beer, swallows it and looks at Paddy, who is beginning to doze off again.

"Some hope of lighting your way to heaven, eh, Paddy?" he says, reaching over with his free hand to tweak Paddy's grey-socked foot. "Eh, Paddy? Might work out in California. But not in Newfoundland. Not on this bloody rock. That damn candle will gutter out just from the wind that's whistling around the window casings in Dad's room. Like I said downstairs, what you need here is a smudge pot. Like they use on the highways. Won't even go out in a hurricane."

He tweaks Paddy's foot again, this time more roughly.

"Listen to me, Paddy! Don't you dare fall asleep! Listen to me! When I'm dying I want you to get me a smudge pot. Two if you can get hold of them. I could use an extra bit of light to find wherever the hell it is I'll be going."

He laughs at his own nonsense. "Yes siree, imagine that! Old Danny Boy all lit up, and not on Black Horse. And on his way to paradise, no less." He holds his bottle over his head like a beacon. "I hope there's a brewery up there. Lots of Black Horse. I'm not going otherwise, I'll say 'Let me stay on this damn rock. That's hell enough.'"

"Shh, Danny!" Greg warns as Danny's voice rises. "How many times do I have to tell you, you'll wake Mom, even if she has a couple of those pills into her. She'll be up and tearing strips off all of us."

Once more we all fall into silence, so much silence in fact that I become conscious of my own breathing. With every gust of wind the house gives a little, making the ceiling light swing back and forth on its long cord. In this slanted, naked light the rows of water lilies race up and down the wallpaper, forming grotesque shapes. To distract myself and to calm my nerves, I concentrate on these shapes. But the concentrating only unravels my nerves. In each contorted, gruesome configuration I can see the face of Death. In fact, Death is so present, it is as if there are now five of us in the hall waiting for Hubert's last breath. I know Danny, too, feels this eerie presence because he fidgets constantly, pulling the pillow out from underneath him, hauling the sleeves of his sweater down around his hands, glancing towards Hubert's room. Finally, he declares in a voice starting to get thick and fuzzy from the beer. "I don't give a shag, Greg, if we wake up everyone in the Cove, we've got to do something or before this night's over we'll all end up in the Mental. If we keep listening to that poor devil in there choking to death, we'll end up as crazy as old Madeline Fitzpatrick. We'll be hearing voices coming out of the piss pots."

Madeline Fitzpatrick's delusions twig a memory in the dozing Paddy. He shakes himself awake. "Or like Mrs. O'Dearin."

He turns to me. "Remember her, Tess? Used to swear that the buzz coming from the transformers on the telephone poles was the Germans spying on us on account of the American base here. And just before the war started, when that Zeppelin flew over the Cove, she said, 'My God, what a queer world 'tis. The Germans are flying in aeroplanes and the Newfoundlanders are flying in rags.'" He shrugs. "At least they said she said that."

Danny nudges my foot with his. "Come on, Tess. Give out with the dirt in the House. You must have lots of stuff to tell, mixing with those politicians every day of your life. All those members. I still can't believe you're an MHA. Honest to God I can't. The first woman Member of the House of Assembly in Newfoundland. Imagine that! I'm always bragging about you in the camp. About my sister-in-law with all that political pull."

"And did you tell them that I was barely elected when our party got thrown out? Did you tell them that I'm an opposition MHA? That the Liberal Party is in shambles? That I've no more power than a beer bum on George Street?"

"Not true," Paddy says defensively, instantly wide awake now that he has gotten a sniff of politics. "You should hear her whenever she gets a chance to speak. She lambastes those buggers. Saw her the other day on the TV. She was speaking on the floor of the House. Stuck it right to the Premier. Nailed him on the spot. Asked him what he was going to do about those animal rights groups, 'those ignorant people from away,' she called them. Said they were savaging the reputation of the Newfoundland people by saying we enjoys clubbing seals."

He stops talking long enough to take a swallow of beer.

"Yes, b'y," he continues, bringing Danny up to date. "They've been calling us barbarians and thugs and God knows what all. Crucifying us. That's what they're doing. Maybe you read about it out in British Columbia. They say we're not doing the seal hunt fer the money. We're doing it because we enjoys it." He gives a small, sardonic laugh. "As if anyone with a shaggin' dollar to his name would want to be out on an ice pan up to his armpits in blood and guts."

He points with his beer bottle towards me. "But she put it right to the Premier, she did. Told him those do-gooders were out for their own glory, not for the welfare of the seals. And she told him that it's on account of them the seal fishery is banned and the people are out of work. And she told him the multiplying seals are eatin' up all the codfish — now, b'y, that's inshore codfish we're talkin' about. And then she got on him about the Norwegians over-fishing the northern cod and anything else they can scoop up while they're at it. Said if we don't establish a two-hundred-mile off-shore limit to stop them dredging the bottom, within ten years we won't have anything with a fin on it left in the Newfoundland and Labrador waters."

He takes another swallow of beer and then looks across at me. "I loved how you said that, girl. 'Nothing with a fin on it will be left in our waters.'"

He turns back to Danny. "And sure, b'y, that's the God's honest truth. They try to make us believe them seals ent eatin' up the fish. But my God Almighty, what do they think they're eatin'? Those shaggin' things lives thirty or forty miles out to sea, so they sure as hell ent eatin' turnips. They're not likely to be havin' a feed of salt beef and cabbage.

"And girl, I loved it when you told the Premier there'll be nothing left in our waters but the hulks of scuttled fishing vessels because the boats will be no good to the fishermen anymore. And the few fish that'll be left will be so full of splinters they'll only be good for firewood — they'll have nothing else to eat but those scuttled boats."

"Imagine taking on the Premier!" Danny says. "Imagine that!"

"And she'll be back in power before long," Paddy loyally predicts. "All the signs are about that the Liberals are going to make a come-back." He wags a finger at Danny. "She'll be our premier yet. Mark my words."

Again we fall into silence, but after only a few minutes the sounds of Hubert's strangling once more press unmercifully against my eardrums. I gulp for air, and even though the hall is bitterly cold, I break out in a heavy sweat. Paddy Flynn leans against the stair railing, a touch of a smile still on his face. In desperation, I say, "Paddy! Tell us some stories. You never run short of stories. Come on!"

Danny pokes Paddy in the ribs. "Come on, b'y. You're not here for your good looks. Keep talking. Make something up if you have to."

Paddy straightens up, rearranges his legs to get more comfortable and looks towards Greg for permission to keep talking. Greg shrugs. The night is already out of his control.

"Did I ever tell ye about the time me mudder went to Boston to visit my sister, Maggie, and she died up there and they flew her body home to St. John's. And my God Almighty, they lost her?"

"No," Danny and I say in unison. Greg, too, shakes his head. By now even he needs a distraction from Hubert's watery breathing. He has laid his reading material aside and has begun softly drumming his hands on his thighs.

Paddy takes a swallow of beer and swipes his mouth with the back of his hand.

"Well, 'twas like this," he begins, rearranging his legs once more, settling himself in for the telling. "Well, you see, she died early one morning up in Boston. A heart attack. We got a phone call telling us about it and that they were sending her back in the morning on the plane. My sister couldn't come with her because at that time she had so many youngsters at home she practically had to turn them outdoors to count them. So we knew we had to go in to St. John's to pick her up. To the Torbay Airport."

He looks at me. "But, of course, before we could leave home there was stuff we had to do. Like getting the parlour ready." Paddy knows that if anyone can understand about getting parlours ready for wakes, I can, but for the other two he outlines the preparations necessary to convert a room into a funeral parlour. "We brought in the kitchen chairs to lay the coffin on. Four of them. Got out the candles. Just like that candle in there, very same pale colour. Only we had two of them. Got them on Candlemas Day. Mopped and dusted and threw out the flies that had hung around over the winter. And we brought in lilacs. Hardly opened, mind you, even though it was mid-June. Capelin-skull time. You knows what that's like. On top of that we had the coldest damn spring, the harbour still had slob ice. There was even a bloody big iceberg grounded out there, came too close to the shore and got hitched up in the shallow water. Just off the lighthouse. Got some neighbours to come stay with the children so me and Bridey and me brother-in-law, Thomas Kiervan, could go to the Torbay Airport. Mick Riley loaned me his station wagon. See, I only had a Volkswagen. And there's not much space in one of them things for a coffin."

He leans over towards Greg, steadying himself by anchoring one hand on the linoleum. "You knows Mick Riley? Lives up the road a ways."

Greg nods. "Up by Dolph Simmons. Right!"

"Right you are. Damn glad of his offer I was. Didn't have the hearse out here then.

Thanks to our MHA here, we got a hearse now. She weaselled the money out of the government somehow." He turns to Danny. "Don't suppose ye knows this, you being away more than you're home, but a fellow from down the bay set himself up a funeral parlour here not long ago. So fancy 'tis a damn shame you have to be dead to spend the night there. Talk about snazzy! My sonny b'y, 'tis almost as good as the Newfoundland Hotel."

Danny begins searching his clothing for matches, flailing his hands against his pockets. "Hold it! Hold! Hold it right there, Paddy! I'm out of matches." He takes a long drink from his bottle of Black Horse, tipping his head far back to let the last drops run down his throat. "You got matches, Paddy?"

"Not a one, b'y. I've been using yours all night, if ye haven't noticed."

I remember the packet of matches Philomena left on the night table by the death vigil candle. I tell Danny, and he creeps into Hubert's room. Paddy takes advantage of the break, says he's going downstairs to see a man about a dog. Within a few minutes Danny comes back into the hall carrying the lighted candle in its holder, holding it aloft. Greg hurries to get up.

"Oh my God, is it time? Is he going?"

Danny calmly motions him to sit back. "Naw, b'y. Still the same. There was only one match in the packet. So I lit the candle. That way I can have all the cigarette lights I need, and we'll have the candle already lit when the time comes."

Clutching the candleholder in one hand and a cigarette in the other, he gingerly lowers himself to the floor. Once settled, he slips the cigarette between his lips, bends low over the candle and draws flame into the tobacco. He straightens up, exhales a mouthful of smoke and sets the candleholder on the floor. With the side of his hand he carefully shunts it towards the wall, out of harm's way.

Paddy returns, sits down and reclaims his story. "Well anyway, like I said, off we went to St. John's. When I gets to the airport, I goes up to the desk and asks for me mudder. Two fellows there. In uniforms. There wasn't a passenger in sight. Not a soul.

"'It's cleared out,' one of the fellows tells me, as if I can't see for meself. So I tell them I didn't expect to find her in the waiting room. I say, 'She was travellin' in a coffin.' My sonny b'y, as soon as I said that their eyes darted to a sheet of paper they had laid out on the counter with names on it. Passenger list. Maybe it said Mudder's coffin was supposed to be on the plane. Anyway, as soon as they scanned that paper, they took off." He swipes his hands together. "Just like that, they took off. I could see them making phone calls. They went out back to the freight shed. They came back in and made more phone calls. They looked in corners. Finally they admitted they had lost poor Mudder."

Paddy stops the telling long enough to uncap two fresh beer. He passes one to Danny and takes a few gulps from his own bottle. This time before continuing he rubs his mouth dry with his sweater sleeve.

"'Lost Mudder?' I sez. Now I'm thinkin' of all of those people back home in the parlour waitin' fer her. All the people Bridey notified before we left. And I'm thinkin' of the lilacs wiltin' in the water jugs, givin' off a dead smell even without a body. And I'm thinkin' of the fire in the kitchen stove having to be kept low so the wake room won't heat up. And I'm thinkin' of the house being filled with relatives and we'd have to hold them over until we found

Mudder. Even my Uncle Matt said he was goin' to try and make it to the house, and he's so thin you can hear him cuttin' the wind when he walks by. Always sick he is.

"Ye fellows knows how Uncle Matt is. Always something wrong. If 'tis not his heart, 'tis his arthritis, and if 'tis not his arthritis, 'tis a lump here or a bump there. Enjoys poor health, ye might say. But he's me mudder's brudder so I had to ask him.

"So I sez to those fellows at the counter — and I can tell ye I'm pretty steamed up by now — 'Blood of a bitch, buddies,' I sez, 'how could you lose Mudder? She was dead. Nailed in a box. Not like she could wander off or anything. Not like she could belly up to a bar and get plastered and miss the flight.'"

He pauses long enough to take another swallow from his bottle. He burps, mumbles "Beg yer pardon," and begins again. "So when I sez this to the fellows at the desk, this head guy comes out and tells me to go home. They have another plane coming in. They'll get back to me later. Made it seem as if I was kickin' up a fuss over a lost suitcase or somethin'. Well sir, that did it for me. '*Get back to me later!* Me go home? Without Mudder? Because yer too busy to find her?' So I moved in real close to him. Just like this." Paddy slides across the linoleum floor, right up against Danny. "So close I could smell the fish cakes he had for breakfast. I said, 'Look here, buddy, I don't give a shaggin' shit if yer busier than a rooster with two dicks, I'm not leavin' here till you finds me mudder.'"

The three of us break into reckless laughter. Even Greg forgets to muffle his mouth. "I'm tellin' ye right now," Paddy says, pointing at me, "he turned whiter than that blouse of hers. In fact, I've seen corpses with more of a flush."

Sensing he has gone on long enough, Paddy takes a swallow of beer and rounds up his story. "So between the jigs and the reels and the phone calls, the long and the short of it is, they found poor Mudder out in Vancouver. Upended in a hangar. Standing on her head. A fellow from here who works out there told me that. Upended, he told me, like an old lobster pot against a shed."

He takes a deep, shuddering breath. "I'm tellin' ye, b'ys, it was some hard. An awful feelin'. I knows she was dead and all, but to think of her gettin' treated that way. To think . . ."

Tears stream down his face. He swipes them away with his sweater sleeve, tries to distract his emotions by fumbling with his beer bottle, wiping its neck with the heel of his hand. Danny reaches over and claps him on the shoulder.

"I knew yer mother, Paddy me son. Mrs. Agnes was a good woman. And those buggers treated her like an old dog. I know it hurts. I know . . ."

Danny's voice chokes. "Shit! I don't want Dad to die. I never really knew him. Left home too early. Seventeen. And before I left we had words. Never told anyone. Dad never said he was sorry. I didn't either, for that matter. Now 'tis too late. Way too late."

Danny withdraws his hand from Paddy's shoulder and rubs it over his own face in rapid strokes. In the half-light the glowing ash of his cigarette looks like a firefly crawling over him. "Shit!" he says again. "Shit!"

Greg reaches out and awkwardly pats Danny's knee.

"That's all right, Danny boy. Seemed bad at the time, I s'pose, whatever it was. But he never said anything to me. Nor to Mom, for that matter, because I think she would have told me."

Danny keeps his head bent. His eyes stare at his knees. "But he never believed me," he says, barely above his breath. "That's what hurts. Didn't want to believe me. If I was telling the truth then that other blood of a bitch would have to be shown up for what he was. And everything would be brought out in the open. And that's what Dad didn't want to have happen. Didn't want a sniff of scandal to touch his church. I'm certain that was why."

Greg senses peril. He withdraws his hand from Danny's knee and sits up straight. "What are you getting at, Danny? What happened?"

Paddy and I sit up straighter as well. Foreboding cramps my

stomach. Danny looks up at Greg and waves him off. "Nothing, b'y. Nothing at all."

He lays his cigarette on the neck of his empty beer bottle so he can use both hands to swab away the tears that he wants to pretend aren't there. He says, forcing steadiness into his voice. "Just the beer talking. Just foolishness. Childish stuff. Forget it!"

"It's not foolishness if it hurt you that much," Greg insists. "Tell us what it was." He reaches out and places his hand back on Danny's knee. "Come on, Danny. What was it?"

Danny jumps up, muttering he has to go downstairs to get more beer. In his hurry and clumsiness, he tips over the lighted candle he had earlier set aside, the candle all four of us have forgotten about.

"Oh shit!" Danny sputters, seeing the mess of wax beside him. "Look what I've done. I've buggered Dad's candle."

He fumbles the remaining stub of candle upright so that it looks like a miniature lighthouse surrounded by a sea of congealing wax. The three of us rush to help, but our efforts produce only a humped-up mess.

"Do we have any more candles?" Danny asks frantically, looking at me. "Mom'll have my ass."

I shake my head. "I don't think so. Just a red one I gave her for Christmas. It won't do."

"Could we shave off the red?"

"It's too big, as big as a water tumbler."

"Don't let the wick drown!" Paddy instructs." A stub is better than nothing. And you'll never get it relit if it drowns."

I grab a bottle cap and begin baling out the well of liquid that is threatening to snuff out the wick. Greg straightens up, cocks an ear towards Hubert's room and hisses, "Listen! Listen!"

We listen. We hear the wind and the rain. We hear the rattle of the windowpanes. What we don't hear is Hubert's breathing.

"Oh my God! Oh my God!" we all cry, scrambling to our feet.

Greg leaps up and runs to wake Philomena. Danny races into

Hubert's room. I grab the stub of candle and, cupping my hand around its base, follow behind, walking fast but not fast enough to douse the flame. Seconds later, Paddy is beside me, shoving an empty cigarette packet underneath the candle to save the dripping wax from going on the floor or from scorching my hand. I pick up Hubert's cooling, lifeless hand and wrap it around the wax-encrusted candleholder — by now there isn't enough candle left to hold onto all by itself. As soon as I have secured Hubert's hand in place, I look at Paddy, who looks at Danny, who looks at me, each of us knowing what the other is thinking: if Hubert has found his way to heaven, he must have fumbled for it in the darkness.

Greg comes rushing into the room, followed by Philomena. She looks like the apparition of one who has already crossed over. She is dressed in a white flannel nightgown and her head is covered with a baby-blue mesh hairnet. A large red rosary dangles from her fingers. She hurries to Hubert's side and bends down to feel his forehead. "Oh Holy Mother of God, he's gone all right," she says, confirming what we already know. She murmurs to him. "But you had the candle. Thanks be to God fer that much."

She gently draws two fingers down over his eyes and lips so he is no longer staring open-mouthed at the ceiling. I ease the candle holder with the stub of candle out of his stiffening hand and snuff out the tiny flame that is already singeing the soft flesh between my thumb and finger. I lay the flattened remains of the candle along with the holder on the bedside table, making sure they are resting on Paddy's empty cigarette packet. Philomena appears not to have noticed the smallness of the candle. But since I can't be certain, and just in case she brings the subject up later on, I begin to construct a lie. Licking my burnt flesh, I latch on to Danny's excuse — I will say I lit the candle early on so I would be sure to have it ready in time.

I pick up the slop pail to take it out of the room and with a nod of my head I indicate to the others, who are now bunched up in the doorway, that we should give Philomena some time alone with

Hubert. But just as I am crossing the floor, Philomena barks an order that stops me in mid-stride.

"Stay here! All of you! We're saying the rosary! And a prayer for the dead and dying. Not like he'll be having a Requiem Mass. Not like there's a minister here belonging to his religion to give him a church send-off."

Greg, knowing the inebriated state of Paddy and Danny and sensing a fiasco in the making, insists that the funeral parlour should be called right away. If rigor mortis sets in, it will be difficult to get his father's suit coat on him. Philomena flings away his reasoning.

"That's a bunch of horseshit," she says, already dropping to her knees and beckoning over her shoulder for us to do likewise. "Everyone knows that when you're dressing the dead you always slits the coat up the back. After it's on, you reefs it back together with yarn. Or duct tape. I've seen it done hundreds of times."

With a grand gesture she unfurls her rosary to permit her to hold the crucifix in her hand, and with it she makes an expansive sign of the cross from forehead to chest. I watch the red dangling beads. They remind me of the necklaces I used to make out of the blood-red partridgeberries that Grandmother used to pick every fall on the barrens behind the Cove.

"The Sorrowful Mysteries of the Rosary." Philomena intones. "The first Sorrowful Mystery, the Agony in the Garden." Danny and Paddy squat in the doorway. Greg crowds in beside them. After taking time out to put the slop pail in the hall, I kneel just behind Greg. *"Hail Mary full of Grace,"* Philomena says loudly, taking the first ten Hail Marys for herself. She finishes with a flourish, *"Glory be to the Father and to the Son and to the Holy Spirit."* She points with the crucifix at Greg, indicating it is his turn. As soon as he finishes, I rush in to take the next decade, and then it is Paddy's turn. He mumbles his way, fuzzy and indistinct, through the required ten Hail Marys. *"Glory be to the Father and to the Son and to the Holy Spirit,"* he ends, reviving himself to say this part extra loud and extra clear, knowing it is Danny's turn next and hoping to rouse him out of his stupor. As an added precaution, he elbows him in the ribs.

His efforts are wasted. Either Danny has forgotten how to say the Mysteries of the Rosary or the beer has frozen his vocal cords, because when Philomena says, "The Fifth Sorrowful Mystery of the Rosary, the Crucifixion," Danny just stares at his father's corpse, his mouth making sounds his lips don't form. Greg quickly pinch-hits for him and, without missing a beat, begins the last decade of Hail Marys. The minute he finishes, he and I exchange relieved glances; as bedraggled a performance as it was, it, too, seems to have escaped Philomena's censure.

Chapter Two

HUBERT HAS TO BE BURIED in the rarely used Protestant cemetery in the Cove. He had wanted to be buried down the bay beside his parents, but because that community had fallen victim to a government resettlement project, it is now a ghost village, and its cemetery is closed.

On the morning of the funeral I take the dress I intend to wear to the burial out of my suitcase and bring it to the kitchen to iron out the wrinkles. Philomena lets her eyes roam over the dress, sizing it up, and then gives me a look scathing enough to unnerve Jezebel.

"*That's* what yer wearin'? A red flowered dress?" She twists her broad shoulders. "Won't do much mournin' in that gaudy getup."

"What difference?" I say. "I'll have my coat over it."

"You mean your raglan?"

"Yes."

"A tan coat? To Hubert's funeral? Won't do much mournin' in that."

"It's just at the cemetery. Without his minister there we won't even be going in the church."

Her shrug is eloquent. I can break with convention if I want to; she can't be held responsible for her daughter-in-law's lack of decorum.

"Myself," she says loftily, "I'm wearing black. Can't go wrong in black."

After I finish pressing the dress, I take it back upstairs. Greg is still in bed but awake. Callers had kept him up until well after midnight, so I had been careful not to wake him when I got out of bed to go downstairs.

"Is this dress suitable to wear this afternoon?" I ask as he squints at me sleepy-eyed over the layers of quilts.

He takes a long, sober look.

"Maybe a bit on the bright side," he allows. "Those flowers. Nothing bashful about them, I'll say that much. Do you have anything else?"

"No. Nothing more suitable."

"But you'll have a coat on, won't you? Judging by the cold in this room, I'd say it's cold enough outside for a coat."

Not wanting to discuss Philomena's assessment of the tan raglan, I agree. I look around the walls of his old room for a hook to hang up the dress so it won't get wrinkled again. But there is none. That leaves only the tiny, crowded closet. I go to hang the dress in there, knowing it will be as badly wrinkled as when I took it out of the suitcase, and Philomena will have to contend not only with a gaudy daughter-in-law, but with a gaudy and slovenly daughter-in-law.

I can't even find a spare hanger in the closet, so I rob Peter to pay Paul, taking an overcoat of Hubert's and hanging it over a sweater of Philomena's which had been hanging over a shirt of Hubert's. As I pull and tug on the hangers, Hubert's hunting gun, which he had leaned in the corner of the closet, falls to the floor, missing my slipper-shod toes by inches.

"What in the name of heaven is *that* doing in here?" I gingerly pick up the gun and stash it back in place. "He hasn't used that thing in years. Why isn't it out in the shed?"

"Because Dad always thought it was safer in there. You never know when someone could break into the shed and steal it. And one of these days I'm going to teach Brendan how to shoot."

"Over my dead body," I say, only half joking. I put my weight against the closet door to push it shut. "Anyway, he won't be around long enough for you to teach him how to use it. He's going out to British Columbia. Danny told him this morning he would teach him how to operate a tree harvester if he came out. So now he wants to pack his bag and go to British Columbia." I laugh. "Don't know which is less life-threatening — gun or tree harvester. Especially if Danny is behind the wheel of the harvester."

"So Danny's up already?"

"Not only up, he's gone to the store to get sugar for your mother and taken Brendan with him."

"Well, I'm up, too." He throws back the mound of quilts and steps out on the floor. He hurriedly looks around for the heavy socks he had taken off the night before, pulls them on, shivering, and then goes to the window and stares down the lane to see if Danny is returning.

"I'm worried about that fellow," he says. "I wish he'd open up. I get the feeling he's keeping something from me. I get the feeling there's something tormenting him."

"Perhaps after the funeral," I say as I reach across the bed to tidy the quilts back in place. "There'll be time to draw him out then."

"Yes, perhaps," Greg responds absently, turning away from the window to haul on the jeans he had laid on the bureau last night for lack of closet space. "Right now I've got enough on my mind. I have to get in touch with Paddy to see if everything is lined up with the pallbearers. And if there's been any hitch with the hearse. Paddy says it breaks down a lot. And I have to phone Josie at the office. And I have to . . ."

He reels off a list of other have-to-do's while he rushes himself into his shirt, shoes and sweater, all yesterday's clothes which will have to be replaced by more sombre funeral attire before the day is over.

The burial is set for two o'clock, and the weather favours me by getting nastier and nastier by the hour. The wind has shifted and has come on strong and blustery, bringing with it a cold, drizzly rain that Philomena says looks raw enough to pierce through oil skins. Perfect weather for a raglan, tan or otherwise.

But it is far from perfect weather for the black summer-weight coat Philomena has set aside to wear. When Bridey drops by to see if we are in need of anything, she tells Philomena she will freeze to death at the cemetery and offers her the loan of a wool full-length black cape she has made herself in a sewing course at the new high school. Another neighbour insists she has just the right cap to go with the cape — one that will stay on in the wind. She goes home and brings back a black tam-o'-shanter.

Because Paddy is a pallbearer and has to ride in the car immediately behind the hearse, Danny offers to drive Bridey to the cemetery in Paddy's car. Her children and Brendan stay at home with a neighbour. Danny and Bridey arrive at the cemetery a few minutes after we do, and when I see Danny coming in through the gate, I hardly recognize him, dressed up as he is in the clothes Greg and Philomena insisted he had to wear. He has on Hubert's navy blue raglan which, Philomena said, was much more suitable than his own leather bomber jacket, and a white shirt and a tie, also Hubert's. Even at a distance I can see that the unbuttoned raglan is hanging lopsided on him, and when he gets nearer I notice his tie is unknotted, simply looped over like a scarf. In the unfamiliar attire he looks as uncomfortable as if his toe is poking out of his sock and he can't wait to get his shoe off to fix it. Even his gait is different, as stiff as a wooden clothespin. But his wit is intact. When he sees his mother standing at the edge of the grave, legs braced against the wind, cape billowing, tam-o'-shanter askew, he sidles up to me and, giving Philomena an under-the-eyebrows look, says in a voice just loud enough for Philomena to hear, "Is that Mom or John Cabot? She looks for all the world like himself standing on the bow of the *Matthew* just before he spied Bonavista."

Philomena tells him to keep a civil tongue in his mouth. "And stay away from the drop for the rest of this day."

"God in heaven!" he retorts, stung that she would even entertain such a thought. "Do you think I've got a mickey of screech in my pocket and I'm going to start guzzling it right now? Right in front of my dead father?"

Philomena gives him the once-over and, by way of apology, says,

"Yer a sight fer sore eyes, me son. Ye looks some good in that rig. Yer fadder must be smiling — that's if he can recognize you, yer so fancy looking. He might even mistake you for the undertaker."

When we return from the cemetery, we — Rose and Frank Clarke, Bridey and Paddy, Greg, Philomena, Danny and myself — gather in Philomena's dining room, lately converted into a den. Two winters earlier, Greg had installed a small oil stove in the seldom-used dining room so Philomena and Hubert could watch television in comfort. The room is warm because a neighbour tended the stove while we were at the cemetery.

We bunch up around the stove and discuss the burial, and I confess that when I stood at the edge of Hubert's grave and watched him being lowered into the ground I felt as traitorous as Benedict Arnold. I admit that I had known several days before Hubert's death what the family only found out afterwards: that he couldn't be buried in his birthplace. I had checked the government records, but I didn't let even Greg know this because I didn't want him feeling obliged to tell Hubert that he couldn't have his wish to be buried beside his parents.

Philomena is still wearing the borrowed cap and cape, which she hauls close around her even though she is so near the stove she is practically touching it. She sits in Hubert's chair and lets her index finger idly trace the groove in its wooden arm, a groove worn by Hubert's years of match-striking to light his pipe. After I admit I dodged the truth, Philomena laments that when she mix-married Hubert almost fifty years earlier it had never entered her mind that one day she would be lying high and dry on the cliff-top cemetery on Dickson's Hill while poor Hubert would be down below in the Cove in the Protestant cemetery, drenched to the skin in the salty water that swamps the place every spring.

"If anyone had said to me back then that such a thing would bother me," she says, "I would have said, 'Don't be ridiculous! Who cares where yer buried once yer dead?' But then ye gets old and ye finds ye do care."

In the morning Greg and Brendan gather their belongings together to return to St. John's. Brendan has school and Greg has a court case that can't be delayed. As well, Danny is going back to British Columbia. He has a drive to the Torbay Airport with a friend of his. I am going to stay on for an extra day to help Philomena sort Hubert's clothes.

Before the brothers go their separate ways, Greg tries to get Danny to tell him about the argument he had with his father, the memory of which upset him so much on the night of Hubert's death.

"Beer talk," Danny again says, "just beer talk. I already told you that." He diverts the conversation by turning his attention to prying open one of the swollen kitchen windows, saying as he grunts over it that the place smells like the inside of an old suitcase that has been kept in a damp shed. "Should open some windows upstairs, too. In fact, if you ask me, the whole house has death breath."

Philomena, coming in from the clothesline carrying an armful of still-damp dishtowels, overhears Danny's remarks. "And who asked you, anyway? Besides, if the house has any kind of breath it's cigarette breath from you and Paddy and those cursed American cigarettes you smuggled in from Seattle." She tosses the dishtowels on the table. "As if the Canadian cigarettes don't stink enough. Maybe you think American cancer is not as bad as Canadian cancer."

She goes to the window that Danny just opened and pulls it closed. "June or not," she grumbles, "I have to keep the fire going, and I don't intend to heat up the whole Cove."

Shortly after noon, as soon as we get the house to ourselves, Philomena and I begin sorting Hubert's clothes. As we sort, Philomena keeps up a steady prattle, as if only the sound of her voice can distance her from what she is doing. When we come to Hubert's shoes, she gets out the polish and brushes and puts a shine on each pair. She tells me about a woman in St. John's who didn't want her husband's clothes to be worn by anyone else, so she put all of his right shoes out for garbage pick-up one week and all of his left shoes the following week. Philomena thinks this is a sinful lack of charity. Just because Hubert can't wear his shoes doesn't mean they can't be useful to some other poor devil. And, she tells me, Hubert's death is the worst heartache she has had to endure so far.

"God knows I've had me share," she says as she tosses an old shirt in the direction of a green plastic garbage bag. "I thought I'd never live through losing little Bridget. And the heartaches with Danny. Leaving home so early, leaving the Church even before that, never really pulling his life together. Restless to the bone. Can't keep track of how many jobs he's had."

She pauses, not sure whether this is the time to mention the heartache I have caused her. She decides to add it to her list. "And when I found out that Greg was going to marry you, a divorced woman, and he wouldn't be able to receive the full benefits of the Church, well, I was sure that was God's punishment for me because I mix-married Hubert and broke me parents' hearts in the bargain."

She sighs heavily and tosses a bundle of mated socks into a pile. "I s'pose sorrow is the price we have to pay for living. And death is, too. None of us is spared. No one gets to go up above without first going down below."

She picks up a glove and absently smoothes out the worn leather fingers, an exact mould of Hubert's hand, even to the crooked little finger. "But God help me, I hopes I'm not around when yer sorrows comes to you, when you learns that the price of living is death. 'Tis easier to bear your own sorrows than to witness someone else's. Especially someone that's close to you."

I refrain from reminding her that sorrow has already barged through my door on several occasions, that death has become almost commonplace to me. Funerals process through my mind: Uncle Martin's, Grandmother's, Mother's. And Dennis's. Each one carries its own pain. Dennis's is the freshest, the cruellest. The memory of it can still shear me to the bone.

Around two o'clock we come to the end of the sorting, and then we put the bags, stuffed to the hilt, in my car and take them to people who, according to Philomena, can make good use of Hubert's things. When we return, Philomena goes upstairs to take her afternoon nap and I sit in the den and think about Hubert. Even though his belongings have been removed from every room in the house, the essence of him remains: the groove in the arm of the chair, the smell of his pipe, the sound of his cough. I recall how good he had always been to me, how he had taken my side in any brush with Philomena, especially when she would get a choke-hold on some notion, like searching for my biological father, and refuse to let go of it no matter how much I tried to make her see reason.

After about half an hour of this recalling and remembering, retracing the years, the everlasting absence of Hubert becomes so crushing I have to get away from the house. A walk is what I need, and I leave immediately, stopping in the porch long enough to put on a heavy jacket. Even if it is mid-June, the wind is still winter cold and the fog is pea-soup thick. I close the back door quietly behind me so as not to wake Philomena.

I saunter through the Cove, something I rarely have time to do. When I rush out for a weekend, I usually have to go see this one or that one about some problem they want solved. Through gaps in the fog, I see how ragged the village has become. With the fishing long gone and the American base all but withdrawn, the young people have moved away to find work. I pass abandoned houses, steps sagging, front yards gone wild, the palings enclosing the yards gap-toothed. Where there used to be windows, there are now shabby boards or in some cases just gaping holes. The once-upon-a-time painted clapboards have been licked to the bone by the northeasters. The fences surrounding the rocky meadows that climb the hills behind the houses have fallen in upon themselves, and the lanes are gullied and rutted from spring runoff. A heartbreaking sight, especially since I know that most of the occupants of these houses had no choice but to leave.

And I know not only why the people left, but also where they were headed when they pulled out of the village. As I walk along, I wonder about the ones who left and whether anyone who has been weaned on salt air and sea can ever be happy in the tar sands of Alberta, in a factory in Toronto, in the timber woods of British Columbia. And I wonder if at night these expatriates from the Cove long to hear the roar of an angry tide battering the side of a cliff? Or the blatting of a foghorn. Or the scrape of a dory being hauled up over beach rocks. I wonder, too, whether the weight of their loneliness will one day become too heavy to endure, and then, like the whale that couldn't support its own weight on land, they will return once again to the sea looking for it to bear them up.

Verses from a song composed by a mother whose son had to leave the Cove for the tar sands of Alberta come to mind, and I hum as I walk along.

> *Are you ever lonely, Neddie,*
> *For the life that you once had,*
> *Walking on the beach rocks*
> *And fishing with your dad?*

> *And are you ever angry*
> *That they led you to believe*
> *There'd be work right here for all of you,*
> *No one would have to leave?*

Despite all the signs of decline in the village, I notice a comforting sameness. Spruce trees still cover the back hills, even if they are a little more scraggly and wind-whipped than I remember. The pond is still there, holding the separate parts of the village together although its landwash has changed. No longer is it edged with purple flagroots. Years ago, the Americans dug these up to replant them on their army base, eight miles away; surrounded by asphalt and dry ground, they parched to death. And the strip of narrow beach is still there, as always appearing inadequate for the task of keeping such an expanse of ocean at bay.

When I left Philomena's house to go walking through the village, it hadn't been my intention to go to the beach, but after only a few minutes, I find myself veering in the direction of the shortcut over the cliff. The path is so overgrown, I tell myself as I push aside young birches, spruce saplings and skinny poplars, that I might as well be blazing a new trail, that I would have been better off taking the road. I recall what Grandmother used to say to me about taking shortcuts: "The longest way round is the shortest way home." She would say this as if I were supposed to understand what she meant. However, as I push through the underbrush and feel the sting of young junipers snapping back at me, I understand that the shortest way is not necessarily the easiest way. I regret not having taken the road to the lighthouse, from where I could have doubled back across the long stretch of rocky beach.

The struggle through the underbrush makes me recall a trip I took with a friend to Cape St. Francis a few weeks earlier. It was her mother's birthplace, and although the tiny, isolated community no longer exists, she wanted to see for herself the nooks and crannies her mother had so often spoken about. The road that led down to the shore was rutted and potholed and so leached out from running water that rocks as sharp as axe blades jutted up every few feet, gouging the tires on the car. And its undercarriage also took a walloping from the road's raised centre. At the end of the day the car was in such bad shape we were barely able to hobble it back to St. John's. For the next several days, especially after she received the repair bill, my friend questioned the folly of that journey.

Now I, too, question the folly of this journey that takes me over the cliff to the beach. The undergrowth is so dense, so snarled and so tangled that it snags my hair, and I leave telltale strands of it on the branches like sheep's wool on a break in a fence. I haven't been near this beach since the day of Dennis's funeral, almost fourteen years earlier, and as I push forward I can't help wondering what possessed me to come to this place on this day of all days, a day sad in its own right, a day that doesn't need to be further burdened with memories. However, once I break out into the clearing and I am able to see the beach stretching before me, bleak and abandoned except for a few sheep grazing on the salty tufts of grass that grow beside the larger rocks, I feel so light-headed with my success that I'm glad I persevered.

From my lookout point I can tell from the way the water lips its way into the landwash that the tide is low, although on this beach it isn't easy to tell the difference. It appears to rise and fall without any great fanfare, much like the seasons in these parts, which begin and end in a loose, inexact and haphazard way. Now it's spring. Now it isn't. Now it's spring again. Here the concern is with rough tides and gentle ones, rather than with high or low tides. Today the tide is not only low, it is also gentle, a rare condition not to be under-appreciated. The waves lap at the shore like a cat washing itself on a sunny windowsill, as if the effort is almost more than the job is worth.

Once I step out upon the beach, I walk quickly towards the rock behind which Dennis and I used to take shelter from the wind whenever the tide was low but the waves were spitting spray in all directions. The smooth grey rock is faithful to my memory of it. The face of it is so tide-smooth it could pass for polished marble. I immediately search out the initials I chiselled into it on the day of Dennis's funeral. I run my fingers over them, much like Philomena did over the groove in the arm of Hubert's chair. Although time and the elements have sanded the edges and rounded the corners of my crudely carved letters, they are still readable: 1970. D.W. SFM. 1970. T.C. MHA.

I take off the jacket and lay it on the damp sand and then crouch on its fake fur lining. I close my eyes, and in the shelter of the rock and in the warmth of the mid-June sun I let my mind gallivant

across meadows and hills and oceans and years, searching for
yesterday's faces and yesterday's voices.

"Stop slapping the Lord in the face with yer lack of gratitude!"

This is the spare voice of Grandmother the evening she found
me lying face down on my bed, a huddled mass of misery, wishing I
could die because Dennis Walsh had just left for Ontario with his
uncle, the Jesuit priest. From his uncle's house he was to go to a
seminary that would lead to his ordination to the priesthood, which
would put him beyond my reach forever.

"The Almighty gave you life and be thankful for it." Without
invitation, Grandmother sat on the edge of my bed and insisted that
I take my face out of the patchwork quilt and look at her while she
scolded me. She cast her eyes up at the crucified Jesus hanging on
the wooden cross on the wall beside my bed and gorged me with
guilt.

"Do you know how many children there are who have never
been born? Do you ever ask why you were chosen to see the light of
day?"

"That's some foolish question to ask anyone!" I had churlishly
replied. "How am I supposed to know how many children have
never been born? And I never ask why I was born. Never!" The heat
of this bald-faced lie flushed my face.

The truth was that I had asked this very question every time the
Redemptorist Fathers delivered a hell-and-brimstone mission
sermon in the parish, although I never asked it in the grateful way of
which Grandmother would have approved. *Why me, Lord? Why did
you pick me to be born? If you hadn't picked me, I wouldn't have to live
with the fear of going to hell after I died.* And there were other
questions on this same subject, questions that I had felt were too
fearsome to put even to God, so I just let them fly around in my
mind, free and unhindered like the puffins on Bird Island.

These questions were always the same, although not necessarily
asked in the same order. *Is it better to have been born facing the
possibility of hell, or not to have been born at all, forfeiting forever the*

possibility of heaven? If you have never been given the opportunity to know God, should you be kept out of heaven? If you can't be kept out for not having had the opportunity of knowing God, should we be Christianizing the heathens, thereby placing them in jeopardy of going to hell? Is it better to die an amoral heathen or an immoral Catholic?

Sitting on my bed, Grandmother had delivered a chastisement that was a lot less lofty in nature. "Girl," she said, smoothing out the quilt that I had bunched up underneath me, "yer acting as if Dennis Walsh is the only bit of spawn in the ocean. Let him become Pope if that's what he wants. Don't you know that nothing less will satisfy that mother of his? Eileen's hell bent on a gold and white mitre for poor Dennis so she can say 'My son, the Pope.' She sure as blazes don't want you mooning over him to sway him in another direction."

She had paused a moment before attempting to quench my grief with a dose of even stronger reality. "And besides, girl, even if he never went to the priesthood, Eileen wouldn't think you were good enough fer her one ram lamb simply on account of you being Poor Carmel's Tessie. She'd keep at him until he broke up with you. So stop this foolishness right now!"

On her way out of my room to go downstairs, she had looked out through the window at the greying evening sky that was on the cusp of turning into night, and she tipped one of her maxims on its head, something she was wont to do when it suited her purpose. "Weep before dark," she had said, thinking she was giving me comfort, "laugh before dawn. Things will look brighter in the morning."

I was certain she was dead wrong. I would not be laughing before dawn. In fact, I knew I would never laugh again. Dennis's departure had seen to that. It had turned the Cove into a grey abyss, even greyer than usual. The sky, the dories, the fences, the beach rocks, even the clapboards on the stables all had turned a leaden grey the moment he left, a mournful grey that would never give rise to laughter. And the usual village sounds that in their familiarity had become merely comforting background noises — the fog horn, the squeal of clotheslines being reeled in, the voices of men spreading manure on the meadows, the bleating of sheep — now grated on my nerves like the rusty hinges on the sheep house door. The screeching seagulls as they battled the wind seemed to be an echo of my own anguished cries, and whenever the train was pulling out of the village, its whistle, which I had hardly noticed before, took on the melancholy sound of departure.

As it turned out, however, Grandmother's prophecy contained more than a grain of truth, although it took some time for this to become apparent. For sure, Dennis Walsh wasn't the only bit of spawn in the ocean. I found this out later when I moved to Montreal and met Leonard — or more precisely, when I met and married and divorced Leonard. The divorce came about soon after I found out that not all spawn is created equal. After my divorce I returned to Newfoundland, where Dennis's life and mine interlocked once again.

At the time of our reunion I was the Liberal candidate for the Cove with a campaign well under way, and Dennis was home on holidays from his missionary posting in Peru. Coincidentally, it was his brother-in-law, Dolph, who was my political opponent and whose own campaign was in full swing. Soon we began secretly meeting on this very beach and in the shelter of this very same rock where I now crouch in the hope of making peace with Hubert's death. In adolescence our love had been sweet and delicate. When we met again as adults our love was even sweeter and even more delicate because it was now a secret love, an unsanctionable love. And because it was also a chaste love, it was all the more carnal.

One rainy, windy evening, the day before polling day, less than twenty-four hours before I was to find out I had won the seat for the Cove riding, Dennis and I walked the landwash together. We walked, arms around each other's waists, until long after dark had closed in, until long after the far shore had disappeared from our sight, until long after the trees could no longer be distinguished from the cliffs they clung to. Sometimes Dennis related marvellous tales about his work in Peru, but mostly we walked in a silence that was broken only by the sounds of the choppy sea as it flung fresh kelp ashore with each grumbling wave. The kelp slithered green and slippery beneath our sandaled feet. And because it was June and because in those years the seals hadn't yet devoured all of the capelin, we could smell these small silvery fish as they schooled by the thousands, just offshore, unaware that they, like the kelp, would soon be pitched high and dry upon the landwash.

Later that night, when I was back home and cuddled into Grandmother's big feather bed, I composed a love poem to Dennis. "For Dennis," I wrote, "whose love for me is as infinite as my love for him." Other lines followed this inscription, but my mind has since erased them, taped over them, perhaps with a lullaby for Brendan. Or maybe with a prayer for the repose of Dennis's soul.

The morning following our walk on the beach — election day morning — I had jumped out of bed the minute I woke up, not wanting to miss one exquisite moment of this incomparable day. There was much work still to be done before the polls opened. Greg, who was then my campaign manager, and Frank Clarke had drafted a victory speech for me, but I still had to add my own thoughts.

I ran to the window and grabbed the tail of the cream-coloured vinyl blind intending to raise it as far as it would go to let in every bit of daylight. In my haste, however, I forgot to keep a grip on it. With a crack and a thump it scrambled up the window like a cat up a tree, and it didn't stop scrambling until it had flipped several times around the spring-held roller at the top of the casing. In my rush to get going, I left it as it was, hanging unevenly, cavalierly ignoring echoes of Grandmother's admonishment that any woman whose blinds list like a Lunenburg schooner heading into harbour is a sorry excuse for a homemaker. With equal conceit I tossed aside her oft-repeated omen that blinds that go up in a hurry come down in a hurry — this referring to the custom in the Cove of lowering every blind in every house for every funeral that processed through the village.

I began working on my victory speech even before I had finished breakfast, adding and deleting words and phrases between bites of homemade bread that Rose Clarke, Frank's wife, had brought to me. Because all signs pointed to an easy victory for me, I concentrated on my victory speech. However, in case of a surprise at the polls, on the off-chance that my opponent, Dennis's brother-in-law, Dolph, would win, I half-heartedly put some effort into a speech conceding defeat.

When I had honed both speeches to my satisfaction, I poured myself a second cup of tea and sat at the kitchen table and looked out through the window at the reddish sun inching its way into the Cove. I pulled my pink chenille bathrobe closer around me to keep out the early morning chill and wallowed in my good fortune, reminding myself out loud in the empty kitchen that by the end of the day I would be the Cove's first female Member of the House of Assembly. Indeed, I would be the first female Member of the House of Assembly in Newfoundland. And best of all, Dennis Walsh was back in my life, and I would be with him as soon as we both could discharge our day's duties, mine to my constituents, his to Dolph.

To be favoured so magnificently, I was certain I had to be the darling of the gods. In fact, I was so sure I had fate clasped tightly in my fist that I neglected to hedge my bets. I didn't knock on wood, say God willing, throw salt over my shoulder or make the sign of the cross over the single crow that sat on the telephone pole waiting for the Cove to wake up. Grandmother would not have been so smug. She would have known that such cockiness would offend the gods, or the saints or the angels or whoever keeps tabs on the unbridled conceit of human beings.

Before the day was over I came to believe that my cockiness must have been exceedingly offensive to those who tally up sins of conceit; otherwise they would not have brought me to the ground so mercilessly, would not have trounced me so savagely. Surely it wasn't simply a stroke of bad luck that had placed that car from St. John's en route to a village beyond the Cove, its driver and passenger intoxicated, on the same road and at the same time as the car Dennis was in as he drove to Dolph's headquarters.

Chapter Three

SITTING BEHIND THE SHELTERED ROCK at the beach, my mind leaping across meadows and hills and oceans and years, searching for yesterday's faces and voices, I forget time. I forget that Philomena has no idea where I went when I left the house. I am even oblivious to the fact that it has turned very cold, and I am chilled to the bone by the time I arrive back at Philomena's house and grateful for the warmth of her kitchen.

"What happened to ye?" she asks even before I'm fully in the door. "I wondered where ye'd gone. I was worried."

"Just out for a walk," I dodge, feeling guilty. "Just wandered around. Just wanted to get away from the house for a while."

"I know how it 'tis," she says, foregoing her usual cross-examination. "I knows you loved Hube, too, and the packing away of his things must have hit you as hard as it hit me. Meself, I put me head down but I couldn't sleep a wink. The house is so bare with him gone. Not even an old shirt of his hanging on a nail. I sat in the den and tried to smell his tobacco. Couldn't even do that with all the airing out that's been done, so I decided instead to do some baking."

She pulls open the oven door and, using a dishcloth for an oven mitt, hauls out a pan of jam-jams and brings it to the table, setting it on a Simpson's catalogue that she always uses as a trivet. The scent of allspice and molasses is inviting to my nostrils after the cold tang of the salty beach air.

"Sit yerself down, girl, and we'll have a bite to eat. Looks like yer half-frozen. Tea's already on the table. And fresh biscuits made. I was goin' to help meself if you didn't show up soon."

Philomena always makes a great cup of tea, and I tell her so after the first swallow.

"Ye only have to do it right, that's all," she says modestly. "Boil the water until 'tis lurching back and forth in the kettle like a big swell. Heat up the teapot with water first. Throw that out. Then add the tea and more water. Let it steep for a few minutes. And loose tea. Never those tea bags. I always keeps King Cole on hand. Wouldn't use any other brand, although every time I goes to the store there's a new brand on the market that they're flauntin' in front of yer face. 'Try this! Try that!'" She twists her mouth. "And those perfume teas. Rose hips. Apple blossoms. Chamomile. Poison stuff, if you ask me. Don't know whether to drink it or splash it over you to fight off the BO."

I remind her that I have to go back to St. John's in the morning, and I repeat Greg's invitation before he left: that she should consider coming back with me and staying with us for a few weeks.

"Never!" she says. "Like I said to Greg, much as I'd love to be close to Brendan, much as I'd love to see that child every day of me life, I couldn't live in St. John's. I'd smother to death in there. Houses piled on top of one another, scrunched together. Cramped up like hens on a roost. Hills so steep ye have to tack like a schooner to get up them."

She waves her hands to take in the fields and cliffs and beach that stretch out beyond her kitchen window. "Here I can breathe. Here I can have a clothesline stretching halfway across the meadow if I wants to. I can let me drawers flap in the wind fer days on end. Can't do that in St. John's, certainly not on those lots as small as a postage stamp. Yer drawers would be flapping up against yer neighbour's window."

I understand her need for space and fresh air because I spend my days in a building with sealed windows, recycled air and a foyer filled with trees that have a perpetual hangdog look. I once told Greg that if the save-the-seals gang wanted a real cause they should hijack the trees in my foyer and carry them back to Botswana or whatever exotic homeland they're pining for.

"All jokin' aside, girl," Philomena says, as if long before this moment she has given a lot of thought to the subject, "there's no place like home. Nothing like yer own bit of sod."

She sets aside her partly eaten jam-jam, dusts the crumbs from her hands and says, "Now, girl, I've been meanin' to talk to you about somethin'."

Her tone, solemn and weighty, makes me think she is finally going to agree to have a will drawn up, something Greg had been trying to get both his parents to do to no avail. What she says is even more surprising.

"I've been meanin' to tell you yer a good daughter-in-law. A good daughter, really."

Taken off guard by her compliment, I can't think of a response. To cover my confusion I reach for a jam-jam, hoping that by the time I take a bite she will have swerved the conversation in another direction. But Philomena has another intention: to go down Memory Lane and bring me along with her.

"For the life of me," she says, "I can't understand now why I kicked up such a fuss when you and Greg said you were going to get married. Don't make that much sense to me now. And it all seems so long ago."

"You did what you felt you had to do," I reply, absolving her. "I understood that even back then."

"I knows that. But it seemed so important at the time. And I'm wonderin' now, wondered fer some time in fact, but especially now that Hube has died and Danny is gone back, whether it was all worth it. All that fuss about you and Greg. All that sparrin' with poor Hube about the children goin' to this church and not to that one. I feels so bad about that now. What the hell odds, I say to myself today, where ye goes to church, jest so long as ye goes. And even if ye goes to no church as long as yer good to yer neighbour. That's all that counts. Jest so long as yer willin' to haul somebody's cow out of the muck or give some poor child a pair of mitts to keep his fingers from gettin' frostbit. That's all that counts. That's what Christianity is about. Not about churches.

"That's all very well for me to say now, but 'tis not what I could say back then. Wasn't brought up that way, I guess. Those changes Pope John brought in during the sixties really should have made me think. But they didn't. He turned the Catholic Church ass over kettle, I say. Even unsainted St. Philomena. Hard to know what to believe anymore.

"Did you know that about Philomena? Me namesake! They unsainted her. Only a few months ago I read about what they did to her, although apparently they did it years ago. And to think I've been praying to her all along and she with no more pull with the Lord than meself. I don't even know if she is Miss or Mrs. Or fer that matter, Ms, like the liberateds."

"I remember reading about that," I say. "Saw it in a church bulletin, I believe. It happened in the sixties, I think. But they didn't unsaint her exactly. I don't think you can do that once someone has been canonized. I think they just took her off the liturgical calendar. Sidelined her, you might say. Much like being a backbencher, don't you think? Or a member of the Opposition. You don't get the same respect."

She laughs mischievously — Danny's mischievous laugh. Although she always maintains she doesn't know where Danny comes by his scampish nature, anyone can see he gets a lot of it from her.

"Yer dead on, girl." She pours herself a second cup of tea and offers to refill mine. I pass my cup over to her. "That's just the way I sees it." She gets up to put the teapot on the back burner of the stove where it will continue to steep. Danny has always maintained she makes the tea so strong you can float the anchor of the Queen Mary in it.

"And poor St. Christopher. Just Mr. Christopher now. They didn't have enough facts on him. You have to have so many documented miracles in order to be sainted. So they must have rushed him through. Probably somebody with pull did it because Christopher had done something for him. You know how it goes, you scratch my back and I'll scratch yours. It's the same with everything."

She takes a sip of tea, savours it before swallowing it. "A shame really. And all those people with him hanging in their cars to protect them. Might as well have had one of those stinky fir trees — you know, those paper things ye hangs on the mirror — fer all the good St. Christopher could do if he was just Mr. Christopher."

She laughs, takes a bite of a jam-jam and wipes crumbs from the side of her mouth with the tail of her apron. "Shockin' to do that sort of thing to people. They had such faith in him. Poor old Mrs. Chassie Bailey used to say it was St. Christopher who protected Chassie when he'd get a snoutful in the taverns in St. John's and drive out over that narrow road in that old truck of his. But I never believed it. I said all along it was that old dog of his that he used to take everywhere with him in the cab. I swear to God that crackie could drive the truck as good as Chassie any day. Even without a snoutful Chassie was a menace on the road. One time he lost his headlights, and he drove out from St. John's with a flashlight strapped to the front bumper."

Sobering, she veers to another topic. "And I wanted to tell you that I knows that candle stuff is being done away with. I knew that all along. Yes, I did, girl. Mind you, it hasn't been done away with completely. Some people still do it. But I like the custom and I wasn't about to give it up just because someone said it was time to give it up. Just as I still prays once in a while to St. Philomena, no matter what I'm told." She smiles, Danny-style. "Ye might say, covering me bets. If the church fathers were wrong in one direction, that's not saying they can't be wrong in another, and fifty years from now they'll be admitting they were wrong when they un-sainted her. Mark my words."

She wipes her mouth again with her apron, this time patting her forehead and cheeks that glisten with perspiration from the heat of the open oven door. "But back to the candle, girl. Everyone always said it gave comfort to have a loved one holding that candle at the end. And it must give comfort to the dying one, too. I knows it would comfort me. And I wanted to give that comfort to Hube."

I am about to agree that there was no harm done by putting the candle in Mr. Hube's hand whether the custom is in or out when she abruptly switches back to the subject of Greg and me.

"But to think I made such a holy to-do about you and Greg getting married. And you've been so good fer Greg. Couldn't have picked a better wife. You really loves him, I can tell that." She lets that statement hang in the air for a second or so before adding, "But still and all I often wonders if he would have gotten a look-in if Dennis Walsh had lived. Priest or not. I've heard tell you were pretty fond of each other."

"Greg's a good man," I say, by way of sidestepping her implied question. "He's a good father. He's easy to love."

Just as she had done, I switch without notice to another topic, one far removed from the subject of Dennis, in the hope that she won't chase after me for it.

While it is not the sort of information you can easily share with others, particularly with your mother-in-law, I have to admit, if only to myself, that I never loved Greg, nor for that matter any man, in the same extravagant way I loved Dennis. Ours was an enchanted love, and I have often wondered whether it would have endured — could have endured — if fate hadn't taken such a grievous hand in bringing it to a close. As heady as it was, I think it would have eventually collapsed had it been allowed to run its full course. It would have fallen in upon itself like the fences around the meadows in the Cove. And it would have collapsed not because of flaws specific to us but because mere mortals are incapable of sustaining a prolonged ecstasy. I remember reading somewhere that for love to endure it must have a future, not just moments. Dennis and I had only moments. Unsanctioned moments at that.

My love for Greg had always been more earthbound, and from the very beginning I was sure it held just the right mix of heat and desire, admiration and companionship for a long-lasting marriage. At the time, however, Philomena hoped otherwise, hoped there would be no marriage at all, not merely one with a short shelf life. Always an uncompromising sort of woman, she was particularly uncompromising when it came to the spiritual well-being of her children.

"This marriage will not only be a scandal," she had declared. "It will be the death of Greg's soul."

It was a Sunday afternoon when we told her. We had just come back from church and we were standing in her kitchen waiting for the water in the kettle to finish boiling. The minute the news hit her ears, she yanked off her sweater as if readying herself for a scuffle.

"Count me out!" she had said, "I won't take hand, act or part in a mockery of religion or the undoing of me son. I've got nothing against you, Tess. Not personally. Not a blessed thing. In fact, the first time Greg brought you to meet us — that was right after he became your campaign manager — I said to Hube that I hoped you two could hit it off because you were just the person I'd have wanted for a daughter-in-law. That shows you how aware I was of things. I had no idea in the wide world that you were divorced."

She tossed up her hands. "But how was I to know? When we moved into the Cove in the early sixties because the government uprooted us from our own place and this was the closest I wanted to live to St. John's, you had already left. And when I heard you were running in the election, all I knew about you was that you used to live here and had moved away. And just because it wasn't your fault that yer marriage to that fellow up in Montreal fell asunder, that makes no difference."

She looked at Greg and from him back to me. "At least *he* says it wasn't your fault. But like I said, it don't make a thimbleful of difference. It don't change the water on the beans one iota. It don't alter the fact you *are* a divorced woman. *Divorced!* I certainly can't approve of my son marrying a *divorced* woman."

She leaned harder on the word with each repetition. If she had been writing it, she would have torn through the paper.

I could offer her little comfort that day except to tell her that I loved Greg, that I wished I had never married Leonard, that I wished I could have gotten an annulment instead of a divorce, but that I didn't have the grounds for an annulment nor the stomach for trumping up grounds for one if that's what she had in mind. I said I came to believe that Leonard only married me on the rebound after his paralegal fiancée had broken their engagement and run off to California with a young graduate student, but that he hadn't done it with malice aforethought. He simply believed he could live with the substitution and then found out he couldn't. I neglected to tell her, because it didn't seem pertinent to this conversation, that I had also come to understand that I had married Leonard not so much out of love as out of need. Mother had just died, and I didn't have another living relative to my name. Besides, I wanted to prove to someone — myself, probably — that at least one of the Corrigan women could marry solid, and Leonard was nothing if not solid.

Hubert had rallied to my aid that day. He scolded Philomena for carrying on with nonsense, and after Greg and I left he continued to lobby on my behalf until finally Philomena came around to at least accepting the inevitability of Greg's and my union. A couple of weeks later she told us grudgingly, wanting to make sure we understood her position, that just because she accepted the letter of our marriage, it didn't mean she accepted the spirit of it. And it certainly didn't mean she wasn't disappointed that her firstborn son was marrying someone whose slate was unclean and whose life wasn't suited to having a Nuptial Mass in the Sacred Heart Church in the Cove.

Her own marriage, mixed as it was, had had to be a low-key affair, a side-altar "do" without adornment or decoration, without pomp or circumstance. Worst of all, she had had to forego the

Nuptial Mass and with it the prayer she had wanted so badly. She had fervently hoped her sons' weddings could have all the flounces and frills to make up for her own spare ceremony.

We had been sitting at her table when she confessed this, as usual drinking her strong tea, and she immediately rose and hurried up to her bedroom and returned to the table with her Sunday missal. She sat back down beside her half-empty teacup and, after a few minutes of searching through the book, came upon the page she was looking for.

"'Tis the prayer I had hoped to have at me own wedding, but it was considered out of place for the occasion. A bit too high-toned. At least that's what my mother thought, so I never pushed for it. I wasn't the type then to push things."

She began reading the prayer, and I could tell from the smooth way she read it that she had gone over this passage many times over many years. "*Look, in Your mercy, O Lord, upon this Your handmaid, about to be joined in wedlock, who entreats You to protect and strengthen her. Let the yoke of marriage to her be one of love and peace. Faithful and chaste, let her marry in Christ. Let her ever follow the model of the holy women. Let her be dear to her husband like Rachel; wise like Rebecca; long-lived and faithful like Sara. Let the author of sin work none of his evil deeds within her; let her ever keep the Faith and the Commandments. Let her be true to one wedlock and shun all sinful embraces . . .*"

She broke off at this point, shut the missal and asked, "Would you consider having this lovely prayer included in your service? Rules have slackened so much, you could probably get away with it. Anything goes now. They even makes up their own vows. Twists and turns the old vows around to suit their purpose. I even heard them saying on one of the soaps the other day, 'Till love does depart.' Gives them a lot more leeway, I s'pose. Don't have to put up with each other until the grave sets them free."

She passed the open missal to me so I could read the prayer for myself.

"I don't like that prayer as much as you do," I confessed, taking the book but not attempting to read it. I didn't need a second reading or time to mull over her request. "But I'm sure we can find one we'll all like." I could tell from the heavy way she closed the missal when I passed it back to her and by the way the lines around her mouth deepened that her disappointment was severe, and for a moment or two I considered retracting my refusal.

Later, when we were alone, Greg asked me why I had been so adamant in my refusal and whether I would reconsider including the prayer in our service. "Can't you humour her by doing that for her?"

"Just read the words!" I said. "Just hear them! Just take in the message. It's as if the burden of keeping our marriage together will depend upon my virtues. Or in my case, my lack of virtues — I'm certainly no Sara or Rachel or Rebecca."

I recited the last line for him, slowly and clearly. "'*Let her be true to one wedlock.*' Can't you see that I'm already one marriage and one divorce too late for being true to one wedlock? We'd be a laughingstock if I read that out loud at the altar. Your mother is so used to reading those words, she no longer listens to their meaning."

As it turned out, my acceptance or refusal of that particular prayer became of no consequence. When Philomena learned the following week that we were getting married in St. John's in the Unitarian Church, she fiercely rescinded her earlier capitulation. She would not be coming to our wedding; the whole thing was a blasphemy.

She had been standing beside her kitchen stove, a dishcloth in her hand, ready to attack the stack of dinner dishes when Greg told her our church plans. For several seconds she was stunned into silence. When she recovered her composure, she tossed the dish-cloth on the counter with a swing that said now she had heard everything.

"What? Not even Anglican or United? Not even a regular Protestant church?" She squared her shoulders and hiked her bosom, readying herself for the fight of her life. "Over my dead body. Not while I'm on this side of the grave."

We hurriedly explained that we had tried but not succeeded in arranging for a United or an Anglican wedding. One difficulty was my divorce. Another was that churches were already booked; we hadn't given enough lead time. Finally, we had chosen the Unitarian Church because good friends of ours belonged to it, and they were going to be our witnesses.

"Might as well get married in a park. Or in a hot air balloon, like those Hollywood people I saw on that thing the other day." She pointed to the television in the den. "And if they want to do that, that's fine by me. That's their folly. 'Tis jest not fine fer my son." She looked me squarely in the eye, as if the plans were mine alone. "Surely ye must know you're not only flying in the face of God by this marriage. Yer going to make Hube and me the disgrace of the Cove."

On the way back to St. John's that evening, Greg explained to me why his mother was so hard-headed about our marriage.

"You have to realize it has more to do with her own marriage than with ours. And it has a lot to do with Danny and the guilt she feels over his leaving the Church. She blames herself for going against her parents' wishes and marrying Dad, and she blames Dad because he never insisted that Danny come with her and me to our church."

He told me how the two religions had slept fitfully between his parents throughout most of their marriage. "She used to throw it up to him that he had signed papers before they got married saying he wouldn't interfere in her bringing up the children in the Catholic religion, and yet he acted as if he had signed nothing. She felt he was always looking for ways to skirt around his sacred promise."

I found it difficult to imagine a stubborn, stonewalling Hubert. "That doesn't sound like a thing your dad would do," I said. "It doesn't sound like Mr. Hube at all. He doesn't seem the type who wouldn't live up to his word."

"Oh, he had his ways back then," Greg said, giving me a tight, wry smile. "They both did, for that matter. I used to hate Sundays because they either argued before church or became silent afterwards. The silence sometimes lasted all day."

"But what would cause the fuss?" I inquired, not fully understanding the circumstances. "Would your dad want you and Danny to go to his church with him instead of both of you going with your mom?"

"Nothing that outright. Danny used to want to go to church with Dad, and Dad wouldn't say no to him. She wanted him to say 'No, go with your mother.' That's how it went. It used to drive Mom crazy. Especially since she surmised that Danny was doing it just to get her goat. But that wasn't the case at all. Danny just felt sorry for Dad going to church alone. And I used to feel sorry for him, too, for that matter. I just didn't have Danny's courage to run counter to Mom. I took the cowardly way out. I used to go to Mass and spend the time praying that the Anglican Church and the Catholic Church would merge so it would be impossible to tell one from the other, and then I'd come home feeling like Judas for my seditious prayers. On Sundays I always felt I was on the rack. Only it was my heart, not my limbs, being jerked in two directions.

"But that's about the only thing they ever seriously argued about. So I don't want to give you the idea that I was hard done by or anything. And even the religion issue settled down after a while. Once we got to be teenagers. Danny gave up going to any church. After we moved into the Cove and there wasn't a regular Anglican minister on hand, religion stopped being such a problem. She goes to Mass, and whenever the Anglican minister comes to the Cove, he goes to his church. Other times he goes fishing. And sometimes while she's at her church, he will turn on one of those evangelical programs on television. Seems to work for them, so I let it go at that."

I married Greg on a sultry August afternoon, the first fine day in a long string of wet days. I married him less than a year after I met him, less than a year after he had successfully managed my political campaign and gotten me elected to the House of Assembly. And I married him without Philomena's blessing. All of Mr. Hube's crusading on our behalf, all of Greg's imploring, all of my apologies didn't make a dent in her resolve. Even telling her that we both intended to keep on going to the Catholic Church even if we couldn't partake of the Sacraments didn't mollify her the slightest bit.

"Some grand day!" the guests said when they met in the dark-by-contrast vestibule of the Unitarian Hall on Empire Avenue in downtown St. John's where Greg and I had just merged our lives. When I came outside after the brief ceremony, I could smell the carnations bedded beside the low iron railing surrounding the front of the building. Their heavy pink and white blooms drooped in the sun and threw soft shadows on the grass. As I breathed in the headiness of the flowers, and as I tasted the air that smelled like fresh green kelp, and as I felt the silkiness of the sun on my bare arms, I told myself that this was indeed a grand day for a wedding. Even though I had no family to witness this marriage, and even though Hubert and Philomena were conspicuously absent, I still felt it was a grand day for my second venture into matrimony.

But just as I was thinking these thoughts, a seagull circled the churchyard, barely clearing our heads, scanning the grounds for food. After a few circles it realized it had been duped — there was nothing but paper confetti on the ground — and it gave a loud, shrill screech and flew off towards the harbour.

That screech, as it faded out into the Narrows, took with it the joy that had drenched me just moments earlier. Memories came at me, indistinct and clouded, as if from a great distance. The more I tried to push them back, the more they crowded in, jostling one another for elbow room. It was as if the screech of that gull had awakened in me old sorrows. Dennis Walsh's face slipped into my mind.

I reached out and gripped Greg's arm tightly, trying to reassure myself that just because the happiness that had lived in me once had died, there was no reason to believe it would die a second time. As if he understood my need, he unfurled my hand from his arm and clasped it tightly in his own as we walked about the church grounds mingling with our guests.

As soon as good manners permitted, we slipped away and drove to the Cove. Although Philomena had refused to attend our wedding and Hubert had refused to defy her and come by himself, they both insisted we go out to see them before we left for our honeymoon in Europe. It was early evening before we arrived. The weather was still sultry, and no wind at all. Not even enough to make a ripple on the pond. Even the sea was calm, and the sun that was dropping down into it over beside Red Island was the colour of blood, promising another good day to follow.

The whole village smelled of freshly washed clothes. Philomena's clothesline was filled cheek to jowl with towels and sheets and underwear and socks, the underwear discreetly pinned to hide any remaining stains, the socks spooned together heel to shin in pairs of blacks and browns and greys. Hubert's socks. The clothes hung on the line without a stir or a flutter, and I knew that before nightfall Philomena would be complaining that everything had dried as stiff as a board and as rough as sandpaper. She liked it much better when the sheets bellied out like wind-bloated sails and when Hubert's shirts flew off the line and strangled themselves on the pasture fence.

Philomena's clothesline had always reminded me of Grand-mother's clothesline. Grandmother's was in the back yard, gallowsed between two gangly spruce trees. The midway point was always propped up with a forked stick so the clothes wouldn't droop on the ground. Many times during the day she would go to the line and grab a handful of blue-bordered flannel sheet and bring it to her nose to glut herself on the scent of salty air mixed with whatever flowers were blooming: lilacs, honeysuckle, wild roses, goldenrod.

"Some good!" she would purr and let the sheet trail away from her hand, reluctant to let it go. She would move slowly down the line to the towels, capture the tail of one and smile as she crumpled a fistful, satisfied the brisk wind had dried it as soft as one of her cotton aprons.

When we got out of the car, my wedding dress, my sedate and non-virginal beige linen dress, was wilted and wrinkled, and Greg's white shirt had a high water mark of sweat where his back had pressed up against the vinyl-covered seat. I could tell from the heat in Philomena's kitchen and from the mucky air that hung in her porch that the day had been an unusually hot one in the Cove as well as in St. John's. I suspected, though, that some of the heat in the house had come from Philomena's baking. I also suspected that Hubert had spent most of his day carrying in wood from the yard to keep the kitchen fire going so Philomena could bake the bread that she now had bottomed-up to cool on the oilcloth-covered table.

After the meal — a boiled dinner of salt beef and cabbage, turnips and potatoes, with a fig pudding for dessert — Greg and his father went to Cleary's Garage to get windshield wiper fluid for the car. Philomena took advantage of their absence to have a mother-in-law / daughter-in-law talk.

Since I was now Greg's wife, she wanted me to forget she had ever been against our marriage. "Let bygones be bygones, that's my motto," she said. "Yesterday has hightailed it over the hill like Lundrigan's government ram." She reiterated what she had said earlier: that her objections had been solely religious, not personal. And she felt compelled to tell me about her own marriage, as if my hearing about it would make me better able to understand her objections to Greg's and my union.

There hadn't been a hitch in her and Hubert's relationship for ten years — that's how long it took her, with the assistance of many litanies to Saint Jude, the patron saint of impossible cases, to produce Greg. No litanies were needed to bring Danny into the world. And later little Bridget, although, as it turned out, little Bridget was a gift that had to be returned after only two weeks.

"I'll never forget the pain of losing little Bridget. And I'll also never forget the goodness of Hubert during that time. We were so poor. Hubert had to leave his job in the Buchans mines because he had sores that got infected with the lead dust. So we had no money coming in. We lived on wild ducks that Hubert shot at the beach and capelin that we got out of the landwash in June, just like here in the Cove, and salted them down for winter. And, of course, handouts from my parents, the Lord have mercy on them. They were so good to us."

After a time the wild ducks began to taste like capelin and the capelin began to taste like wild ducks. But the worst thing of all was that they couldn't afford a proper coffin for little Bridget, and Hubert had had to make one for her out of a couple of discarded lobster pots a neighbour had given him. Philomena said she loved Hubert most when he was making that lobster pot coffin. He had padded the inside of the rough laths with sheep's wool and lined it with a pillowcase her mother had contributed, and she had dressed little Bridget in a pretty pink silk dress another neighbour had donated. A few years earlier, when her own baby was born, this neighbour had received the dress from a relative in Boston, and it was still spic and span because the child had been born in the winter, and God Himself knew you didn't put silk dresses on a baby in the wintertime, especially in an unheated house. "So," she said, her voice as soft as it must have been on that day when she dressed her daughter for the last time, "my little Bridget looked as pretty as any baby that ever entered Heaven."

Then Philomena sighed heavily, remembering how life had continued to batter them. Hubert had gone back to fishing, a job he hated worse than the devil hates holy water. The children began to grow, and they had wants and needs that the parents had a hard time filling. And then pretty soon the mixed marriage issue reared its head. And it kept on rearing its head so it even blemished the good times. It was plain as the nose on her face, she said, it was even blemishing this very day — her first-born's wedding day. This day should not have been tinged with sorrow. And it wouldn't have been if Greg had been given a stronger foundation in his religion.

She acknowledged that the situation was partly of her own doing. She should have known better than to mix-marry. Even at the time, she was aware that a mixed marriage could cause all kinds of grief for a couple, not to mention watering down the faith of the next generation. Her mother had told her this, but she had paid her no heed, madly in love as she was with Hubert. Now that she had paid the price — was, in fact, still paying the price — she did, indeed, know better. If Greg had grown up in a solidly Catholic family, he would never have considered marrying a divorced woman. And now he was totally lost to his religion.

At least with Danny she still had some hope. As far removed as he was from his religion, he could turn a corner any day. There was no canonical impediment to his returning to the Church. But Greg's marriage left no hope for him at all. At least not as long as he stayed married to me, which she hoped he would. And that, she said, was the contradiction she now had to live with, that was the quandary she was steeped in. It was enough to break a mother's heart wide open. However, with the help of God and with the help of Hube, who always had a way of making her see that she was making mountains out of molehills, she would bear up. Hubert, for all that he was a Protestant, was the best thing that had ever come her way, and she hoped that the good Lord, if He had any warm feelings toward her at all, would put her into the ground before He took Hube. Life without Hube was hardly worth talking about.

Chapter Four

WHEN, DESPITE HER PRAYERS, Hubert goes into the ground before her, Philomena gives God the benefit of the doubt. He must have recognized that she was the stronger of the two, and He had kept her around to look after Hube. Hube, for all that he was kind and good, would have been useless tending to a sick woman. He had never made as much as a cup of tea for himself in his whole lifetime, and he would have starved to death sitting on a bag of flour.

In the months following Hubert's death, we go to the Cove as often as possible, particularly for special occasions. The Cemetery Mass is one of these. Weather permitting, it is always celebrated in the cemetery on Dickson's Hill on the Sunday closest to the fifteenth of August, the proceeds from the offertory going towards the upkeep of the cemetery.

Greg, Brendan and I go to the Cove on Saturday afternoon so Philomena will know with certainty that we will be with her. Unlike all of the others who will be at the Mass, she has no connection with Dickson's Hill, since her parents and little Bridget are buried down the bay in the settlement of her birth and Hubert is in the Protestant Cemetery on the flat land of the Cove. She wants us on hand to help her ward off her loneliness and her sense of not belonging.

On Sunday morning, Philomena gets us up long before we need to get up, insisting she wants to be at the cemetery early. As it turns out, we are so early we have the cemetery almost to ourselves. I use the extra time to check on the Corrigan family plots to see how the grave markers have fared over the winter. Greg, Brendan and

Philomena follow after me as I pick my way down the steep slope of the cemetery hill. I walk carefully, watching my step so as to dodge the foundered graves and the sharp rocks that have been thrust to the surface by frost heaves. When I reach the spot where my uncle Martin, my grandmother and my mother lie side by side, I stop and stare across these graves to a grave isolated from the others by several feet. Ned Corrigan's grave, the great-uncle who had always been passed off to me as my grandfather.

"My oh my, I never knew yer Grandfather," Philomena says, catching up and following my gaze, breaking into my thoughts. I am thinking, as I have before, what a fluke it is that Ned is now buried on the inside of the cemetery fence instead of on the outside of it. If the parish hadn't needed extra burial space, the cemetery fence would not have been moved out beyond Ned's plot, and it would still separate him, he who had died by his own hand, from those others, they who had died by an act of God.

"An awful thing, suicide," Philomena acknowledges, remembering the story from years past. Her all-out-of-breath voice carries in the cemetery stillness. Even though the morning isn't cold, Philomena shivers and rubs her sweater-covered arms to brush away the goose bumps.

"Makes ye wonder how anyone could do such a thing. Such a cross fer them unfortunate enough to be left behind. But the poor fellow must have had his reasons. No one would do such a thing without a shockin' good reason. No one would want to string himself up on the back of a stable door unless he saw no other way out of his misery."

Remembering she is amongst the dead, she has interjected a touch of charity on Ned's behalf, but she is still unable to fathom such an ungodly action. She shivers again as if chilled to the bone by the mere contemplation of the pain that must have been left behind in the wake of Ned's death, yet she can't seem to let go of the subject. Her words are whispery thin because she is still out of breath from the walk. "Meself, I don't see how I could bear it. I mean, being the one left behind to take the blame. And right or wrong, I know I'd be the kind to take the blame. I'd be the kind to ask meself all those questions about why I didn't notice there was trouble brewing."

As we head back up the hill, retracing our steps to the top of the cemetery where the Mass is to be held, we make small talk about the graves that we pass along the way. We note how this grave marker hasn't fared so well while that one is still standing upright, how this person died so young, how that one lived so long. Here and there I fill in information that Philomena is lacking on account of her not having lived her whole life in the Cove. By the time we make it back to the top of the hill, Mass is just getting underway.

Immediately after the service, we go back to Philomena's house. Brendan and Greg grab a snack and then go fishing for trout in a brook on the outskirts of the Cove. Philomena and I take our tea into her parlour, which she has opened up for the summer and where she has temporarily hooked up the television set. Because the den gets the heat from the kitchen stove, Philomena thinks being able to sit in the cool parlour is well worth the nuisance of having wires strung along the floor and having to constantly caution people not to trip over them.

Because this room faces the ocean it always holds a dampness that no amount of airing out or window opening or spraying with Lily of the Valley air freshener can fully camouflage. And no number of whatnots or crocheted doilies or petit point samplers with gold letters asking God to bless the house or save the king can totally mask the musty smell of mildew burrowed deep into the windowsills. And not even an outdated calendar of the Dionne quintuplets smiling identical teenage smiles can hide the water stain on the wild fern wallpaper.

As soon as I sit down, Philomena switches on the television and positions herself on the couch in direct view of the screen. In a secretive voice, a male announcer discloses the plays of a golf tournament in Phoenix, Arizona.

"Loves looking at golf," she says, "even if I don't know the first thing about the game. It's so easy on the nerves. Not like that foolish hockey everyone is crazy over. Out to kill each other."

As always, Philomena sits with her legs wrapped in a granny-square afghan that she pulls from the back of a chair. The first time Danny saw her cuddle the afghan around her legs he had accused her of believing the announcers could look up her skirt. "I won't stand fer ye playing me fer a fool, young man," she had said, the fire in her eyes negating any notion that she could be played for a fool. "I wasn't born on a barge, I'll have ye know."

Once the afghan is in place to her satisfaction, she shifts around to make herself comfortable in the velour-covered chair, shuffling a pillow behind her shoulders and heeling in a footstool for her legs, more as if she is settling in for a nap rather than preparing to watch television. Actually, neither a nap nor a golf game is on her agenda.

"So Tess," she says, twisting around to face me. In her eyes I see the resolute look of a dogfish caught in a seine. "'Tis now mid-summer. The House has been prorogued for a few months. When do you intend to look up Brendan's grandfather?"

Taken off guard, I hedge. "Soon. Real soon. I promise."

"That's what you said last fall, you said you'd look him up when the House prorogued in the spring. Well, the spring has come and the spring has gone, and the House has prorogued, and you're still no closer to looking up your father than you ever were."

Because it has been almost a year since she last brought up this subject, I wonder what has triggered the thought now. At first, I put it down to the peacefulness of the parlour. The windows are open, propped up with Hubert's homemade two-foot screens, and the warm air filters in through the polyester lace curtains. With every breath of wind — and for a rare change the wind is gentle — a branch from a blooming rose bush rubs up against the screens, perfuming the room. The moment holds the sort of deep peace-fulness that makes you fear it won't last. Or it could be the trip to the cemetery that has sent her mind spiralling in the direction of Ed

Strominski. Seeing the freshly turned sod of the new graves may have reminded her that at best life is provisional. Then it strikes me that the golf tournament is taking place in Arizona, the last known home of my biological father.

"Soon," I repeat, aware that I no longer have Hubert to act as a buffer for me. "I'll get on it real soon."

Hubert always told Philomena to stop pestering me about finding "that man," and although she seldom listened to anyone's admonishments for any length of time, she would always lay off for a few months. Hubert's sickness and death had given me a longer reprieve than usual. But I now realize it was just that: a reprieve.

"I've already found out he lives in Arizona. I've done that much," I say.

"Don't you think I already know that!" she snaps. "But finding out he lives in Arizona is no bloody good unless you go to see him."

Two years earlier I had traced Ed Strominski's whereabouts to Scottsdale, or rather, I should say, Greg with his lawyer know-how had traced him. At any rate, having gone that far, I lacked the will, or maybe the courage, to go any further.

When Greg began the initial search, I gave him whatever information I could recall about the man I knew only through a dog-eared black and white snapshot. However, the fact that I didn't know him in the flesh didn't mean I knew nothing about him. I knew that his home town was Portland, Oregon, and that he had been a construction worker. He had come in the early 1940s to Argentia, a seaport village eight miles from the Cove, with a shipload of American construction workers to turn Argentia into a naval and army base for Uncle Sam. And from research I had done years earlier, I knew that all US military base construction workers had later been formed into a group known as the Seabees, and that this group had obtained official navy status. This meant that there were official US naval records for all of the Seabees, including Ed Strominski.

Most of the unofficial information I had gathered on Ed Strominski had come my way through deliberate eavesdropping upon whispered, hand-over-mouth conversations. But some of it had come to me through serendipity. When I was eight or nine and rummaging through my mother's possessions in her bedroom, I found a postcard that proclaimed on its front FOR YOU A ROSE IN PORTLAND GROWS. There was no message on the card. There wasn't even a postage stamp. But on the back, in the left-hand corner, the words "Portland, Oregon" were printed.

Scanty as this information was, it was enough to tell me that Ed Strominski had given this card to Mother. I intuitively knew this. Indeed, my senses in all things having to do with the man who had bigamously married my mother had become so fine-tuned over the years that from a word or a sentence, or even from a covert look, I could fashion a biography. On that very same occasion I had also come upon a snapshot of a construction worker leaning against a khaki-coloured piece of construction equipment, a bulldozer or a steam shovel. Although, like the card, the snapshot bore nothing to identify this person staring back at me, I instantly knew that I was looking into the face of my begetter. I knew it was him by the way my whole being reacted: by the way my breath escaped my lips — loud and jerky, as if a wild animal had grabbed me by the collar and flailed me this way and that way, shaking the life out of me — and by the pain that seared my insides. Had a volcano erupted in some deep cavern within me and belched molten ash over my vital organs I would not have been more scorched. Above all, though, I knew it was him because of the delicious fear that circled my heart and forced its way outside in the form of cold perspiration.

I remember standing beside my mother's white-painted bureau, its drawer gaping open, as I looked down into the palm of my hand into the face of Ed Strominski staring back at me. Sweat drenched the hair at the back of my neck and trickled under my chin.

Underneath my long-sleeved convent school uniform, the flesh on my arms felt damp and cold. At first I had looked at the snapshot through tentative, squinted eyes, as if I were looking at an object as eye-damaging as an eclipse of the sun. If I had stumbled upon a pharaoh's grave I would not have been any more timid of risking its curse than I was of looking full strength into the face of Ed Strominski. After a few seconds, though, curiosity overcame my fear, and I summoned the courage to stare at the snapshot with eyes fully opened. For the next several minutes my eyes refused to focus anywhere else but on the smiling man who leaned against the khaki-coloured piece of earth-moving equipment.

I continued to stand in that one spot in Mother's room, on the little oval rug in front of her bureau. I stood as if riveted on the belly of the home-hooked rooster whose open beak crowed "Good Morning" in red wool letters, the red of the letters perfectly matching the red of the rooster's comb and wattle. Past incidents, snippets of whispers and fragments of almost forgotten conversations forked and zigzagged around me like chain lightning. My heart raced wildly, and I was certain that if I had tried to speak, I would not have had the breath for it.

After what seemed like a very long time I finally came out of my stupor. Grandmother was shouting from the kitchen that I was taking entirely too long to fetch the envelope of pictures that Carmel had sent home from Boston. With a cunning developed over years of whispers and anxious looks and veiled words, I quickly hid the picture, tucked it up the tight, wrist-length black serge sleeve of my uniform so that I could have it later, all to myself, out of Grandmother's sight. For several days I kept it hidden under my pillow at night and in a special compartment in my school bag during the day. It was the closest I had ever come to meeting the man who had married my mother and who was half responsible for my existence.

"Ye'd better get to him soon, girl," Philomena goads me as she turns down the voice on the television set. She sits back and rearranges the afghan around her legs. If Hubert were alive he would by this time be asking her why it was necessary for me to go traipsing across the United States looking for someone I wouldn't know if I fell over him. And she would retort, as she always did, that if, like herself, he had his grandson's best interest at heart, he wouldn't be so anxious to take my side.

"Ye'd better get to him before he dies," she now warns, no longer even pretending to look at the television screen. "Dies like Poor Hube. From what ye tells me, yer father must be in his late eighties. Can't expect him to hang on much longer."

"He was alive two years ago," I reply uselessly, hoping she will lose interest. "And besides, he's not my father. He's just a man in a snapshot. I've told you a thousand times, I've no desire to see him."

She whips around and says, "Your desire? Who cares about your desire? 'Tis for Brendan. Ye never knows, girl, and as they say, God be between us and all harm, but one day that child, who is no longer that much of a child, may come down with something, and it would be important to know if it ran in the family."

"I know! I know!" I say, and use an excuse I've used many times before, one that had always worked with Hubert. "It's a matter of finding the time. Things are in an uproar in the House. I have all I can do to get my work done."

She waves her hand as if she is shooing away a fly. "Things are always in an uproar in the House of Assembly. A bunch of shit disturbers, that's what they are. They create a hullabaloo just to get their names in the *Evening Telegram* to con the voters into thinking they're getting their money's worth. But like I said before, think of Brendan. Weaknesses can run in families. Ye'd be surprised what can be passed on. Stuff can show up in the teenage years. And those years are coming right up on him."

Because she isn't at ease acknowledging that a defective gene may already be lurking in Brendan's system, poised to leap out and manifest itself in a terrible, uncontrollable disease, she offers the possibility of a more benign defect, one easily overcome with foreknowledge. "Might be able to prevent something, or it jest might be something simple. People die all the time because their systems can't handle some kind of food. Or maybe a bumblebee sting." She looks toward the rose bush and the mass of ruby blooms swarming with bumblebees. "But ye got to know these things beforehand. I knew a fellow at home once. He died in minutes after he got bit by a wasp. And I heard of a young girl, not more than three or four, died from eatin' salt fish. Her system couldn't handle all that salt. Things like that could be fatal if not known beforehand. If ye knew beforehand, ye'd be able to do something."

She hugs her sweater around her body, just as she had done on Dickson's Hill. It is unthinkable to her that a weakness in the Strominski line might pose such a threat to her precious Brendan. I want to tell her to stop badgering me, but I find it difficult to fault her for her lobbying on her grandson's behalf. Everyone in the family knows she gave her heart to Brendan as she has never been able to give it to another human being, her own sons included.

She keeps up the pestering until she extorts a promise from me — and this time a 'pon-my-soul promise, like Danny's promise about the deathwatch candle — that I will search for, find and go see the man who I know only through a snapshot, an unsigned postcard from Portland, Oregon, and a gaggle of family whispers that always jolted to full stops whenever I veered into sight.

"Brendan's welfare aside, girl, which I'm glad you're not setting aside," she says, and it is her way of putting a temporary stop to the subject, "I'll never understand why you haven't been inquisitive about what he really looks like. I mean in the flesh. Not just in a picture. Something like that would prey on me day and night. I'd be picturing him all the time. Looking for him in crowds."

She starts to pay attention again to the golf game. As she pulls the afghan around her legs, she adds, "You're sure different from me, girl. I'd never know a minute's peace until I was standing before him, sizing him up."

She says this with surety, certain that my mind hasn't already sized him up. But she is dead wrong. I have sized him up, although not in the flesh. On the day when I came upon that black and white snapshot, I chiselled Ed Strominski's features into my memory, chiselled them as deep and enduring as the names on the gravestones on Dickson's Hill, as deep and enduring as Dennis's and my initials on the rock at the beach. And once I had chiselled his features into my brain, I was no longer content with the snippets of information about him that had randomly come my way. I begged my uncle Martin unmercifully for details.

"Tell me about my father," I would ask him unfairly, knowing he had been forbidden to talk about Ed Strominski to me. "Does he know about me?"

Martin would furtively glance around him to see if Grandmother was in hearing distance and then chance an answer. "I don't know that much about him either, girl," he would hedge nervously, anxious to bring the conversation to an end. "None of us did. And in all likelihood he knows nothing about you."

I would persevere. "Does he have children?"

"I haven't the slightest idea, girl. Not the slightest." Martin would hold his hand over his heart. "'Pon my soul," he would say, with every bit as much sincerity as Danny, "I really don't know whether he has children or not."

As I continued to probe, Martin would become testy, either because he was tired of being quizzed or because he was concerned about Grandmother's overhearing him.

"But then, so what if he does have children?" he would say crossly, a hint to me that he knew more than he was willing to tell. "It won't change the water on the beans. We think he's somewhere back in the United States. But we really don't know where the son of a bitch is now. And not to make you a saucy answer, girl, we don't care, either."

He would then veer the conversation in another direction, usually toward the topic of school, which was always guaranteed to divert my attention temporarily. However, the bits and pieces of information he would supply always left me with plenty of room to manufacture bits and pieces of my own. And from these and from others that had come to me through more indirect means, I was able to fashion a marauding pirate out of Ed Strominski. He had come from the United States, and on solid rock instead of on the high seas he had commandeered the lives of the Corrigan family and plundered their happiness. I imagined that one summer day he had come to our village. Why he had come to our village and, specifically, why to our door were questions I never posed to myself. It was simply that he did come, and Grandmother invited him in for a cup of tea and a Purity caraway biscuit, like she did with peddlers whose suitcases were filled with stuff she couldn't afford, beggars with empty stomachs, and children selling raffle tickets.

After I had pooled all the bits and pieces of information regarding Ed Strominski's visit to our house, collated it, synthesised it, analysed it, I came to believe that on the day he arrived, Carmel had been sitting by the kitchen stove crocheting, as usual, a Star of Bethlehem doily for one of the parlour chairs or perhaps for a donation to the church bazaar. He took one look at her — at her neat and clean dress, at her long red hair, at her ability to whip the crochet hook in and out through the little loops of white thread — and he knew he could not leave the house without taking her with him. So he simply shanghaied her. He dragged her out of the house while Uncle Martin, Grandmother and I looked on in; while Carmel shouted for us to help her; while the ball of white crochet cotton trailed after her like a fishing line floating downstream.

There was just one problem with this scene. It wasn't in Martin's makeup to stand by and let anyone bully his family. Or, for that matter, to allow anyone to bully another person, family or not. I reconciled this contradiction by telling myself that the shanghaiing must have occurred during one of the times when Martin had a setback with his tuberculosis and was bed-bound. Or perhaps it had occurred when he was away in that sanatorium on the outskirts of St. John's.

However, despite the fact that bits and pieces of Ed Strominski were chiselled into my mind, despite the fact that morsels and fragments of him were scratched into my soul, there were still times during my childhood when I could almost convince myself that he was a figment of my imagination. He was a character in a book Martin had read to me, like *Ali Baba and the Forty Thieves,* or I had him mixed up with Barabbas, the thief I learned about in Catechism. But even on those few occasions when he almost vanished from my reality, there had always been someone to remind me that Ed Strominski was very much alive. Sometimes it would be my childhood playmate, Sarah Walsh, who would sing-song,

> *Spoons, forks, cup and knives,*
> *Her Yankee father had two wives.*

Or perhaps it would be Sister Rita, my teacher, who would whisper my special conception to our parish priest, Monsignor Myrick, whenever he visited our classroom. Unless she jogged his memory, Monsignor would forget my unholy beginnings and ask me where my father worked, or some other question involving a father in residence.

In fact, even Grandmother's voice held this same sorry information whenever she would fold me into her great aproned lap and croon,

> *Bye baby bunting, Martin's gone a-hunting,*
> *Gone to get a rabbit skin to wrap the baby bunting in.*

I knew that when other children had this rhyme sung to them, it was always Daddy who had gone a-hunting.

And there were other times when I could feel the reality of Ed Strominski rushing blood-red up my neck and filling my eyes with thick shame. Whenever anyone referred to me as Poor Carmel's Tessie or asked me about Poor Carmel, I would stare at the floor, hoping an earthquake or a tidal wave or some other catastrophe would instantly befall the Cove and the ensuing ruckus would jerk all eyes away from me. No such calamity ever rescued me, however, and I always had to stand there helplessly and inform people that Poor Carmel was fine, that she worked in a factory in Boston, and, God willing, she would be home in the summer for two weeks.

When I promised Philomena that I would search for Ed Strominski, I think I was also hoping for the equivalent of an earthquake or a tidal wave to liberate me from the promise. But, as before, I'm not rescued, so, with the help of Greg, I begin the search. In a surprisingly short time we locate the man in a semi-retirement complex in Scottsdale.

Finding him permits me no recourse other than to follow through with my promise to contact him. My quandary is whether to do this by telephone or by letter. After to-ing and fro-ing for a couple of days, I settle on writing, preferring the distance a letter will allow me. I stress that I want to meet him for my son's sake, and my insistence that I do not intend to encroach upon his life also implies that he is not to encroach upon mine. I give him possible dates for my visit.

His reply, also by letter, comes swiftly. In his shaky and hurried handwriting I detect sincerity, although I remind myself that Carmel also had presumed sincerity and had been soundly duped. He says his health won't permit him to meet me at the airport, but he gives me directions to get to his place via airport shuttle. Because of his hospital commitments and my work commitments, the earliest we can meet is the second weekend in March.

Between obligations to work and family, the time goes by so quickly that the second weekend in March is upon me almost without my awareness of time having passed. Just hours before I am to leave for the airport, I begin to pull my travel wardrobe together. As my hands toss articles of clothing into my travel case, my mind frantically tosses around questions that I must put to Ed Strominski before I leave Arizona to come back home. I line them up, each one having to do with the suffering he had inflicted upon us. Why had he so heedlessly brought so much pain upon the Corrigan family? I become so intent on my tally of these wounds and bruises that I pack my clothes helter skelter and forget that my sole purpose in meeting with Ed Strominski is to obtain his medical history. It is as if at the last moment the central purpose of my quest has changed from information to reparation. I tick off the wounds and bruises, and with each check mark my anger plumps up. I can barely wait to lather this man with Carmel's pain, with my shame, with Martin's disgust and with Grandmother's weary acceptance of what was instead of what could have been. My flesh itches with the need to weight him down with a lifetime of culpability. Only incidentally do I remember that I am meeting with this man for the benefit of my son.

Chapter Five

My plane lands at the Phoenix airport in the late afternoon, and I take the shuttle bus to Scottsdale. All during the ride, I fret about the moment when I will first set eyes on Ed Strominski. Like the three holy women on their way to anoint Jesus in the tomb, worried over what they would see when they rolled back the stone, I worry about what I will see when Ed Strominski pulls open his door. And I worry about what I will say to him. For that matter, about what he will say to me. I wonder whether he will be the one to speak first. And, if so, will he say, "Hello, I'm your father"? If I speak first, will I say, "Hello, I'm Tess, your daughter"? Or will I say instead, "Hello, I'm Tess Corrigan"? Will we shake hands? If he extends his hand, can I bear to have his flesh touch mine even in such a cursory manner?

I get out of the shuttle bus at the entrance to the gated complex, and as I walk up the flagstone path to his building, my travel case slung over my shoulder, I can hear my heart beating deep inside my ears, beating as if it is going to burst out through my breastbone. When I press my hand against my chest to try and slow it down, I leave a sweaty wet stain on my blouse pocket. Because I'm not accustomed to such heat, or maybe because I am nervously gulping air and taking in too much oxygen, I begin to feel light-headed. The flagstones on the path start to heave and swell as if I am out on the mid-Atlantic, and I have to cup both hands over my mouth and breathe into them to regain my equilibrium.

Ed Strominski's apartment is on the second floor of the two-story building. A handwritten sign on his door says, No Solicitors. I read the sign, recheck the number on the door, swipe my sweaty hands across the thighs of my cotton slacks and snag one more mouthful of air before I press the bell.

A great deal of time seems to pass without a response, and I am just about to recheck the door number again when it is pulled open by a stooped, pale-fleshed, sunken-jawed old man in beige cotton pants and a white shirt buttoned to the neck. The pants hang slackly on his hips, and his shirt is buttoned crookedly, so that one side jibs upwards towards his chin. There is a wide gulch between his neck and the collar of his shirt.

Over the years I fantasized many meetings with Ed Strominski, but in all of those meetings I never took into account the intervening years. The man I always met was the jaunty construction worker of the black and white snapshot, the man who could bulldoze a navy base out of windswept rock, the handsome scoundrel who could flimflam Carmel with romantic postcards, Evening in Paris perfume and a disarming, roguish smile.

At the sight of the threadbare old man standing in the doorway, I am so certain I have rung the wrong doorbell that I am about to excuse my intrusion when he says, "Tess? You must be Tess Corrigan."

When he speaks my name he hesitantly extends a pallid hand towards me. My own hand refuses to budge from the shoulder strap of my carrying case. It might just as well be welded there. For a few seconds his fingers flounder, and then he stuffs them into his pants pocket as if that has been his intent all along.

"Yes," I manage to squeeze out. "I'm Tess." My mind, however, is intent on reconciling this frail old man with the Walter Pidgeon look-alike in the dog-eared snapshot.

His eyes rake over my face like the searchlights that during the war had reached out from the bases in Argentia, frisking our sky, ferreting out enemies. I surmise he is searching for resemblances. To Carmel perhaps. Or maybe to himself.

In those early moments, despite the fluster of my thoughts, I, too, begin to search for resemblances, and I gratefully recall Martin's constant reassurance that I am Corrigan through and through. Certainly I have no desire to harbour any likeness to the transparent old man who stands aslant in this doorway.

"Sorry I couldn't meet you at the airport," he says in a voice that is surprisingly substantial for such an insubstantial frame, "but, like I said, I've been in and out of the hospital a lot this winter, and I thought that standing around and waiting would be too much." He pauses before adding, "But if I had gone I would have been able to pick you out in the crowd because . . ."

He turns quickly and leads the way into his apartment, beckoning me to follow. As he walks along he touches things for support, the door frame, a wall, a chair.

I jabber nervously to his retreating back. "I had no problem at the airport. It's an easy airport to find your way around. But when I saw your apartment complex, it's so big I was certain I'd never find you."

In contrast to the brightness outside, his tiny apartment is dark. Although it is only late afternoon, he has two lamps lit, and the slatted window shutters are closed tight. He directs me to sit on the couch and says, "Eats up everything in its sight. The sun does. I keep the shutters shut most of the time. Easier on the air conditioning, too."

He anchors both hands on the arms of a sofa chair and lowers himself into it.

When I see him glancing at my travel bag, which I have placed on the floor by my feet, I hurry to assure him that I have my own accommodations, something I should have made clear to him in my letter. "I have a motel just up the street. The Sequoia," I tell him. "The travel agent said it was no more than ten minutes away. I asked the shuttle driver to drop me off here first. Save me the walk in the heat."

He crosses his legs and lets a brown felt slipper dangle from his bare foot. "Good idea," he says, and his tone relaxes. I take this to mean he has wondered whether he would have to be my host. "The Sequoia. So that's where you're staying. Everything out here is called after a cactus or an Indian tribe. I would have offered to put you up, but it's so cramped here. You'd have to sleep on the couch."

He asks if I would like a drink of juice or cold water. I decline, mostly because I want to spare him the struggle of hoisting himself out of the wing-backed chair. He advises me to drink lots of water while I am in Arizona, otherwise I'll get dehydrated in the hot sun. He asks me what airlines I flew with and what airports I stopped at, so I give him my itinerary.

He tells me he had triple bypass heart surgery ten years ago and even traces a line on his shirt to show the length of his incision. He has been having a little trouble with his heart lately; it races madly, like a chuckwagon going down a canyon, and this was the reason for his last hospital stay. I say that it is marvellous what doctors can do nowadays, but I don't ask him how he's feeling. He asks me whether I am married and if I have children, and seems satisfied with my skeletal answer.

Each splinter of small talk is punctuated with long silent spaces, as if we have difficulty tying sentences together into a meaningful thought. In between the bits and pieces of conversation the room fills with dead air. I can actually hear the silence, as if the motor in the refrigerator has suddenly cut out, or as if the television has been turned to an inactive channel, with nothing but hissing snow on the screen. Neither of us can make it easier for the other by opening up substantial conversation. Or perhaps it is too soon for substantial conversation.

After less than twenty minutes of this sidestepping and word shuffling, I am exhausted from keeping the conversation afloat, and I suppose he must be feeling the same. I get up to go on the pretext that I want to get to the motel before dark. He doesn't counter by saying there is still plenty of light.

As he creeps me to the door, his breath labouring, his walk wobbly, a rush of compassion ambushes me. I want to plead with him to go back and sit down, that I can find my own way out. I want to sew the missing buttons on his shirt, and when he teeters and has to clutch his cane for support, my hand automatically darts out to steady him. I jerk it back as if from a flame.

"The old legs aren't what they used to be," he apologizes, quickly righting himself. "It's that last spell in the hospital. Took the strength out of my legs. They get tired so easily now. Especially towards evening."

I tell him I am going back home on Sunday and ask him what time will be suitable to come to see him the following day.

"In the morning," he says without a halt or a shake in his voice. "I'm always up by seven. My best times are the mornings. Before the sun gets too hot. We'll sit outside." He leans out the door and points to the area beside the swimming pool where there are chairs and some shade. "Over there. We'll talk then."

"Yes," I reply. "We'll talk then." I am already starting down the steps to the flagstone pathway before I finish.

I walk slowly back to the motel along the seemingly endless stretch of flat street, absorbing the foreign landscape. Camelback Mountain, which the shuttle driver had pointed out on the way from the airport, is straight ahead of me, and in the fading sun its raw flanks and humped spine are turning a deep shade of lilac. Both sides of the street are lined with blossoming citrus trees and milky petals fall softly to the sidewalk. Some of them land on my shoulders and some on my hair. In almost every yard there are blooming rose bushes, salmon and pink and white, and scarlet bougainvillea cascade over back yard privacy walls, tumbling over the adobe brick like waterfalls of blood. In the midst of this summery landscape, it is hard for me to grasp that back in Newfoundland spring hasn't even begun to try to push winter out of the way, or that when I return home it will be to snow squalls and ice-covered streets and sightings of icebergs in the Narrows.

In this unfamiliar environment I feel as alien as Ruth in the land of Naomi, a stranger amongst the parched sheaves, a foreigner under the beating Palestinian sun. Everything is so strange I might as well have tumbled down a rabbit hole. I have to keep reminding myself that I am actually in Arizona, that I have just met my father and, indeed, that I have come away from this meeting without pelting him with accusations of betrayal and deception.

I walk past a group of young men clumped in a driveway tinkering with a motorbike. Music blares from a radio they have propped up beside them, and the sultry voice of a female singer asks do I know where I'm going and do I know why I'm here. I presume the singer has the planet in mind, but I apply her questions to my trip to Scottsdale. Why am I here? Am I hoping to learn that there is no terrible disease in the Strominski genes that can be passed along to Philomena's grandchild? Am I hoping to learn, strictly for the sake of satisfying my curiosity, why the faded old man in the sunless apartment had married my mother while he was still married to the woman in Oregon? Or am I hoping that his mere telling, even if it is without remorse, will be enough to fill the wounded emptiness inside me, an emptiness that so far no one's love has been able to fill — not Greg's, not Brendan's, not Carmel's, not Grandmother's, not Martin's, not even Dennis's.

I undo another button at the neck of my blouse and take a couple more turns on my full-length sleeves, rolling them above my elbows. I regret not having paid more attention to my packing, and I wish I had worn a cotton shift dress instead of pants so I would be able to expose more of my flesh to the soft desert air. As I trudge towards my motel, I vow to wear my walking shorts in the morning.

Although I arrive at the motel shortly after six o'clock, only a wash of sunset remains on the horizon, and the last traces of red and lilac and orange sky are dropping into the desert. It jolts me into remembering that despite the heat of the day, it is only March, and the long daylight hours of summer are still months away.

I am bone weary and want only to sleep, but I force myself to stay awake long enough to telephone Greg to let him know I have arrived safe and sound.

"I can't understand what Mother saw in him," I blurt out almost as soon as Greg comes on the line. "He's so . . . he's" — I stretch my mind looking for a word that will describe Ed Strominski and express my stunned disillusionment, but I can't find one — "so ordinary. So unimpressive. Like the old snowbirds you see on the Florida beaches. Pale and frail and lurching along on resocketted hip joints. You know the type. I can't understand what Mother ever saw in him."

Greg laughs his hearty Hubert-type laugh. "What were you expecting, my dear? Robert Redford?"

"But it's not just his physique," I say, rankled that Greg can't sense how cheated I feel. "It's his whole presence. There's no flaunt. No swagger. And it's not that it's gone. I don't think it was ever there."

"Tess," he says, as patiently as if he is explaining to a small child why the Big Dipper has to stay in the sky, "the man is pushing ninety. Even Helen of Troy's face wouldn't have launched a thousand ships when she was pushing ninety."

After I hang up, I lie face-down on the motel bed and try to reconcile the Ed Strominski of the black and white photograph with the old man in the apartment. Severe disappointment settles in the pit of my stomach as I admit that I wanted him to have the exact rakish smile and swaggering walk that I had fashioned for him. And I also reluctantly admit that I had coveted both that smile and that swagger, the outward signs of the assurance, certitude, confidence and conviction that I believed were mine simply because they were his and because I always knew, Martin's exhortations to the contrary, that I was not all Corrigan.

As agreed, in the morning I go to the swimming pool at Ed Strominski's apartment complex shortly before eight. He is already there by the time I arrive. In fact, he has been there long enough to set our lawn chairs in place, off to one side in a shaded area under a clump of lemon trees and facing a concrete privacy wall with blood-red bougainvillea spilling over it. He has placed a jug of water, along with two plastic glasses, between our chairs. Considering how slowly he walks, I wonder how long he has been out getting the area ready.

"We'd die of thirst out here without water," he says, holding on to the back of a chair. "And I added a little lemon to give it more of a kick."

This morning he wears a T-shirt instead of a dress shirt. However, the trousers are the same ones he wore last evening, and they are wrinkled at the crotch and buckled at the knees. A ball cap is stuffed in his hip pocket.

Other complex dwellers are already seated around the pool, some chatting, others playing cards. When he sees me eyeing the group, he says, "They're all old here. A raisin farm, that's what these places are called. On account of the wrinkles. Lots of raisin farms in Arizona."

He signs for me to sit down in the chair closest to the blossoming lemon tree and lowers himself into the other one.

"It looks so pleasant and summery," I say, surveying the lemon trees and bougainvillea. "It's difficult to believe that back home they're shovelling out driveways."

As I had done the evening before, I duck calling him by name. Before I left home I had ruminated over how I should address him. "Father" and "Dad" I dismissed out of hand, and the diminutive "Ed" seemed to be too chummy for someone who was fifty percent responsible for my being. On the other hand, "Mr. Strominski" seemed too respectful for the feelings in my heart. I even experimented with fusing both names — "Edstrominski" — like Grandmother did on those few occasions when I had overheard her speak of him directly.

As if he can read my mind, he says, "Call me Ski. Everyone calls me Ski." He turns his back to me to show me the three embossed black letters on his shirt: SKI. "See! Everyone calls me Ski. Except my mother. I was always Ed to her." He pauses, and his next words are so low and muffled that they almost evaporate before they reach me. "And Carmel. Your mother. She always called me Ed."

If he expects me to respond, I disappoint him, although I am sure he hears my sharp intake of breath. He reaches into his back pocket and takes out his wallet. He rummages through it, pulls out a picture and passes it to me. Just as I had instinctively known who he was the moment I found his snapshot in Mother's bureau drawer, I now know it is a picture of Carmel that he is passing between our chairs.

My spine stiffens. I have no intention of allowing him to pull me down into his guilt. And I certainly have no intention of permitting him a time and a place for reliving his past — especially a reliving that will be tilted in his favour.

Still, I automatically reach for the picture. I guardedly grip it between thumb and finger, my hand trembling and my breath sticking in my throat much as it had done on the day I had come upon his picture. The only difference is that I can look at Mother's likeness open-eyed, not with a tentative squint. However, the person in the picture is a Carmel I have never known. She is standing on the steps of the Sacred Heart Church in the Cove. She is dressed in a light-coloured suit and is wearing a hat with a wisp of a veil — a 1940s-style hat. One hand clutches it to keep it from blowing off and the other holds a missal with streamers of flowers falling from it. Visible in the background is the white picket fence that surrounds the Presentation Convent garden next door to the church. Behind this fence I can see two lilac trees — full-leafed but without blooms. Behind the lilac trees a silver maple bends in the wind.

"Her wedding day," I say.

Although no one ever told me what mother wore on her wedding day, or for that matter the month in which she was married, I know all of this. I know it just as I know so many other scraps of information having to do with her marriage, even though none of it was ever told to me — at least not straightforwardly. I continue to hold the picture in my sweating, trembling hand. Carmel looks so innocent. So trusting. So sure of the future. And so very, very young!

A few seconds pass before I feel red-hot rage course through my body, rising even as I struggle to keep it under control. I recognize this rage. It is not new. It is a rage that seeded itself deep inside me early in childhood. It is a rage against this man who has deprived me not only of a father but of a mother as well.

Up until this moment, my memory bank of my mother held a picture of a mature woman, strong and determined and capable of tossing off adversity with the ease with which she would toss my cat off the parlour furniture. It held the picture of her coming home every summer and tackling domestic jobs, jobs that would never get done unless she did them — lengthening or shortening my school uniforms, making jam, cleaning cupboards. And it held a picture of her that was laced with resentment: if she had really loved me she would have found a way to stay in the Cove! If she had really loved me she would not have turned the responsibility for my upbringing over to my grandmother! None of my pictures were of a girl so young, so innocent and so trusting that she was ripe for being duped by a fast-talking American construction worker with the unnerving good looks of a Walter Pidgeon.

I pass the snapshot back to Ed Strominski. I pass it back without comment, scrupulously avoiding eye contact. The trembling of my fingers is the only giveaway that my mind is searching for scourging words to hurl at this marauder who had pillaged the innocence of a young woman and swindled an unsuspecting family out of happiness.

He takes the snapshot from my outstretched hand, and as soon as it is out of my possession, I squirm about on my chair to unstick my bare legs from the sun-heated vinyl seat strapping. In doing so, I inadvertently look his way. I see that he is still holding the snapshot, and his fingers are trembling just as much as mine had trembled when I had held it. Oblivious to my presence, unaware of my scrutiny, he continues to stare at it.

In the morning light he seems even frailer than he had the day before, even more unkempt. His uncombed hair is pushed up towards the crown of his head as if he had stood back on to the wind. His white T-shirt has the grey-blue cast to it that white takes on when it has been washed with jeans and other coloured clothes.

Just as on the evening before, a surge of compassion — or something akin to compassion — douses my escalating rage. I want to take hold of this scruffy old man and shake him out. I want to shake out his wrinkles, his creases, his uneven folds so that he will no longer look like something pulled from the bottom of a laundry basket. I want to turn him back into that jaunty construction worker who could build a base out of rocky pastureland and push a road through a cliff of solid granite. I want to turn him back into someone who is strong enough to take my fury, a fury heightened by seeing Carmel in her wedding dress but now beginning to flag.

I refuse to allow this surfacing compassion to scuttle my fury. I frantically try to pump steam into it, racing through the storehouse of slights and bruises and open wounds that I have stored over the years to let loose upon a fast-talking scoundrel called Ed Strominski. That they now have to be let loose on a dishevelled old man is of minor consequence.

My mind swiftly scans the years I have spent hating this man, all the years I spent needing him, dreaming that one day he would turn up on our doorstep and I would hear Grandmother's gasp as she pulled open the porch door — "Oh my God Almighty, if it ent Edstrominski!" And then, all out of breath and in a fluster, she would shout to me, "Come here, child! Come here, Carmel's Tessie. Yer fauder's here."

"Why did you do it? Why did you marry her when you already had a wife back in the States?" The words shoot out of my mouth like a volley of arrows, rupturing his reverie and even flabbergasting myself. My question is so fierce and unexpected that he jerks his gaze from the picture and turns to me, so startled that even after a few seconds he can't rally. Had I stuck an ice pick in his back he wouldn't be more shocked. His chest heaves inside his T-shirt, and I spare a moment of concern for his runaway chuckwagon heart.

He fastens his gaze on the bougainvillea-covered fence, stares at it as if he has to memorize every detail of the scarlet blooms.

"Why? Why did you destroy us?" I prod, letting the words sink in deep as daggers.

He makes no response, simply moves his eyes from the bougainvillea back to the picture. Something in this gesture deflates my fury, reduces its bloat. Once more, I feel the nippy edges of my rage dissolving. Against all of my defences, my breath takes on the hitch that always told Grandmother that Sarah Walsh had been taunting me again about my unholy beginnings, the sound that always told her that within a few minutes I would be sobbing into her big apron. But I refuse to shed tears in the presence of Ed Strominski. I bridle them while I wait for his excuses, excuses that I am prepared to shoot down with one explosive negation after another.

"She was a wonderful woman, your mother," he says after an interminably long time. His features slacken as if he is relieved that the worst is now over with, as if he has been waiting for my question ever since I arrived. Indeed, I am willing to grant that he may have been waiting to hear it for even more years that I have been waiting to hurl it at him.

"Yes, a wonderful woman," he repeats. His gentle words fall so lightly that he might have been tossing away the stray blossoms of the lemon tree that are falling on our shoulders. "She deserved more."

He puts the picture back in his wallet. He squints into the sun, takes the ball cap out of his hip pocket and pulls it on over his tangled hair, tugging the visor down hard against the sun. The cap is maroon-coloured, and just behind the visor in heavy gold letters are the words "Sun Devils." The cap triggers thoughts that have nothing to do with Carmel. Or perhaps it offers him a conversational escape from thoughts of Carmel.

"My team," he says, fingering the lettering on the cap. "After I retired from the Seabees I came out here just for a visit. I went to see the Sun Devils play, and that did it. I've been here ever since."

There is now a cocksureness about him, a cocksureness reminiscent of the Ed Strominski in the snapshot. He leans back in his chair in much the same way as he had leaned back against the piece of earthmoving equipment. His body no longer seems so shrunken. It is as if he feels that he has given out all that he needs to give out on his bigamous marriage, and he can go blithely on to ordinary conversation.

A gust of wind, hot and breathy, forces him to grab his cap. Just as suddenly as it sprang up, it dies down again and eddies the loose sand and dirt around at our feet. Seconds later it pelts this grit into our faces. The few moments it takes me to brush the lemon blossoms, grains of sand and fragments of tumbleweed out of my face are enough to allow Carmel in her wedding dress to parade before my eyes, to allow Sarah Walsh to sing,

> *Spoons, forks, cups and knives,*
> *Her Yankee father had two wives.*

Still wiping my face, I pull my chair around so Ed Strominski and I are facing each other directly, like two passengers on a train. I am so close to him that my knees almost brush up against his, although I am careful not to let this happen.

"Is that all you have to say? She was a *wonderful woman*! You start talking about your damn football team just like that" — I snap my fingers — "just as if I didn't grow up being called Poor Carmel's Tessie." My hands flail and my voice rises even higher in pitch. "You spoiled our lives. Mother's! Martin's! Grandmother's! Mine!"

In the once-again still Arizona air, my voice carries beyond our chairs. The card players stop their game and stare at us. Embarrassed, I lower my voice, calm my hands. But because my insides are still raging, I can't stop the accusations.

"Carmel never remarried. Do you know that? After her experience with you she couldn't trust another man. She had to leave the Cove to get away from the scandal. And to earn a living to support me — a little something you happened to leave behind."

Past hurts spin through me. They suck the breath out of me, and I have to stop talking to snag air, as I had to do before ringing his doorbell. Once again I look directly at him. He has wilted back into being an old man, his body sagged back into its creases. Again I have to stifle an urge to reach out and touch him, to try and shuffle him back into the Ed Strominski of the black and white snapshot, the Sun Devils fan so venturesome he could move his life to Arizona on a whim. I especially want to shuffle him back into being the Ed Strominski strong enough to command my rage, not the Ed Strominski frail enough to spur me to pity.

"I'm sorry," I say. "I came here to find out your medical history for my child's sake. I'm sorry."

"I'm sorry, too," he says. "Sorrier that I can find the words to tell you." He pauses, wiping his eyes with the sleeve of his T-shirt. The sun is getting high and very hot. I'm certain it is perspiration that he is wiping away, although I'm willing to allow there could be some tears mixed in with it.

"I never intended to hurt anyone," he says. "It just happened that way. And I always wanted to find Carmel to tell her that. But I never got the courage." He reaches out his hand to touch mine but quickly reconsiders and pulls it back. "She was the love of my life, but I never even told her. It would have given her too much of a hold on me. After Christine, I vowed never to let another woman get a hold on me."

Once again my spine stiffens. My voice becomes an icicle. "What do you mean, *hold on you?* You married her, didn't you? Or at least pretended to? If you didn't want her to have a hold on you, you shouldn't have gone through that bogus marriage ceremony."

"I know. I know." He shuffles his cap on and off his head. "But after my troubles with Christine, my wife, I never wanted to get tangled up with a woman again. Christine wouldn't give me a divorce even though the marriage was over. You could really say it had never begun because it was a shotgun marriage. She was pregnant with our son. We had four children in all. I loved them very much. She held that love over my head. Said if I divorced her she would never let me see the children."

"But if the marriage was so bad, why didn't she want a divorce? Why didn't she want out just as much as you did?"

"She didn't want to be a divorcée. Back then that would have been a real stigma. Not like now. And she liked my salary coming in every month. I was in construction — a heavy equipment operator. I made good money. But as soon as the war broke out in Europe and Uncle Sam began building bases outside the States, I joined a construction crew to get away. That's how I got shipped to Newfoundland."

He stops talking long enough to wipe more perspiration from his face. The sun is getting higher, and the airy-leafed lemon trees offer little defence against it.

"Do you want to go inside?" I ask partly out of compassion and partly out of selfishness. I don't want to be responsible for an old man dying of heat exhaustion.

He counters, "Do you? I'm conditioned to the heat."

"No. I'm fine," I lie, although I'm practically at the point of seeing a mirage of icebergs in the Narrows. I feel that what he has to say and what I have to hear is better said and heard out of doors, without the confinement and intimacy of walls. I judge that he feels likewise because he makes no attempt to get up out of his chair.

"When I went to Newfoundland," he continues, "I felt single and, for the first time in years, alive. And I was filled with a recklessness I had never before known." He shrugs, not expecting me to understand. "You had to live those times, the world foundering underneath your feet."

By the time he met Carmel his marriage seemed to be behind him and, besides, there was a lot of talk about Uncle Sam entering the war, making his world even less certain than it already was. And he was madly in love with Carmel, but she wouldn't consent to live with him unless they were married. So between the ups and the downs and the ins and the outs, he said, he decided to go through with a bogus marriage — an act he can't explain now even to himself, much less to me.

"How did you get caught?" I rush in, feeling queasy over so much confession even though I had commissioned it. Besides, I can see that he is relishing the telling — not what I intended. I want his explanation capsuled and paraphrased, not made into a glorious epic.

"I'm not sure to this day how I was found out. I applied for base housing in the married quarters. They may have contacted Christine regarding that. And I slacked off on sending her the money we'd agreed on. I needed it to keep the second household going. So she may have smelled a rat. Or maybe someone who worked on the base from my hometown found out and told Christine when he was back on leave. The upshot of it is that I got careless about covering my tracks. With the world out of kilter and the threat of being swallowed up in a war, ordinary ways of behaving went out the window. And it wasn't as if I was all that conniving. I was just a simple construction worker from the wrong side of the tracks in Portland. Maybe if . . ."

"Did you go to jail for bigamy? Did you get court martialled? Is that why you never got in touch with Carmel? Is that why you never came back? Or was it because she annulled you?"

"Annulled!" He jerks up straight in his chair. "She had the marriage annulled?"

"Right from Rome! *Void ab initio*, that was the term. From the beginning it never was." I disappoint myself because I feel no pleasure in this revelation or in the fact that it seems to disturb him. "Did you have to sign papers?"

He shakes his head slowly, thinking back. "Don't recall. I signed lots of papers back then. For a while there, with my divorce from Christine and child support and joining the Seabees, someone was always shoving a legal paper in front of me. I signed everything, I didn't want to do anything to make the situation worse than it already was. But I don't remember papers about an annulment."

"Maybe you didn't have to sign anything," I say, rushing him along. "She had enough legal evidence to make her case. And what about jail? Were you court martialled?"

"No. No. Nothing like that," he says, negating the rumours. "I wasn't part of the military at the time, so it wouldn't have been a military concern. Became part of the navy later on when the Seabees were formed. Christine divorced me in exchange for most of my salary. And as far as I can tell, Carmel never pressed charges. I just thought the marriage would be wiped out once it was uncovered that I was already married. I didn't know she had to get it off the records like that. I didn't know she had to get it officially annulled."

"Maybe she wanted it that way. The slate wiped clean."

"Maybe so. And as I said, there was the war, and I was needed to build bases, not to fill up a jail cell. Anyway, nothing came of it. I carried on working for Uncle Sam."

He looks away, and his shaky hand wipes his eyes. This time I am certain it is tears that he wipes away, but he regroups quickly. "I didn't get off without a price, if that's what you think. I gave up the children. Never saw them again until they were grown."

He had gone to Europe around the time the bogus marriage was exposed. "Anywhere," he says, his arms wide-arcing the space between us to take in even the remotest parts of the world. "Anywhere there was a base to be built." His enthusiasm rises as he leaves the episode of Carmel behind. "Joined the Seabees a short time after that. Like I said, we were a construction battalion that was formed to build bases. A branch of the navy. When the war heated up, they thought we'd be more secure in combat zones if we were part of a military unit. I went to Bora Bora in the Pacific. Constructed a fuel tank farm there. I was with the first Seabee unit in a combat zone — September 1, 1942. I'll never forget it."

He stoops and picks up his half-full glass of lemon water and drinks it. He refills my empty glass, and when he passes it to me he no longer looks old and frail. Pride in himself and in his unit is transparent on his face. And it is transparent in his voice as he resumes his story.

"We were part of the 6th Naval Construction Battalion. We went ashore at Guadalcanal. We had to use captured Japanese equipment, but we finished Henderson Field. It was a hellhole, I tell you that much. A real hellhole. Rain, mud, sniper fire, artillery and bombing. But we finished it. After that I took part in almost every island invasion in the Pacific. We were always working under fire. Always right up there with the Marines. We were afraid of nothing. Nothing! Absolutely nothing!"

He squares his shoulders and holds his head high, confirming his lack of fear, his dedication, his conceit. Irritation once more circles my stomach and creeps up my spine. I didn't come to Arizona to listen to him tell succulent war stories.

"It's awfully hot," I say in the hope of sidetracking him. "Think we should go in?"

"Nonsense! A dry heat. I don't mind it if you don't. But then, like I said, I'm used to it." Impervious, he takes up where he left off. "We hauled artillery guns up mountains, repaired bomb-damaged runways while we were being shot at from all sides. We built an artificial harbour in Normandy immediately after the invasion. We were older than the fellows in other branches of the service. I don't believe there was anyone in the Seabees under thirty-five. We joined the Seabees because we wanted to. Not because we had too. They respected us for that. In fact, the Marines put up a sign at Bougain-ville to tell us how much we were needed."

He shuts his eyes and recites the words on the sign as if he were reading them for the first time.

So when we reach the Isle of Japan,
With our caps at a jaunty tilt,

We'll enter the city of Tokyo,
On the roads the Seabees built.

"Yes ma'am," he says, rousing himself. He gives his own cap a jaunty tilt. "On the roads the Seabees built."

I recall from whispers and unguarded conversations in our household that at this very same time — at the height of his war adventures — Carmel was home in the Cove refusing to leave the house, ashamed of her marriage, ashamed of her pregnancy, ashamed of the passion that had led her so astray.

"What about Mother?" I ask. "Didn't you ever try to get in touch with her? To explain?"

My questions unnerve him, and he looks as dazed as if I had just rousted him out of Bougainville or Normandy. He wipes his face once more, wiping away the sweat brought on by hauling artillery up a mountain.

"I did try," he says, "I truly did. But just once. I wrote to her. Years afterwards. But it came back. From what you told me last evening, your grandmother was dead by then. And Martin, too. And you had moved away. I don't even know now what I said in the letter. I knew it was no good expecting her to marry me even if she was still single, even if she could forgive me. You know very well that in her books a divorced man was no different than a married man. But I wish now I had tried harder."

He removes his cap, rakes his fingers through his sweat-matted hair and then replaces the cap. "I would have liked to have had you for a daughter. I really would have."

I am as unnerved as he was earlier. I hear truth in his words, and when I look at him I see truth in his face. In that same face, I can also see traces of myself: nose not as straight as the Corrigan nose. Lips not as full as the Corrigan lips. Hair suggesting it was once black. Only the eyes are different. His are dark grey, the colour of a sky hunkering down for a rainstorm. Mine are Corrigan blue, the colour of the wild blueberries that grow on the hills behind the Cove.

"If you're thinking I got off scot-free, you're dead wrong," he says, inaccurately reading my thoughts. "Like I said a while ago, I lost my children, and I spent a lifetime trying to bury ghosts. And I never managed to get them buried. Or at least I never managed to keep them buried." He lets his breath out in a heavy sigh. "Sometimes I even think I'm the ghost."

He touches my hand with his index finger as if he is nudging me to pay attention. His finger barely skims my knuckles. My flesh burns.

"Do you know that ghosts are dead people who can't cross over because they have some unfinished sorrow? They can't get from here to there because of some incompleteness in this world, something unforgiven or unabsolved."

"I don't believe that," I counter, although a shudder passes through my body like the one that had wrapped itself around Philomena when she stood beside Uncle Ned's grave. Ed Strominski looks so flimsy it would be easy to believe that he has spent his life amongst ghosts or that he himself is a ghost. He looks so insubstantial it is easy to believe that the spirit world has sucked the soul out of him and turned him into this ramshackle old man whose face carries traces of my own. What is not easy to believe — what I don't want to believe — is that if I persist with my steadfast unforgiveness he will be forced to wander forever on this earth, forever in the company of deceased but not departed souls.

"Believe it or not," he says, "it's true nevertheless."

Again he looks away. I am certain he has returned to Bougainville or Normandy, or he may have gone back to the Cove. At any rate, when he speaks his voice sounds far away and years ago.

"I'd give anything to be able to undo some of the things I've done in my life and to do some of the things I never did. I'd give forty years of my life to be able to do that. Even more. That's the God's honest truth."

When I leave Arizona early Sunday morning, my emotions are gutted, splayed like a slaughtered sheep. But at least I have good news to carry back to Philomena. There is nothing lurking in the Strominski gene pool readying itself to spring out to harm her grandson.

Apart from our memories of Carmel, the only link between Ed Strominski and me is to be the knowledge that we shared in the burial of ghosts. Before I leave Arizona I offer him my forgiveness. It is a stingy, selfishly motivated forgiveness meant to allow him to cross over when his time comes. I want for him what he wants for himself: his bones to dry brittle under the relentless Arizona sun and his spirit to settle wherever spirits settle. I have no wish for ghostly sightings of him wandering through the Cove, shuffling along the foggy landwash, crisscrossing the manure-covered meadows while he waits upon absolution from the last of the Corrigan women.

Chapter Six

BY EIGHT-THIRTY Monday morning I am back at work, suffering only from climate shock. During the night an ice storm moved inland, and when I woke up it was to a city covered in icicles.

When the House of Assembly opens, it opens in an uproar, and the uproar continues throughout the day. Indeed, it is easy to predict that this uproar will continue until the House prorogues in mid-June. Part of it has to do with rumours revolving around Hibernia, the offshore oil-seeking project that is getting underway in the Grand Banks area. The juiciest of these is that workers from other provinces are going to be brought in to take over the most coveted jobs. Island workers lack the expertise to fill these jobs. Members from both the party in power and the opposition are demanding that institutions be set up to train Newfoundlanders and keep out workers from away.

Early on in the development of Hibernia, I had registered my concern over just such a problem, and at the time I proposed that the trade school in the Cove be enlarged for this advanced training. I used question period after question period to drive home the point that if the government wouldn't act immediately, qualified help would have to be imported and Newfoundland workers would be idle.

On top of the Hibernia situation, blame is being heaped on the government for not forcing the federal government to establish a two-hundred-mile offshore limit for foreign trawlers, which still gouge the northern cod despite the fact that the stocks are almost depleted.

Because I am my party's official fisheries critic, I am front and centre in the burgeoning conflict. This morning someone told me that late Friday afternoon, just after I left for Arizona, fishermen dumped their catches to protest the government's inaction. The fish they are catching are too small to fillet, and they are too small because foreign trawlers have scooped up anything bigger than a capelin. A moratorium is now being called for to keep the resource from being totally plundered.

The afternoon session opens as a Tory member discloses that "Burn Your Boat" protest rallies are being organized around the island, and he calls for a Royal Commission on the fishery. I shout out — at the risk of being called to order by the speaker — that fishermen cannot feed their families on Royal Commissions, that something constructive has be done. Applause bursts from both sides of the floor.

Later on in the afternoon, a group of fisherwomen and wives of fishermen sneak into the House as visitors. When they're all in the gallery, they stand and begin to sing protest songs for a way of life that is unjustly being taken from them. They don't stop even as they are being hustled from the House. Once outside, they give a loud rendering of "Ode to Newfoundland" and start chanting "Fisheries package — another kind of dole!" The whole House applauds them, too.

Just before the session ends for the day, the seal problem flares up, probably lit by the women's protest. It's a problem that keeps surfacing but never gets resolved. Fishermen and members on both sides of the floor view the ban on sealing and the now-enormous seal population as a major cause of the ruined inshore fishery. When this ban was enforced, the fishermen predicted the outcome, but no one paid attention. Now the problem is too vast to ignore, and hardly a day goes by that it isn't brought to the floor.

Fortunately for me, I no longer have to fight this problem alone. Conservatives as well my fellow Liberals have come alongside. In fact, the first person whom the speaker acknowledges is the Tory member from Capelin Head.

"Mr. Speaker," she says, "the Member from Capelin Head rises to tell you that there are no capelin heads in Capelin Head. There aren't any capelin heads because the seals have gobbled them up. And, Mr. Speaker, they've gobbled up the tails as well, and if we don't soon do something about culling those seals, there won't be any voters left in Capelin Head. The seals will have gobbled them up, too."

The members laugh so hard that the Speaker has to call for order several times. When the Member from Capelin Head begins again, she points out that between the yelping of the seal saviours from away and the unrestrained whelping of the seals, we're in big trouble. If the government doesn't hurry up and do something about this problem, she predicts, the people of Newfoundland, just like the cod, will become infested with parasites and worms from having to eat seal excrement. There won't be anything else left to eat — the seals will see to that.

Again laughter, again a call for order. She turns more serious. The government must counter the propaganda that the seals are being bludgeoned solely for their penises, which are then sent to Asia. And it must do so immediately. The government also must dispel the myth that seals weep for their killed offspring, the myth that inspires the "bleeding hearts." Tell the truth, she charges the House: seals shed copious tears, not out of sorrow, but to protect their eyes against the harsh, cold air.

Despite the day's commotion, the spring session holds a promise of good fortune for my party. There are definite signs that our period of dormancy is ending, signs that the Tories are falling into such disfavour with the voters that the next election, expected in the spring, will destroy their majority. In the foreseeable future, we will take back the government.

In the weeks before I went to Arizona, the notion of a Liberal leadership race had circulated, and it was understood that the new leader might well become premier. I was approached to allow my name to stand. Although I was flattered and honoured, my first reaction was to refuse, but after much encouragement from Greg and Brendan, I finally had agreed. My main concern over assuming the leadership — especially if this leadership were to be converted into premiership — was the increased amount of time I would have to spend away from home. Greg and Brendan both scoffed: they were quite capable of looking after both themselves and each other while I was away. Brendan assured me that he was so busy between his school work and his Altar Servers' Association duties that he would hardly know I was gone.

That Brendan has a full and busy life cannot be argued. Shortly after the New Year began, a young priest by the name of Tom Haley came to our parish, and he breathed new life into the Altar Servers' Association, a group of boys twelve and upwards who serve the altar during Mass. Brendan joined right after his twelfth birthday and he instantly became involved in one activity or another: bottle drives to make money for camping trips, food drives for the soup kitchens, visits to shut-ins, singsongs at the old age homes, jamborees.

From its onset, Brendan's newly acquired full life has caused the first serious dissension that Greg and I have experienced in our marriage. To say that Greg does not share my delight in Brendan's involvement in the association is at best an understatement.

"Why does it have to be an either-or situation?" Greg had demanded one evening when I had rather simple-mindedly asked, "Would you rather have him hanging around malls or going to the Association?"

"Why does it have to be either-or?" he had repeated irritably when my silence told him I was refusing to argue. "Isn't there a third option? He used to love playing hockey. He doesn't even play road hockey anymore. All I ever see of him now is the back of his neck as he goes tearing out the door to go to something or other for that association."

With no response from me, the dispute had ended there, and since I was leaving for Arizona the next day, there wasn't time to pick it up again.

When I leave the House at the end of my first day back, worn out by the uproar, I am feeling the effects of jet lag and the emotional drain of having met with Ed Strominski in Arizona, and I am looking forward to a peaceful supper and early to bed. Greg is already home in the kitchen, getting a salad underway. I can sense his tension by the arch of his shoulders as he stands by the sink, his back to the door. Almost before he says hello, he says, "Guess what? You won't believe this."

"Believe what?" I say, my own shoulders tensing.

"The firm gave me two tickets to that semi-pro hockey game tonight, but Brendan says he can't come with me. Father Tom has arranged for the Altar Servers' Association to go over to Holy Heart to see the play the students are putting on to raise money for gym equipment."

"Well, if he's already promised . . ." I stop in mid-sentence as Brendan races past the kitchen, announcing on his way by that Father Tom is in the driveway waiting for him. "Can't wait for supper," he calls out from the porch as he grabs his coat and tears out the door.

Brendan's hurried departure only fuels Greg's grievance, and long after Brendan has gone, he grumbles over and over again how the Altar Servers' Association is dominating Brendan's life.

"Like I've said before, we used to go to hockey games together. And like I said, he used to play road hockey with the guys on the street. He used to go skating with them. Now there's always this or that going on with that damn association. And what's even worse, you don't see anything wrong with what's going on. In fact, you encourage it."

Too tired to think up something original, I fall back on my hackneyed defence. "It's better than hanging around the malls."

"That same stupid comparison. As if there's only two choices, hanging around in the malls or hanging around with that priest. I want my son to have a touch of balance in his life, something you don't seem to be concerned over."

His tone implies that Brendan's life is so far out of balance that even hanging out in the malls would be a welcome leveller.

"And I *don't* want his life to be balanced? You make it sound as if I've been scheming to have him locked up in a monastery or something."

"I only said what I said," he snaps, the muscle in his jaw flexing, drawing it taut. "Take it whatever way you want."

Just at that moment the telephone rings and Greg goes to answer it. He has to go back to the office. The hockey ticket issue is left unresolved, like many others on this same subject. I go upstairs to the bathroom to see if a shower will revive my energy. I am bone weary — not only from the trip, not only from the day at the House of Assembly, but also from defending Greg to Brendan and Brendan to Greg. Under the pelting water I reflect that no matter which path I take, I am going to end up lost in the same forest. I think of a woman I once met when I lived in Montreal. Newly divorced, she had come to Montreal for a visit. She told me that her husband had been a US Marine and her son — their son — was a conscientious objector to the Vietnam war. Somewhere in the process of defending her husband to her son and her son to her husband, she had ended up losing the love and respect of both of them. It is not a prospect I relish for myself.

March folds into April and April folds gently into summer and summer folds into autumn. Seven months since I went to Arizona and met with my biological father. One year and eleven months since Hubert's death and a little over nine months from the time Brendan joined the Altar Servers' Association.

The days, the weeks, the months pass, little problems ebb and flow, but for the most part there are few creases or crinkles in our lives. They mirror the passing months, no unbridled highs, no unsettling lows. Even the conflict over the Altar Servers' Association appears to have reached *détente*. Greg tolerates Brendan's involvement in the association and Brendan manages to take enough time away from it to go to a few sports events with Greg.

The autumn of 1986 comes to us like all autumns on the Avalon Peninsula. It comes without strut or boast. No maple leaf reds, no chokecherry oranges, just here and there a few splashes of water birch yellow interspersed with the garnet clusters of berries that droop from the dogberry bushes. The South Side Hills in St. John's are a haze of magenta, the remains of withering blueberry bushes.

Philomena is well and adjusting to Hubert's death far better than we would have thought. Danny is still working in the lumber woods in British Columbia. Greg is in line for partnership in his firm. Brendan is busy and content. I am preparing myself for the leadership of my party.

Someone once said to me in the course of an otherwise unmemorable conversation that a family tragedy, especially one of cataclysmic proportion, is usually set in motion by the most improbable circumstance, the most innocuous situation, the most benign word or the most inoffensive statement. At the time I had agreed wholeheartedly. The remark brought to mind two brothers in the Cove by the name of O'Connor whose lives were forever changed by a word, by all accounts benign: "turnips." Apparently, one day as they sat across the supper table from each other, one O'Connor brother said to the other, "Turnips! Let's talk turnips," and thereby started a feud that got passed down through several generations, ending when one branch of the family dropped the "O" from O'Connor to distance themselves from the other branch.

Apparently, the brother who initiated the conversation had recently read an article in a farmer's almanac that someone had brought home from the States. The article said that for best results, crops should be rotated every so many years, and he, believing what he had read, suggested that they stop growing turnips for a few years and grow cabbage instead. The other O'Connor brother refused to go along with this idea. He maintained that for the past ten years they had grown wonderful turnips on their jointly owned piece of rocky land, and he saw no reason to make a change. Indeed, he said, he wasn't going to be persuaded by any folderol in a farmer's almanac printed in the United States. What, he asked of anyone who would listen, did people in the United States know about working a piece of hilly ground in Newfoundland? Sides were soon drawn, words were hurled, land was divided and brothers and cousins and nieces and nephews split apart, never to come together again.

One Wednesday evening as October is winding down, a tragedy in our family begins its slow, circuitous unfolding with the words "Here's the *Globe and Mail,*" and it keeps on unfolding until it breaks our hearts into pieces smaller than the putty mounds of a tinkers dam, finer than the ashes from a stick of wet spruce.

Greg, who is sitting at the kitchen table finishing off his second cup of coffee, pulls a newspaper out off his briefcase and passes it to me.

"Here's the *Globe and Mail,*" he says, handing over the neatly folded paper. "Don't throw it out. I haven't read it yet."

Greg and I are alone in the house, Brendan having already left with Father Tom to set up tables in the church hall for a bazaar that the Catholic Women's League is hosting. I take the newspaper from Greg's outstretched hand and go up to our bedroom, where I settle myself into the big rose-coloured chair by the window. I switch on the lamp beside the chair and proceed to organize the sections of the paper into the order in which I will read them. After the organization is complete, I begin reading. Half way down page one of the business section, I come upon a column that makes me gasp.

"Oh, my God," I exclaim to the empty bedroom — the Toronto

law firm that is the subject of the column is owned by my ex-father-in-law; my ex-husband became the senior partner. The column speculates about the fate of the dynasty-controlled firm now that the only son and senior partner is no longer there, he having been killed in a twin-engine plane crash in Northern Ontario.

"It's Leonard. That's Leonard. Oh my God, he was killed."

I jump up out of my chair to take the paper downstairs to show Greg, but then I quickly sit back down again, my legs too weak to hold me upright. That I am so affected by the news of Leonard's death perplexes me. Certainly it has nothing to do with residual love for him. Any love that Leonard and I had shared disappeared long ago — many, many months before the divorce proceedings had gotten underway. It had disappeared one argument at a time, one deception at a time, and particularly with one stabbing word at a time. In fact, on occasion Leonard had battered me with such wounding words that even yet when I recall them I feel as if I've been pierced.

In fairness to him, though, he had hurled the harshest words at me only at the end of the marriage. He had hurled them at a time when he desperately wanted the union dissolved and I desperately wanted it kept intact, convinced as I was that if the marriage dissolved, I, too, would dissolve, would melt into nothing like a snowman under an April sun.

As I continue to sit in my chair, unable or unwilling to go downstairs and share this news with Greg, I concentrate solely on Leonard. I need this time to myself to mourn a husband I did not love, to mourn a husband who, towards the end of the marriage, I did not even like. And as I let my thoughts run backwards to recall the Leonard of my marriage, I wonder what pressing business would have taken him to the sky over Kirkland Lake in weather that, according to the article, was unfit for flying. The Leonard of my marriage — the meticulous, exacting Leonard, the cautious, vigilant Leonard — would not have flown under such conditions.

I reluctantly accept that Monica, the "other woman," had transformed him into a caring, considerate person, a person who would be likely to say, "I promised I would be on hand for the meeting, so I can't let a little bad weather stop me." I reluctantly accept that under Monica's loving tutelage he might have become more impetuous, even a tad reckless. Perhaps even a mite less acerbic. And I reluctantly accept that I failed Leonard as grievously as he failed me. I failed him by never being able to make him more than he was, and he failed me by always being able to make me less than I was. In fact, whenever I am in a gathering of people and see a woman's body choke up at the approach of her husband, see her fidget with her hair or her rings or her nails, or hear her conversation slide away as he comes close, afraid she will say the wrong word or express an unsupportable opinion or be too solicitous or not solicitous enough, I recognize myself when I was Leonard's wife.

I reread the article several times to make certain I have the details correct, and, once I have calmed myself down, I go to tell Greg. In typical Greg fashion, compassionate and considerate always, he asks me whether I would like him to tell Brendan the news. He thinks that perhaps it would be easier for him than for me to pass it along, and he is right. Although I don't anticipate the news to make any impact upon Brendan — he has always known that I had been married to someone else before I married his father — it comforts me that Greg will tell him.

On the weekend we go out to the Cove, and I tell Philomena.

"God help his poor mother," she says, crossing herself. "There's no sorrow for a mother like the sorrow of a child going first." On the heels of this compassion, the implication of Leonard's death dawns on her. Her face lights up. "Sure, girl, the Lord have mercy on his soul and all, but it means yer now a sod widow, not a grass one. Now ye can have yer marriage blessed by the Church."

She rushes to make herself clear: she wants the blight removed from our marriage post-haste. The sooner Greg can be fully reinstated into the Church, the sooner her heart will be free of the bruise that our unsanctioned union has placed upon it. Apparently, the sooner her pride will be assuaged as well; she immediately launches into plans for the ceremony that will let everyone in the Cove know her son is returning to the fold. After years and years of illicit union, Greg and I can now properly be united, and after the ceremony she will put on a scoff in the Star of the Sea church hall the likes of which won't have been seen since her sister Madeline got married in Herring Head fifty years ago.

I quash her plans as gently as I can.

"Sorry, Mrs. Phil," I say, "but all that fuss is out. We're not having any of it." I speak firmly so as not to give her a wedge to help her wheedle me into giving in. "We don't want any fuss. We've already talked it over. We're going to get our marriage blessed in our own parish in St. John's."

I turn to Greg for his support. "Isn't that right? It's just going to be a very quiet affair."

He solidly confirms my plans, and then I elaborate upon them, adding that I have been thinking that we should ask Father Tom Haley to officiate. I'm certain Brendan will like that, especially since he will be our altar server.

"Did you mention to Brendan about serving the altar?" Greg asks, surprised that I am taking Brendan's participation for granted. "Did he agree?"

"I didn't ask him yet," I reply, equally surprised that he could even entertain the thought that Brendan might refuse to be our Mass server. "I'm just assuming. Why wouldn't he agree?"

Greg shrugs. "I don't know. It's just that lately he's changed so much. Can't take anything for granted with him anymore. Seems he has his own agenda." He shrugs again. "But if Mom comes in and we have this Father Tom he's so fond of, he'll agree. I don't see why not."

On Monday night, I arrive home from work before either Greg or Brendan, and I hurriedly prepare supper. My intention is to discuss the arrangements for the upcoming blessing of our marriage during the meal. And I want to broach serving the Mass to Brendan.

As a rule, Brendan gets home before Greg, and although my original plan was to wait until after supper and the three of us were seated at the table, I blurt out my request to Brendan as soon as he gets in the door.

"Dad and I were talking at your grandmother's yesterday, and we thought you might like to ask Father Tom to officiate at our marriage blessing. We can do that now because of my ex-husband's death, and we thought that, with you serving, you'd like to have Father Tom rather than another priest from the parish."

"No way! I'm not asking him," he retorts, his voice flat and his tone brooking no negotiation. "And I won't serve the altar for the Mass, either. A bunch of foolishness, that's what that is."

He tosses his book bag on a chair, slips from the room and hunkers down in front of the television in the den. Confounded by his reaction, I follow him.

"That was rude of you to stomp off like that. What's wrong with you? Did something bad happen at school?"

"Nothing's wrong. Why should anything be wrong? Right away you think something's wrong if I don't agree with you."

He barely takes his eyes from the television screen to acknowledge my presence, although I know he has no interest in the program. I cross the room and switch off the set, sit down opposite him and begin a cross-examination.

"Why don't you want to ask Father Tom? It would be nice. Especially with you serving on the altar. I thought you'd be delighted."

"Who said I was serving?" he asks, continuing to stare at the blackened television screen. "How many times do I have to tell you, I won't serve on the altar when you get remarried or have your marriage blessed or whatever it is you're having done."

"What do you mean, you won't serve on the altar?" I am sure I am not hearing him correctly. "Certainly you'll serve on the altar. Of course you will."

"Of course I won't."

"You know you will. Stop carrying on like this! I don't have time for such foolishness."

"It's not foolishness. And I'm not doing it. And that's final."

I realize he is not parrying. He is dead serious.

"Why not do this for us? What's your reason? You must have a reason."

"Just because. That's all. I don't have to spell out a reason." He switches the subject. "I'm out of drafting paper. I have to go to the Avalon Mall. Can you or Dad drive me there after supper?" He throws this out scrappily, as if he expects me to say no.

I tell him his father will probably drive him while I clean up the supper dishes. Although I can easily drive him, I am hoping he will open up to Greg along the way and tell him why he is so negative. I switch the television back on and return to the kitchen.

At the supper table, Brendan surprises me by reopening the subject of serving our Mass. As soon as we sit down to eat, he turns to Greg and says, "Mom wants me to serve on the altar when you go to get your marriage redone, but I said no, I won't. Now she's all mad at me. Won't even drive me to the mall."

Unprepared, Greg flounders. "What! What's gone on?" He looks to me for an explanation.

"That's it," I reply. "Just what he said. Except the bit about the mall. I never said I wouldn't drive him. I said you'd drive him while I cleaned up."

Scrambling together the bits of information that Brendan and I have parcelled out to him and adding to this the loaded atmosphere, Greg asks, "What's going on, Brendan? How come you won't serve on the altar? You do it every Sunday. Every funeral. Every wedding. Why not for us? You know what it would mean to us. And to your grandmother."

"A bunch of foolishness!" Brendan repeats, as surly as before. "That's what the Altar Servers' Association is. And serving on the altar is foolishness, too. Never should have joined. I'm going to quit."

"Oh, no, you're not," I cut in tightly and straighten up in my chair to give authority to my words. "You know our rules. No flitting from one thing to another. You commit to an activity, you commit for a year. That's what you agreed to."

"But if he feels so strongly," Greg begins, eager to let him off the hook. He is about to say we can make an exception in this case. A glower from me heads him off.

"One year commitment. Isn't that what we agreed to?" I say pointedly. Greg, after all, was the one who set the rules after Brendan joined the Cub Scouts for all of two weeks. His uniform was still on order when he quit. "No quitting before you've given something an honest try."

Trapped, Greg backs down. "If you don't want to serve on the altar when we get our marriage blessed," he says, "that's okay. But there's no need to quit altogether. Maybe just slack off. No need to spend every waking minute with the association." He is determined not to display his delight at this happy turn of events.

"Can we go now?" Brendan interrupts, not committing himself to either a yes or a no about serving our Mass or about staying in the association. "I'm out of drafting paper."

"Sure, Sport," Greg replies, as eager as Brendan to stop the squabbling. He hunts up his car keys, and as he goes out the door he gives me a bewildered look, stumped by Brendan's intense reaction to our request.

When they return from the mall, Brendan bolts to his bedroom, saying he has lots of homework to do. Even before he is out of earshot, Greg and I exchange another look, and the second I hear the bedroom door closing, I ask, "Did he open up to you? Did he say anything?"

"Nothing. Not a thing. I tried to get him to talk. All he'd say was, 'Stupid rules,' and when I asked whose stupid rules, he said, 'Yours and Mom's.' Then he clammed up. Maybe he's ashamed of us getting married by the Church at this late date. Maybe it embarrasses him. Maybe he doesn't want his friends to know."

"Probably that's it," I agree, eager to grasp at an explanation that is both reasonable and reasonably inoffensive. "And then again, maybe it's because he's almost thirteen. Lately he's been quick to take offence. And he's gotten sullen. My grandmother used to say she hoped some day I'd have a daughter to make my life a Calvary like I made hers. Maybe a son can do the same thing."

Greg laughs. "Maybe it's payback time for both of us. Mom said much the same thing to me."

Greg goes back to his office to catch up on unfinished work. Before he leaves, he says reassuringly, "I'll talk to him before I drop him off at school tomorrow morning. Maybe Father Haley chastised him. Told him to hurry up or something. You know what a slowpoke he can be. He might have gotten chewed out for being late."

This seems to be such a strong probability that as soon as Greg leaves I am able to put Brendan out of my mind and go into the den to finish up leftover work of my own, especially to bone up on a brewing illegal strike by the Association of Public Employees. But after several minutes of aimless paper shuffling, I realize I can't put Brendan out of my mind after all, so I shove the papers back into my briefcase and go up to his room.

I knock on his door. No answer. He can't be asleep because it is much too early. I knock louder.

"Go away! I'm sleeping." His voice sounds muffled, as if it is coming from underneath the covers.

"I want to talk to you," I say, keeping my tone light, trying to withhold censure from my voice. "I'm counting to ten and then I'm coming in." I actually count to twelve, open the door and walk in.

"Did I say come in?" he demands, pulling the sheets away from his mouth just far enough to let the words escape.

I don't switch on the light. I don't have to. Moonlight slants in through his window, cutting a soft shaft through the blackness before dropping down on his bed. He lies crouched into himself, the bedclothes bundled around him as if he is trying to get warm. But the room is sweltering; its windows face west and the afternoon sun has been unusually hot.

I ignore his rudeness, go over and sit beside him on the rumpled bed. I pull the blankets away from his face and reach out my hand to brush his hair back from his forehead. Sensing my intention, he whips his head to the opposite side of the pillow.

"What's wrong, Brendie?" I ask, reverting to my pet name for him. "You act as if you're mad all the time. It can't all be about our marriage getting blessed."

"I'm sleepy," he grumbles. "Can't you see I'm sleepy? And don't call me Brendie. I hate that foolish name."

He pulls the sheets back over his head, hoping to discourage me. I make one last effort to get him to talk, speaking louder to penetrate the covers. "I'll talk this over with Dad, but I'm sure he'll agree. I've been thinking. Instead of us going to the church for the blessing, we'll make it even simpler. We'll get Father Tom to come to the house."

He sits bolt upright. "No way!" he shouts. I feel as if he has struck me, and I jump to my feet. The bedclothes have fallen away from his body, and I see that he hasn't even bothered to remove the shirt he wore to school. Although I make no mention of his being in bed with his clothes on, I'm wondering whether he even bothered to take off his jeans.

I ask angrily, "What's going on with you anyway? Why are you so stubborn?"

"I won't be here when he comes," he says, ignoring my question and staring straight at me, daring me to contradict the pronouncement he is about to make. "And I *am* quitting the altar. I'm not going to serve on it ever again. I've decided on that, and you can't make me change my mind. Christopher O'Connell quit this week. His father said if he wants to quit it's fine with him."

Refusing to be manipulated by the intimation that his friends have far more reasonable parents that he has, I snap. "Well, your quitting is not fine with us. Mr. O'Connell has his rules and we have ours."

"I knew that's what you'd say. I told Christopher that's what you'd say. But I'm quitting anyway." He plops back down in bed and pulls the bedclothes over his head again, allowing just enough space to mumble that he is sleepy and wants me to leave. Bewildered and frustrated, I do his bidding, making certain the door is closed tight so the light in the hall won't seep in.

Greg is home by the time I go downstairs. Like me, he was unable to concentrate. I unfold my conversation with Brendan.

"Let's drop the whole thing about getting the marriage blessed. It's embarrassing to him," Greg suggests. "And for once can't we bend the rules? Can't we let him quit if he wants to so badly?"

Fresh from the scene upstairs, I yield a little. "I'll go along with postponing having the marriage blessed. It was mostly for Philomena anyway. I'll let you square it with her."

"What about letting him quit? Just this once, let's go back on our rules. The world won't self-destruct because we bent a rule. And it's not like he wanted to quit without giving it an honest try."

I have often heard him use such persuasiveness on juries, judges and prosecuting attorneys. I counter with a compromise. "We'll ask him to hang in until the end of the month. If he still wants to quit, I'll go along with it. That will give enough time for the influence of Christopher's quitting to wear off."

"Good," he says. "Let's go tell him right now." He grabs my hand and tugs me in the direction of the stairs. "Let's tell him right now. Maybe this'll get him back to his old self again."

But it doesn't have any impact on him at all. Because he never had any intention of either serving the Mass during our marriage blessing or of continuing with the Altar Servers' Association, he has no reason to be grateful for our compromise, and he is quick to let us know as much.

Chapter Seven

ALTHOUGH WE HAVE MET George O'Connell at a few church functions, we are only nodding acquaintances, and we are surprised the next evening when he and his son Christopher appear at our door. Because George is recently widowed, I assume he wants to discuss Christopher's quitting the association with us, and I surmise that Christopher has told him that Brendan is quitting. Brendan had used this ruse on us a couple of times, and I had used it myself many times on Grandmother.

As soon as we settle in the den I go to the bottom of the stairs and call up to Brendan that Christopher has arrived. When several minutes pass and there is no sign of him, Greg, thinking he must not have heard me, also calls upstairs. "Hey, Brendan! Christopher's here. Come on down."

Within a few minutes Brendan comes into the den, slowly and hesitantly, and the instant he sees that Christopher's father is also in the room, his face blanches. His eyes widen in fear. He hovers near the door, ready for flight. My stomach knots with apprehension. I now know that this visit is not about Christopher's leaving the Altar Servers' Association. The air in the room fills with tension. The boys must have gotten into some kind of mischief. But what kind of mischief would occasion such fear?

"Come on in, Brendan," Greg says, forcing Brendan to come all the way into the room. "You know Mr. O'Connell, don't you?"

Brendan nods uncomfortably towards George and mumbles a barely audible "Hi." He quickly crosses the floor and stands in the opposite doorway, the one that leads to the kitchen, as if he doesn't intend to stay and is just waiting for the attention to move away from him so he can leave.

George O'Connell's firm voice squelches that idea. "Stay, Brendan! Come sit! Whatever I'm going to say to your parents, I want you to hear, too."

Brendan slides himself down on the edge of a chair near the door. He looks so distraught my insides begin to churn, and I start forming excuses, justifications and alibis for whatever misdeed is going to be laid at his feet.

George clears his throat and looks from Greg to me. "I'm here about this priest, Tom Haley."

My hastily concocted excuses to justify a schoolyard fracas are instantly shredded. Whatever the infraction is, and I now believe it has to do with impertinence or disrespect to Father Haley, it is definitely more serious than name-calling or a tussle that got out of hand.

George moves to the edge of his chair, like Brendan, ready for flight. He clears his throat again. "I didn't know what to do except come over here." He turns towards Greg. "In fact, I half expected you to be on my doorstep instead of the other way around. I'm sure you feel like I do. That fellow should be drawn and quartered. I was going to go see him myself before coming here, but I was afraid I'd kill him if I got my hands on him and if there was no one around to stop me." He pummels the palm of one work-hardened hand with the knuckles of the other.

Greg and I stare at him so blankly that he turns to Brendan, who looks as if he is going to throw up. "You didn't tell them, did you Brendan? You told me yesterday that you'd tell them tonight." Brendan is silent, his face desolate. "We have to tell them, Brendan. We can't let it go on any longer."

"Tell us what?" I demand, getting to my feet. My stomach begins to heave, buckling in upon itself in preparation for certain pain.

"What's up? What is it, George?" The tremor in Greg's voice does nothing to pacify my stomach. "What's going on?"

Brendan's head is bowed so low it almost touches his knees. Christopher is squirming and savagely biting his nails. George, who has continued to sit on the edge of his chair, stops pummelling his palm with his fist, stands up, clears his throat and says in a do-or-die manner, "I don't want to be the one to bring this news. It's . . . well, it's . . . it's about Haley. He fooled around with Christopher. And with Brendan. I wormed the truth out of Christopher yesterday."

I look at Brendan, hoping for some sign that George is building something out of nothing. Brendan's eyes never leave the floor.

"Fooled around?" Greg repeats. "What do you mean, fooled around? You mean he was carrying on with them in the sacristy? Acting the fool?"

"No!" George shouts, as if loudness will make his meaning clear. He rams his hands in his pockets, takes them out and shoves them through his hair, lets out a heavy breath, and then coughs up the message he came to deliver. "Not acted the fool. He *fooled around* with them. He jumped them. He's been jumping them. He's a queer box. A young boy queer box. That's what he is."

"No!" Greg yelps, jerking backwards as if he has been pole-axed.

I drop back down into my chair and grab its sides to keep from tumbling to the floor. I feel as if I am careening downhill, my legs trying to outrun the force of gravity pulling me to the ground. No! No! No! I can feel the words strangling in my throat. I can hear them echoing inside my skull. But no sound leaves my lips.

Greg recovers first. He gets up, crosses the floor in one hurried stride and crouches in front of Brendan, who, like Christopher has shrunk into himself and is staring at the floor. "Tell me it's not true, Brendan," he beseeches. "Tell me!"

I know he wants Brendan to say George is mistaken, that it had only happened to Christopher, because that is what I want to hear as well.

"It's true," Brendan murmurs, never raising his eyes.

Greg drops back on his heels, covers his face with his hands and rocks back and forth. "Oh God! Oh God! Oh Jesus Almighty! Help us! Help us! Help us!"

Brendan's shoulders slump even further. His head drops even lower. He begins to whimper. I stumble across the room and squeeze in between Greg and Brendan. Although pain more searing than childbirth is arcing through my body, making me wish I could drop to the floor and die, I put my arms around Brendan and murmur meaningless calming words and non-words. "Shh! Shh! It's all over now. It's all over."

Greg leaps up, his anger revived by my ridiculous comforting. His eyes, glazed with pain, bore into mine. "Stop saying that! Stop that foolishness! It's not over! It'll never be over!" He clenches and unclenches his fists and then lets his mouth spew out his fury, sounding more like Danny than himself. But Danny's words never held such vehemence.

"That black-hearted son of a bitch. I'm going over to the rectory right now to beat the hell out of him," he shouts. "If I get my hands on him, I'll strangle that scum-eating pervert. I'll rip the collar off his neck. And then I'll go to the archbishop and tell him to get that piece of tripe out of our parish before daylight."

He continues to clench and unclench his fists, savouring the thought of his knuckles connecting with Father Tom Haley's flesh. He starts for the door, patting his pants pockets for his car keys and wallet.

Brendan throws off my arms, jumps to his feet to block Greg's way. "No! No! Please Dad, no!" he shrieks. "Please don't go over there! Please!"

"Why not?" Greg shouts back, pushing him aside. "For the love of God, why not? I'm not going to bed this night until I've torn that son of a bitch to shreds."

Christopher begins to cry, whimpering against his father's sleeve.

Brendan shouts and cries and pleads all at once, tearing at my arm. "Please Mom! Please Mom! Stop him. Please stop him! Please!"

"Calm down! Calm down!" George O'Connell shouts at all of us. No one pays any heed, especially Greg, oblivious to everything except his own fury. He takes a step towards the door. I vault upwards and stand in front of him, using my body as a barricade. "You're not going near him!" I shout. "Not tonight! Get control of yourself! This isn't about you. It's about Brendan. Do what he asks!"

As if I have punched him, as if I have kicked him in the stomach and knocked the wind out of him, Greg's hands fall to his sides, and he groans as he drops into a chair beside the door. He looks so beaten I want to put my arms around him, but Brendan's need is greater. He is standing behind his father, tears streaming down his face, mouth gaping. I go to him and put my arm around his shoulder. He doesn't squirm away as he ordinarily would have done, embarrassed at being mothered in the presence of a friend.

Greg remains wilted. He looks to where Brendan is cowering in the shelter of my arm and asks, from the bottom of his soul, "Why, Brendan? Why did we have to hear it from other people? Why couldn't you tell me yourself?" Although his every word accuses the son of having failed the father, the anguish underlying his words recognizes that the father may have failed the son. "Why did you keep this from me?"

Brendan moves out from beneath my arm. He slowly rubs the tears out of his eyes with the heel of his hand, first one eye, then the other, stalling. I am reminded of the times when, as a child in the Cove, I had hoped the sky would fall so I, Poor Carmel's Tessie, wouldn't have to answer questions regarding the whereabouts of Poor Carmel.

"Because they said I'd get everyone in trouble. And I'd get in trouble, too. Big trouble. If I told. They said . . ."

"*They?*" Greg interrupts.

"Willie Farrell and Father Tom."

"Willie Farrell? Who is he?" Greg demands. "Who else is involved?" He wants an immediate enumeration of all of those he will have to tear apart.

"Just Willie. He's in the association. He's almost fifteen. I'm afraid of him."

"Willie Farrell said he'd beat the shit out of us if we told," Christopher says. He sniffles and adds dismally, "And he probably will, too. He even beats up his own dog."

"And this . . . Father Tom? What about *him*? What did *he* say? Did *he* threaten you?" His voice is hopeful; it would be even more justification for beating him up.

In fractured sentences and phrases and in between rubbing his face and pulling his ear, Brendan relates Father Haley's reaction. "He told me I would bring scandal on everyone. On you. And Grandma. Even the Church. A mortal sin. That's what I had committed. A worse sin than . . . you know . . . a worse sin than what he wanted us to do. I said I didn't care, I was going to tell if . . . you know . . . if the stuff didn't stop, and he said okay, it would stop. But it didn't."

Christopher rushes in to verify Brendan's confession. "That's right! I heard him. And he said the same thing to me. He said sex sins are sins of impurity. God forgives them quicker than other sins. But people don't. He told me they'd call me a pervert because I had committed the sin of sodomy, and when I asked him what that meant, he said it meant I had to keep the parties quiet."

"Parties?" Greg interrupts. "Parties?"

Christopher looks at his father. "That's what he called our meetings. Parties. He said there'd be hell to pay if I told." Expecting his father to chide him, he repeats, "That's exactly what he said, 'hell to pay.'"

But if George ever had the will to scold Christopher it has now left him. He slumps in his chair, stunned mute. Christopher blurts more details in a helter-skelter fashion, as if now is the one and only time he will have to unburden himself.

"He asked me if I remembered my catechism, and I said yes,

and then he asked if I knew why God had destroyed the cities of Sodom and Gomorrah, and I said I didn't remember that part, and he said God would be so mad if we brought scandal on the Church by telling about the parties that he might even destroy St. John's like He destroyed Sodom and Gomorrah. I said I didn't care, I was still going to get out of the association, and when I came home I looked up in the catechism about sodomy, but it didn't say what it was except that the sin of Sodom was one of the five sins that cried to heaven for vengeance. But I figured out for myself that sodomy was what we were doing."

He hauls back into himself and waits for the adults to make the next move. But the adults are too clobbered to even exchange glances. Although I have lost all sense of time, it seems that a lot of it passes before George pushes himself out of his chair and makes ready to leave.

"I've got to get back home," he says in the weighted manner of a man having too many responsibilities. "My boss is supposed to call me about a job he's bidding on. He wants me to head up the carpenter work." He turns to Greg. "Why don't you come over to see me later on tonight? We've got to decide how we're going to handle this." He adds, deferring to Greg's lawyer know-how, "Whatever you want to do will be okay with me."

As soon as the three of us are alone, Brendan threatens that if the news of the parties gets out into the open, he will never go to school again. In fact, he will never leave the house again. He might even jump off Hickman's Wharf.

"I swear to you," he says with such desperation that I have no doubt he means every word, "I'll run away. If you lock my bedroom door, I'll jump through the window."

"Don't talk ridiculous!" Greg almost shouts. "This has to be stopped. And right away! If we have to go public, we have to go public. That's final!"

He sees Brendan's stricken face and immediately retrenches, hastily manufacturing an air of quiet and calm. "Mr. O'Connell and I are going to talk over how we should approach this. That's all. Should we go to the archbishop first? Should we go to Haley first and let him know we know? Should we . . ."

"No!" Brendan shrieks. "Don't go over there! Don't get into a fight with him."

Greg's loosely covered fury almost surfaces again. "Who said anything about going over there? I'm cooled down now. I'm not going to do anything foolish. I'm not going to give him any reason to sue me." He spitefully tacks on, "If there's any suing to be done, I'll be the one to do it."

Less than an hour later, Greg leaves to go to George O'Connell's house, and Brendan and I sit silently at the kitchen table, neither of us meeting the other's eyes, neither of us knowing what to say. Brendan makes no attempt to touch the bedtime snack of brownies and milk I put out for him. However, he is the one who finally breaks the silence.

"It won't get out, will it?"

"I don't see why it should." I answer him too quickly because I'm not at all certain of what is going to happen when Greg and George get their heads together. "I think Dad and Mr. O'Connell will take it to the archbishop, and the archbishop certainly won't want it splattered across the *Evening Telegram*."

"Okay. That's good." Relieved enough to reach for a brownie, he settles back in his chair.

"When did these *parties* take place?" I ask, driven to want details but cowering from them even before they are supplied.

"Different times."

"For instance."

"The weekend we went camping."

Although queasiness overwhelms me, I continue to mine for specifics. "And?"

"The time we had the bottle drive. We went back to the rectory afterwards. His housekeeper was away. And when we went to the jamboree on Witless Bay Line."

I swallow back a wave of nausea. It doesn't take much memory scraping to make me realize I had been the one who had insisted on his going to that jamboree. "Is that why you didn't want to go?"

He takes a swallow of milk. With thumb and finger he pushes brownie crumbs into a huddle on the table. He answers without taking his eyes from the crumbs. "Yeah. But you made me go, remember? You said it would do me the world of good."

Each question, each answer makes me agonizingly aware that I have contributed to the scourging of my own son. I have aided and abetted his tormentor. Didn't I bake cookies for sales to raise money for the trips out of town? Drive Brendan to and from these outings? Insist that he go when he balked, when he gave lame reasons for not wanting to take part?

"I want to go to bed now," Brendan says suddenly, sensing my horror and self-disgust, "I don't want to talk anymore."

After he leaves the kitchen I remain at the table, mercilessly flogging myself for helping Tom Haley snare my son into sexual abuse. I ask myself questions I don't want answered. Why had I been so slack? Why had I been so inattentive? Why had I given my time to seal overpopulation, cod underpopulation, the lack of work in the Cove and all those other crises with such passion that I neglected to notice trouble brewing for my child? A mother should have felt a jab of anxiety. A needle prick of distrust. A thimbleful of suspicion. A *good* mother surely would have.

Nausea overtakes me, and I rush to the bathroom to empty my stomach. Sister Rita's voice reaches me there as I squat on the tile floor, my head hanging over the toilet bowl. I am seven years old, and she is teaching a lesson on the Agony in the Garden. "Children," she is asking, "have you any idea how much pain your heart would have to endure in order to sweat blood?" Along with the others, I shake my head, not having the faintest notion of how much pain a body would have to endure before it would be manifested externally in the form of sweated blood. I only know it must be a staggering amount.

When she looks up and down the five rows of wooden desks and sees not even one head nodding, she flicks her waist-length black veil over her shoulders as she does when she is making an infallible statement. "Of course you don't. Only the Saviour knows, the Saviour Who suffered so much pain that it is called the Agony in the Garden. Thank God, none of you will ever know that much pain. None of you will ever come close to enduring that much pain, knowing that much agony."

I push myself away from the toilet and look at the palms of my hands, certain I will see blood. But they are stain free.

Greg returns from George O'Connell's house shortly before nine. If he looked beaten and broken before he left, those words don't even begin to describe his appearance when he returns. His face is chalk-grey, and he slouches in his clothes, much like Danny, only Greg's slouch is from defeat.

We sit at the kitchen table and talk quietly so as not to let Brendan hear us. We know he is awake because he has made several trips to the bathroom even in the short while since Greg came home. This hollowed-out carcass of the man he was a few hours earlier tells me he learned more details about the abuse from George, that Christopher opened up to his father on the way home. I share with him that Brendan confided the times and places to me.

"We tried phoning Haley," he informs me. "We got talking and got so fired up we couldn't wait for the archbishop to do something. But we had no luck, got his housekeeper. She lied, I could tell by the hesitant way she spoke. Said he wasn't home. He must have told her not to let George or me through."

"But how would he know why you were calling?"

"He knew. Sure as I'm sitting here, he knew. And he knew because Willie Farrell told him."

On the way home George had stopped at a corner store so Christopher could pick up a carton of milk. Willie Farrell happened to be in the store at the time, and he had sidled up to Christopher and said, "I saw you and your father going into Brendan Slade's house. You better not have told them anything, or you'll get your face beat in." Greg and George surmised that Willie had warned Father Tom.

"Probably for the best," I say, for the lack of something better. "Neither you nor George are in a fit state to go near the rectory tonight. And besides, you promised Brendan you wouldn't."

"You're probably right. Like I said, we had no intention of going over there. But as we got to talking, it stuck in our craws that he was having a peaceful evening while we were in such a mess. We just wanted him to have to suffer through the night, knowing the jig was up. I never knew I had so much anger in me. Dad used to say you never know a man until you've spent a summer in a fishing dory with him. Now I'd change that to 'you never know a man until someone has hurt his child.'" Once more, he clenches and unclenches his fists. "I still want to tear him apart with my bare hands. I want to hear the sound of my fists connecting with his face. And George feels the same way. But I should know better. Violence isn't the answer. That's why I finally convinced George to let the law take its course."

"Law?" I fairly screech. "What do you mean, let the law take its course? You're not involving the law! I won't let you! We promised Brendan . . ."

"I never promised I wouldn't involve the law. I said I'd do whatever had to be done." But he knows he is splitting hairs because his eyes look almost as sad as Danny's. "Tess, dear, we can't just shuffle this off as if it never happened. It wouldn't be right." Seeing me recoil, he entreats, "We have to, Tess! When we couldn't get hold of Haley, George and I did some serious talking. And we can't put this solely in the hands of the archbishop. Just shipping Haley off somewhere else isn't the answer. The crime against the boys needs to be validated for their sakes. And there's other people's sons . . ."

"No!" I scream, forgetting to keep quiet. "I don't care about other people's children. Just Brendan."

"Can't you see, Tess, if we go to the palace and they send Haley up to that treatment place in Ontario — that place where they send all the scoundrel priests and the high-class drunks and perverts — he'll get the quick fix, and in a year he'll be back in some parish working his perversion on other altar boys."

"Toronto!" I say, my mind rapidly forming defences. "Yes, I remember now, that's where they sent Father O'Riley to dry out, someplace in Toronto. It worked for him. He doesn't touch the stuff anymore."

"It might work for boozers," Greg concedes, "but not for sex perverts. I've seen too many of them in the courtroom."

His indignation and outrage and agitation escalate, and he gets up and paces the floor. His voice, however, remains as controlled as if he were in the courtroom. As he walks back and forth between the stove and the table, outlining for my benefit why treatment isn't an option, he could have been performing before a jury.

"Are you aware that well-heeled perverts — the priests and the doctors and the professors, not your dirty old men — usually get away with their crimes by saying they're going for treatment. They get a little counselling here, a little pep talk there and bingo! They see the light. Go through an epiphany or something. All cured. As right as rain. Next thing you know they're back in the courtroom for having ruined another child or two or four or fifteen." He turns to me, leaving a last thought with the jury. "I can't have the destruction of other children on my conscience, Tess. I just can't. And I don't see how you can either."

"Easy. Because I can't have the destruction of my son on my conscience."

Greg's eyes turn bright with anger. He straightens up, full of fight.

Uncharacteristically, he pounds his fist on the table and shouts, "Don't you dare insinuate that I don't care about Brendan! Don't you dare!" He hesitates only momentarily before saying what he knows will bury an axe in my heart. "And bear in mind that if it wasn't for you he wouldn't be in this mess in the first place. You wanted him in that damn association, not me. You thought you had found another Dennis Walsh. Mr. Perfect Priest. You thought if Brendan hung around Haley, he'd turn out to be just like Dennis Walsh."

Now I am the one who staggers back. Now I am the one who yelps.

Instantly contrite, Greg reaches out to touch me. I flinch. He sees the flinch.

"I'm sorry. I'm so sorry." He dives his hands deep into his pockets and begins pacing the floor again, mumbling, "God Almighty, what's getting into me, I'm so tormented I'm losing my sanity."

He comes and stands in front of me, his eyes pleading. "I didn't mean that. I shouldn't have said that. We've got to keep our wits. We've got to stay focused. We can't waste our energy tearing each other apart."

"I'm not tearing you apart. You're the one who's doing the tearing apart."

"I know, I know. I had no right." He takes several deep breaths. "Tess," he says, pulling out a kitchen chair so that he is sitting opposite me, "you're such an innocent about this. You keep thinking it will all pass away. That it's just a little blip in Brendan's life. A hug and a kiss and a brownie and everything is made better. But that's not the reality of it. I've seen too much of this muck in the courtroom.

"It never goes away for the victims. You've got to understand that. Never! Never! Never! I see the same youngsters ten years later downtown, no longer youngsters, making their way to the taverns, the heart and soul reamed out of them by some son of a bitch like this Father Pervert. They're going nowhere. They're lost souls, the lot of them. Some of them can't keep on dealing with the pain; they just throw themselves over a wharf. Others take the slow way out with drugs and booze. I've seen it all."

He leans in close to me and asks a question that my brain would never be able to form into a thought nor my voice put into words.

"What if we can't salvage Brendan? What if you find out that love and brownies aren't enough. What if . . ."

The sentence hangs in the air, the words too terrible to utter.

"What I don't understand, though," he says, "is why he never confided in us. If he didn't want the situation to continue, why didn't he come to me?"

I snap to Brendan's defence. "I can't believe you said that. You're hinting that he might have wanted to be involved in that mess. He was trapped, Greg, trapped. Can't you see that? He's deathly afraid of Willie Farrell. And, like Christopher said, if they were to tell anyone, they would get so many other people in trouble. They didn't know which way to turn."

At that very instant both of us hear the floor above us creak. Startled, we look towards the ceiling. Awareness dawns on Greg first. He moans, "Oh God! Oh God! Oh God! He's been in our room listening. I've got to explain."

He rushes upstairs. I follow closely behind. Brendan is back in his room. Through his closed door we can hear his muffled sobbing. We go in and crouch beside his bed, our arms enclosing his hunched body.

He pulls his face out from under the bedclothes. Between sobs he says, "I heard you fighting. You're ashamed of me. I knew you would be. That's why I wouldn't tell."

"No, Sport. No, Sport. I'm not ashamed of you. I wish I could take back what I said. It's just that I don't understand how this could have gone on as long as it did."

"I should have lied," Brendan sobs. "I should have said I wasn't in on it. Then you wouldn't be fighting."

"No, you did the right thing to tell the truth. And Mom and I aren't fighting. We're just arguing, more like explaining."

Greg knows he is skimming the truth and he looks towards me, soliciting help with his lie.

"Just wanting to make sure you won't be bothered by Father Tom again," I say, neither supporting nor contradicting Greg. "Dad has his way of making sure and I have mine. We just don't agree."

"What will they do to him?" Brendan's muffled voice is small, tentative. "You said something about the law. I heard you."

"He'll probably go to jail," Greg says. "If it gets into the courts."

"Noooo!" Brendan wails. "Noooo! I don't want him to go to jail. I don't want anything bad to happen to him. He's really nice. Just that one bad thing."

"Nice? You call that child molester *nice?* That pervert!"

Brendan pulls himself up in bed. "Yes, he *is* nice," he says, his voice no longer tentative. "And he is good. He's just bad in that one way."

Greg reins in a nasty retort as Brendan continues, as if now he is the adult and Greg is the angry child who needs to be reasoned with. "He is good, Dad. If you got to know him, you'd see that. He does lots of good things. And it's my fault, too. I should have told. But I was afraid of Willie Farrell. Willie's father is really poor, and Tom used to give Willie money, so Willie wanted to keep on getting money."

He falls back down in bed, the futility of explaining evident to him. "I wish now I had said that Christopher was lying. I wish I had said, 'Speak for yourself, Christopher. Don't try and drag me into anything.' If I had my time back that's just what I'd do."

"That's foolish talk, Brendan," Greg says. "That's stupid talk. That excuse for a priest has to be dealt with. He belongs behind bars, and I'm going to see that he gets there."

Brendan emits another shrill "no" and rolls back and forth on the bed in agony. "I wish I could die. I wish I could die right this minute."

"It's going to be all right, Brendan," I say. "Maybe he won't go to jail. Maybe he'll just have to do community work. I've heard of that kind of thing happening. Maybe Dad and Mr. O'Connell will decide not to take it to court. Maybe they'll get the archbishop to send him away to get cured. Or maybe they'll send him up to . . . "

Greg gets up from where he has been squatting beside the bed. Without even saying goodnight he leaves the room. My pacifying lies are more than he can stomach.

After we are in bed, Greg and I continue to argue, although we make certain our voices are low enough to be out of Brendan's earshot.

"Why can't you settle for letting them send him to that place in Toronto?" I ask for what now must be the tenth time since George O'Connell came to our house. "Maybe he *can* be helped. You're not a doctor. Maybe the scare will be enough to stop him from ever doing the like of this again."

"When hell freezes over, that's when he'll be helped."

He raises himself on his elbow and looks directly into my face. I can almost feel the heat of his eyes. Certainly, I can feel the heat of his words.

"How do you expect Brendan to be able to live with himself if he doesn't show enough backbone to break this wide open? Other boys are going to be molested if he doesn't do something about it. Don't you think he should consider someone else besides himself and that pervert? And don't you think you should stop looking at this disaster through rose-coloured glasses?"

Because I surmise he is right and because I do not want him to be right, I savage him with a counterattack. "My oh my, how moral we are. I think it's your male pride, not your civic duty or high morals that are getting singed here. He despoiled your son, so vengeance is mine, saith Greg Slade."

"And you want to give Haley a break because he reminds you of Dennis Walsh. If Father Perv was some fat old fart, I bet you'd have a different take on things. You'd be telling Brendan he'd have to have the strength to do what is right."

"You're dead wrong," I retort, not at all sure he is. "And I'll thank you not to sully Dennis's name by dragging it in to this sordid mess."

We tear at each other for the best part of an hour. Our good night is strained and perfunctory. Neither of us makes a move to kiss the other. We push out to the far edges of our queen-size bed in case, in turning over, our bodies might inadvertently touch.

Chapter Eight

IN THE MORNING the accusations and denials of the night before hang suspended between us. We pussyfoot around them at breakfast, excessively, coldly polite, each of us aware that what our son needs more than anything else is a united family.

However, all of our pretence, all of our laboured politeness is wasted because it is carried on without an audience. Brendan has refused to get out of bed. When we go up to his bedroom, he claims his stomach is sick. We coax and cajole to no avail, and finally, in exasperation, we tell him he can stay home from school for the morning, but we will re-evaluate the state of his health at noon. He sits up in bed, no longer deathly ill, and asks Greg whether he is still thinking about taking Father Tom to court.

"If it comes to that," Greg replies. "I'm going to go see some people at the palace this morning. I have to make a start somewhere. I just telephoned to get an appointment."

Agony crosses Brendan's face. Without saying a word, he lies back down in bed, turns his face to the wall and pulls the covers up over himself.

Greg and George's appointment at the palace is for ten o'clock. The archbishop is out of the country, and the calendar of the next in line, the vicar general, is booked solidly for the next three days, so they must see a monsignor who is an assistant to the vicar general.

George and Greg talk over the ramifications of waiting for either the archbishop to return or for the vicar general's calendar to clear. They have settled for the monsignor in the hope that once the substance of their visit is revealed, the vicar general will quickly find the time to see them. They know, that without the vicar general, nothing can be done to get Haley out of the parish. At the last minute, on account of an emergency at work, George can't keep the appointment. Greg decides to go alone. I plead with him to accept laicizing Tom Haley.

"And what in the name of God is the good of having him laicized? So they take his collar away. He'll go get himself a government job. Fisheries officer probably. Like Donovan from the West End. One day he's a priest hearing confessions, the next day he's a fisheries officer catching people jacking salmon on the Humber River. And he'll still be out there marauding young boys, collar or no collar."

He walks to the kitchen door, takes hold of the knob but doesn't turn it. "Why won't they admit up front that Haley is a rogue priest? There are rogues in every walk of life, every profession. God knows there are enough rogue lawyers, but that doesn't mean all lawyers are rogues. Or that we'd cover up for the rogues."

"Just listen to yourself." I move towards him, my voice rising in spite of my good intentions to keep Brendan from hearing. I am not only angry with him, I am frustrated with myself because I am unable to make any inroads into his resolve to accept nothing less than courtroom censure. "You're the one who believes people are innocent until proven guilty. Who says they're going to cover up? For all you know, they might stone him out of the parish. They might even hang him on Hickman's Wharf and castrate him with a blunt knife. How can you know beforehand what they'll do?"

He brushes past my sarcastic outburst, slips right over it. "What if they laicize him and he gets a job in the government that has some jurisdiction over children? He might even end up being a youth counsellor. Or a Boy Scout leader."

The word counsellor triggers my thoughts in a different

direction. "I don't know whether you thought of this or not, but we're going to have to get some counselling for Brendan. He'll need help."

Greg lets go of the door knob. "For the love of the Lord Almighty, Tess, what good will that do? If Brendan's not willing for anyone outside of the family to know what happened, he's certainly not going to agree to talk to a counsellor. And a lot of good a counsellor will do if he doesn't know the problem he's dealing with."

He is right. And I know it. A feeling of powerlessness overcomes me. "I don't know what to do. I don't know where to turn. The first time Brendan really needs me, and I feel so useless."

Greg reaches out and puts an arm around my waist, pulls me close. His chin rests on my head.

"I feel the same way," he confesses. "A father should have been able to protect his son from something like this. I'm furious with myself for having allowed it to happen." He straightens up, removes his arm from my waist. "And on top of everything else, it turns my stomach that Brendan is more concerned over betraying that pervert than he is with getting the truth out. It just about tears my guts out to hear him taking up for that scumbag. I want to shake some sense into him."

"Brendan is what we made him," I carefully point out, trying to walk the fine line between defending Brendan's loyalty and understanding Greg's repugnance towards the object of it. "We're the ones who taught him to look for the good in people." I brush my hand over the rough tweed of his suit coat. "And besides, you wouldn't want him to be a tough nut like this Willie Farrell. You know you wouldn't."

"I suppose you're right. But that doesn't alter the fact that it curdles my stomach when he says Tom Haley isn't all bad. A saint with just a little touch of perversion." He glances at his watch. "If I'm going to keep that appointment I'd better get a move on. The quicker I get there, the quicker it will be over with."

Because I decide to work at home for the morning and I do not want Brendan overhearing our conversation when Greg comes back from his meeting at the palace, I ask him to call me as soon as it's over. We arrange to meet at a little café a few minutes' drive down the street from our house, and I leave on the pretext of needing some groceries.

In my anxiousness I arrive at the café before Greg does. I choose a seat with a view of the door. Greg comes in a few minutes later, so haggard and woebegone that my lungs clog with fear at the sight of him. He wears the look I remember from when he was doing family law and had lost a child custody case, a custody case where right had given way to might. I could always tell, even before he came into the house and I was able to see the wilt of his body, that he had lost. I could tell by the way he heaved the car door shut, as if he didn't care whether it closed or not.

"How did it go?" I rush to inquire the instant he sits down, my mind already racing ahead to disastrous conclusions. What if George and Christopher had backed down and Brendan was going to be the only witness? What if the palace had called in Tom Haley, and Greg had pulled the collar off him like he had threatened to do last evening and now he was the one being sued?

I stretch forward across the table, shortening the distance between our voices, and he drops his briefcase on the floor with the thud of the car door closing in the driveway. "How did it go?" I repeat.

"You got your wish," he says. "I settled for the treatment centre and a promise to have him laicized. No court case."

The steel vice which had been squeezing the heart out of me all morning suddenly eases up. "You did?" I say, and then because I fear that the end of one calamity may mean the beginning of another, I hurriedly ask, "What changed your mind? What happened? When you left you were going to push for going to court."

"I caved in. I gave in to them. And don't get the notion I did it for some high-minded reason, either. Because I didn't."

I can't think of anything to say, and silence hovers between us until Greg says, "And I didn't do it for you, I can tell you that much.

And I didn't do it for Brendan, either. And I sure as hell didn't do it for Father Perv."

The waitress comes to our table and we order two coffees. We remain silent while she cleans up the spills left over from the previous customer. In this once again hovering silence, my mind poses a question: if he didn't give in for my sake or for Brendan's sake or for Tom Haley's sake, then for whose?

"I buckled under for my own sake," Greg says as soon as the waitress leaves. "When push came to shove I didn't have the guts to go through with a court case. I wasn't in that monsignor's office more than ten minutes before I realized what I was up against."

"Up against?"

"Everyone in this city thinks Haley is Christ incarnate. And it's not just the Catholics who feel that way. There were two monsignors in the meeting. One was Duffy, the other Collins. Collins has a parish out towards Torbay. Duffy is strictly with the palace."

The waitress brings our coffees. Greg ignores his. I tear open a packet of sweetener and watch the chemical spill into my cup.

"Both of them told me that Haley lives a life that would give Jesus a run for His money. Or words to that effect. They said he practices the Corporal Works of Mercy with a vengeance: feeds the hungry, gives drink to the thirsty, harbours the harbourless, et cetera, et cetera. And ditto the Spiritual Works of Mercy. Comforts the afflicted and all that. And to top it all off he's got this great voice. Sings in a choir at the basilica. And plays the violin better than Itzhak Perlman. He just hasn't walked on water yet. But then, who knows? Maybe no one would know, because according to the palace, Haley would be much too modest to make it public."

"None of this is news to me, " I say. "It was his great reputation that made me think he would be a good role model for Brendan."

"Some role model. A fiddler and a diddler."

"But you're not explaining . . . I don't understand. What happened? If you intended to take him to court, how come you changed your mind? Mind you, I'm glad you did, but . . ."

"Can't you see? Every member of the parish and his dog and cat would be out for our blood if we blemished all that saintliness."

He rips open one of the plastic thimbles of milk. Most of the milk squirts over the table, only some of it hitting his coffee. He doesn't notice.

"And then there's Brendan. I got to thinking about that on the way over. What if he throws the case?"

"*Throws the case!* For the love of God, Greg, you're talking about Brendan! Not some Chicago mobster!"

"You have no idea, do you, about what things can go wrong in a courtroom. You really don't. Not an idea in the world." With his thumb and finger he absently flattens the empty milk container. "What if he breaks on the witness stand? What if he gets up there and starts blubbering that it is his fault, too? What if he says the pervert isn't all bad? I'll be laughed out of the courtroom. That's what I'm up against."

"You're being ridiculous."

"Perhaps yes, perhaps no." He pushes his coffee aside, having lost interest in it. "Anyway, that's not the real reason." He leans in closer so his voice won't carry. "It's not even close to the real reason. The scandal will be bad for the firm. That's the real reason. I got that message loud and clear from the palace. As soon as I told them what I intended to do, both monsignors mentioned the firm. They already knew where I work. Good friends with both partners, they told me. Apparently they checked up as soon as they got my phone call because they were quick to tell me that Murphy and Cadagan were basilica parishioners and neither of them would want the Church scorched on account of one bad apple. Duffy even reminded me that Murphy has a daughter in a convent. The verb is had, actually. She kicked the habit a few weeks ago, but I didn't bother mentioning that. Anyway, they stopped just short of saying I'd never make partner, like I've been promised, and that I might even be let go."

He reaches for his briefcase as though he has wasted too much time on this issue already. "So," he says heavily, tossing the price of the coffees on the table with his free hand and making ready to get up out of his chair, "you might say I sold out Brendan for a lousy job. Afraid to bring his tormentor to justice. Afraid it'll impact on . . ."

He quickly forestalls the comment I'm forming about his capitulation being all for the best. "And don't try and tell me you're glad for Brendan's sake! The day will come when he'll regret that nothing public was done about that pervert." We leave the restaurant and together we walk to where our cars are parked.

"I made it quite clear," he says, "that Haley has to get out of the priesthood ASAP because, I said, I'm sure as hell not going to stand for a pedophile parading around in priest's clothing. Actually, I repeated several times that the collar has to go. I said I'd keep track of things to make sure it did. And I'd give them a week to get Haley shipped off to the treatment centre, although I let them know that none of the literature supports a cure for pedophiles."

As I start to get into my car he adds, "I really think there were other complaints about Haley. I don't think mine was the first one."

"What makes you say that?" I ask eagerly, hoping for strength in numbers.

"They didn't seem overly shocked. They didn't protest my accusations. No one said 'Hold on here! You better have sound reasons for making such a charge.' There was no asking if I had other witnesses. And they had their answers down pat. Off with the collar. Off to the treatment centre. No argument. "

"Sure does seem like they knew," I agree, relieved things have gone as well as they have. "It's certainly not the reaction I would have expected. I expected them to ask if others had been involved."

"Not a peep. Maybe they surmised that's what George O'Connell was coming in about. Anyway, they just kept trying to convince me Haley is a saint. They said he had been one of their most promising seminarians, an archdiocesan seminarian at that. When I asked what that meant, they said he had been incardinated for the archdiocese of St. John's so they could depend on him staying in the parish. And they were delighted to get him because of the priest shortage. Apparently he went to All Hallows in Dublin for his education, training or whatever. And he did a stint at St. Augustine's — I believe that's in Ontario. They said he was active in the archdiocesan vocational recruiting, and on and on and on."

"I'm surprised they didn't say he had discovered the Shroud of Turin," I say. This lifts the tension and Greg smiles, then adds, "Oh yes, something else. They told me that when Haley came to the parish his religious superiors at the seminary said they were certain he was in peaceful possession of his sexuality and that he was prepared to sustain the commitment to chastity and celibacy."

"So much for the perceptiveness of his religious superiors."

"That's what I was thinking. I wanted to say, Bullshit! Monsignors, I bet everyone in the seminary with him knew he had a thing for young boys! But I thought I'd better keep a little respect."

At the supper table Greg relates to Brendan the result of his meeting at the palace — or at least he relates a laundered version of it. He even uses the word *father* when he speaks about Tom Haley, and I know he does this by way of an apology. If the meeting with the monsignors has done nothing else, it has made Greg understand why Brendan can say that Tom Haley isn't all bad.

"There'll be no court case," he says. "And Father Haley will be sent to a treatment centre somewhere on the Mainland."

Brendan's whole body sags in relief. He begins to eat his macaroni and cheese, which he had been merely pushing around on his plate. The tension has started to leave my shoulders as well.

"That makes you happy, eh?" Greg says, taking stock of Brendan's relief.

"Yeah." Brendan detects the bite in his words. He keeps his eyes on his plate and returns to rearranging his macaroni and cheese. He squirms around in his seat.

"It should have been taken to court," Greg says, as if an argument to the contrary is already in progress. "Haley is getting off too easily. And his victims need to see him punished. Healing won't begin for them until their abuse is acknowledged."

"Not me," Brendan mutters. "I don't want to be acknowledged. Whatever that means. I just want to forget about it."

Greg's nostrils flatten out at the base. His jaw clenches. I can almost hear him counting to ten before he asks, "You mean you don't mind that he is getting off as free as a bird?"

Brendan flinches, sensing a trap. "No. Yes. Maybe. I dunno."

"What do you mean 'No, yes, maybe, dunno?' Surely the answer is yes! Why would you want to let him off the hook totally? He's worse than . . . he's . . . ." Greg's ready vocabulary offers no suitable noun or adjective to describe Haley.

"Because he bought us pizzas." Brendan doesn't look up from his plate. "And he helps Willie Farrell with his math. And he makes sandwiches and gives them to bums on the park benches. I've gone with him many times. And he always makes sure to give them juice because, he says, alcohol dehydrates the body and drunks need lots of fluids."

Greg remains silent for a long time. When he speaks his words are turgid with anger and frustration. "For the love of heaven, Brendan, you're making him out to be St. Francis of Assisi instead of Chester the Molester. I just don't understand you, my son. I'd want to see him strung up naked down on Water Street. I'd want . . . ."

"May I be excused?" Brendan gives me a beseeching look. "Please, may I?"

I look at Greg, hoping he will be the one to release him. When he keeps a stony silence, I say, "He has a report he has to finish for school tomorrow. He should get at it right away."

Brendan waits for no further permission. As he scrambles out of his chair, Greg, angry at being thwarted, impotently throws out more words. "I guess I'm not you though. Am I? Because if I had been you, I certainly wouldn't have hung around with that pervert once I knew what he was like. And for the life of me I can't figure out why you did, either."

Brendan rushes from the kitchen and heads for his bedroom. Aghast, I, too, jump up, but I don't leave the room.

"What's gotten into you?" I charge. "Do you know what you just said? That you're ashamed of him. That he's a disgrace to you. You insinuated that he must have encouraged Tom Haley. You might just as well have said that he's as much to blame as Tom Haley is. No wonder he couldn't come and tell you what was going on. No wonder . . ."

Greg almost tips over his chair in his need to get to Brendan.

"Brendan!" he calls out as he runs up the stairs. "Brendan! I'm sorry! I didn't mean that . . . I'm sorry!"

I hurry after him, feeling, as usual, that I have to be the mediator. Halfway up the stairs I turn back, not understanding why but knowing only that I have to get away from both of them. I cannot help one without hurting the other. I am suddenly bone weary from this living nightmare. I feel as if I'm climbing a sandhill, and each time I dig my foot into the face of the hill, I succeed only in dislodging a shower of pebbles. No matter how hard I try, I can make no progress. Filled with a sense of futility, I go back to the kitchen and round up my purse and car keys and the coat I had on when I went to the café to talk to Greg. As I back the car out of the driveway, I have no destination in mind. I simply want to be away from the house.

For a while I drive aimlessly, first going up to Signal Hill in the hope that the brisk, salty air will blow my mind free of Greg's angry words and Brendan's stumbling, hurt ones. But when I get there, I don't even slow down, just circle around for a few minutes and then come back down into the city. I drive down Water Street, back up to Elizabeth Avenue, down Confederation Drive, and from there up and down streets, noticing neither street names nor house numbers.

Without conscious thought, I find myself heading towards St.

Sebastian Church. Our parish church! Father Tom Haley's church! When I get there, I cruise past it once, twice, three times. Each time I slow down almost to a stop and stare at the darkening evening and beyond the dark to the lighted rectory adjacent to the church. Father Haley's car is parked out front. On the fourth pass-by, I brake to a stop and pull into the driveway to park beside the green Toyota that on so many occasions had pulled into our own driveway to pick up Brendan.

As I walk up to the rectory door, I fleetingly wonder whether driving by the church has been totally accidental or whether some part of my tormented mind planned it with precision and purpose. However, at this point it no longer matters. All I know is that I have a compelling need to confront the person who has been the source of terrible conflict in my family, the person who is responsible for the scourging of my son. Hesitating only a moment, I ring his doorbell.

His housekeeper, Mrs. Crawley, pulls open the door and stands in the vestibule wiping her hands on her apron, which bears the signs of jam making. Partridgeberry jam, judging from the smell reaching me from the kitchen. I ask to see Father Haley.

"Have you an appointment?" she asks, wiping her hands up and down her aproned sides, first to clean them, then to smooth out the wrinkles she has made while swiping upward and downward along the flowered cotton.

"No. Sorry," I say, and smile apologetically. "No appointment. But I'll only take up a few minutes of his time."

"He's too busy now. Could you come back in the morning? You see, he's been at the palace most of the day, and now he's gone into his study to prepare a homily for a funeral Mass in the morning. He asked me not to disturb him except if he got an emergency phone call from one of the hospitals."

She expects me to begin a retreat, but I hold firm. "No, I must see him *now*."

My calm insistence annoys her, and she says with a nip in her voice. "Father don't like people coming in off the street unless in an emergency. He's tired and busy and don't need to be disturbed." She scrutinizes me and recognition dawns. "Haven't I seen you on the TV? You're *that woman Member*. In the House."

I extend my hand. "I'm Tess Corrigan. Tess Corrigan Slade, and my son, Brendan Slade, comes here sometimes for the Altar Servers' Association meetings."

"Oh yes, indeed," she says brightly, the nippiness gone from her voice. "Brendan Slade. A nice young man. Polite." She nervously brushes her hands down along her apron again, still ironing out the imaginary wrinkles. "I'll go speak to Father," she says. "Maybe he'll be able to spare a minute."

She leaves me standing in the vestibule while she hurries away, tiptoeing down the hall so her leather shoes won't click-clack on the hardwood floor. I'm certain that "Father" will know the reason for my visit because he *had* spent the day at the palace, probably called there the minute Greg left.

In just a few minutes, Mrs. Crawley comes tiptoeing back to me, smiling a sort of mission-accomplished smile. She says deferentially, "Father will see you now." Fleetingly, I wonder whether the deference is for Father or for *that woman Member*. Either way, of course, it's of no consequence. She points towards the priest's study.

My rubber-soled shoes muffle my footsteps, so even though he is expecting me, I catch him unawares. His chair is turned towards the window, and he is staring out at the rectory's well-cared-for lawn, which in the light from the window is now a soft black green.

"Good evening." I speak louder than necessary, partly because I feel clumsy leaving off the reverential "Father" at the end of my greeting and partly because I'm embarrassed at taking him off guard. Startled, he swivels his chair around to face me. He is wearing a black suit, complete with Roman collar, a change from the pullover sweater he usually wore whenever he came for Brendan. In the bright light of his desk lamp, I can see beads of perspiration on his forehead and around his hairline. His glasses have slipped down his nose. Embarrassed himself, he fumbles with his hands — pushes his glasses into place, touches his collar, gropes for a handkerchief to wipe his forehead. He looks like a man about to face his mortal enemy.

He clumsily stands up and nods toward the leather chair where he wishes me to sit, and then he glances at the open door behind me. Caught in a Hobson's choice of whether to break the unwritten rule of never being closeted with a lone female or chance having Mrs. Crawley overhear a conversation that may become heated and loud, he comes around his desk, walks to the door and eases it shut. It slides across my mind that he may have done this very same thing when the altar boys met with him. My stomach somersaults at the thought.

When he sits back down, he steeples his elbows on his desk, places his interlocked hands underneath his chin and looks towards me, although not at me. Spare, gangly, clean-shaven and fresh from being reprimanded by his superiors, he doesn't look much older than Brendan.

Just as I am wondering how I should open the conversation, he says, "The palace called after your husband's visit. I was in to see them this afternoon. I just got back. It looks like I'll be leaving here."

"So they're at least going to take some action." I strive for a corrosive tone on the off-chance that he might try to arouse my pity by telling me he is losing his parish. I also want to squelch any notion my heart may be harbouring of equating him with Dennis. "You destroyed Brendan and God knows how many other mothers' sons. The least they can do is get you out of here."

"Yes, I know that." He speaks so matter-of-factly I might just as easily be telling him his front steps need repainting.

I am not sure what I expected from him when I decided to call on him, but it definitely wasn't this calm acceptance, this detached passivity. Perhaps I hoped he would beg or plead. Or accuse. Or deny. Or that he would rage at Greg for going to the palace. Or even at Brendan for tattling. I have a battery of fighting words at the ready, but his submissiveness disarms me. I take a moment to regroup, unbutton my suit jacket, place my purse on the floor. When I straighten up, I speak the first thought that comes to my mind.

"Have you any idea of the extent of human destruction you have caused? Have you any idea of the heartache that you have handed out?" I feel a surge of Greg's anger, a swell of his frustration. With painful clarity it strikes me that Greg has been right all along. Nothing can ever be enough to undo what he has done. No matter what answer Tom Haley will give me, it will not be enough. And no matter what punishment his superiors hand out to him, it will not be enough. And no matter what we do to him, even tearing him limb from limb, as Greg has threatened, will not be enough. Canonical censure will not be enough. Public disgrace will not be enough. Nothing will ever be enough to give Brendan back his innocence. Nothing will ever be enough to allow our lives to return to where they were before George O'Connell's visit last night.

He slowly unsteeples his elbows, unlocks his hands, picks up a paper clip from the desk, turns it over, pries it open, presses it together. As I search for scalding words in the face of his complacency, he tosses the paper clip aside, looks squarely at me and, in a voice as dead as his eyes, says as if he has just read my mind, "I wish to God there were some punishment for me that would give you the satisfaction you need." He hangs his head. "Such punishment doesn't exist, does it? Nothing in this world can help you. And nothing in this world can help me. For that matter, as far as I'm concerned, nothing in the next one can help me, either."

His jaw slackens. His shoulders slump. Perspiration oozes out of his skin. His abject despair is almost enough to douse my rage. He clears his throat several times, a nervous habit that I had noticed before whenever I had spoken to him. "They're going to laicize me. Did you know that?"

"I hoped they would," I reply, striving for composure.

He stares at his fingers and quotes, *"You are a priest forever, according to the order of Melchizedek. This is the priest whom the Lord has crowned."* He runs his fingertips along the edge of his collar. "That's all I ever wanted to be. A priest. Ever since I was ten or eleven."

"You should have thought of that before you destroyed the children." I have no intention of allowing him to wallow in vocational passion.

He makes no attempt to refute my chastisement, just absently rubs one hand over the other on the desk. Aware that I am beating the beaten, I persist. "Greg is all for you going to jail. Do you know that? He wants to take you to court. He wants public censure. Public flogging, if it were allowed. And as soon as he found out what you had done, he wanted to come over here and beat you up himself. I had to block the doorway with my body."

When he gives me a grateful look, I squelch his gratitude.

"I did it for Brendan's sake. He begged me to keep his father from hurting you. And he begged his father not to have you put in jail. Or harm you in any way."

He recoils, drops his head into his hands and mumbles, "Oh God Almighty. Oh God Almighty. I'm so sorry. I never asked to be this way. I never intended to hurt anyone. Especially not Brendan." He adds, as if it is supposed to make a difference, "And I never bullied anyone to be with me. I may have enticed. But I never bullied."

"*Enticed!* You mean lured! Snared! Is that supposed to justify your behaviour? You never *bullied* them? They're just children, for the love of God. You took advantage of them. That's what you did. They revered you. If you had told them to jump into a snake pit, they would have done it for you.

"Do you know that I left Greg at home right now disgusted with Brendan because he knows in his heart that despite everything you've done to that child, Brendan will still defend you. And worst of all, part of Greg believes Brendan wanted to be abused.

Greg won't admit that, but I can see it's true. I can see it in his eyes. I can hear it in his voice. And it's tearing me apart. It's tearing all of us apart. We're a family destroyed. That's what we are."

He claps his hands over his ears. "Don't! Don't! I don't want to hear any more."

He jumps up and begins pacing the floor. He rips his collar off as he walks, tosses it on the desk beside the mangled paper clip. Tears roll down his face, and he brushes them away, childlike, with the back of his hand.

"Like I said, I never meant to hurt anyone! As God is my judge. Especially not Brendan." He stops his pacing. There is a chair beside the wall, heaped with pamphlets. He heaves the pamphlets to the floor and brings the chair close to mine.

He stares at me until I can no longer avoid meeting his eyes. They remind me of Danny's. "Listen to what I'm going to say," he says softly. "Brendan isn't flawed like me. You must make Greg understand that. Brendan got led along because he admired me. I knew that, and God help me, I used it. But he also liked the camaraderie, being around boys his own age. And he loved the charity work. He loved helping the needy. What happened after those events was my fault. All my fault."

He looks away, focuses his gaze on a point distant from me, clears his throat again, and, once he has his emotions solidly in check, he begins to explain the hold his perversion has upon him.

"I've tried to control this beast inside of me. That's how I think of it. A raging, untamed beast. God alone knows how I've tried to get it under control. And if you think your husband hates me, he doesn't hate me nearly as much as I hate myself."

He stands up. Paces some more. Goes to his desk and sits down again.

"I'm telling you, I hate myself so much I have anxiety attacks. Blackouts even. Sometimes it's all I can do to catch my breath. I get dizzy. Break out in a cold sweat. My heart pounds. Sometimes I'm certain I'm going to die, right at that very moment. And that puts me in a worse state — if I die I'm certain I'll go straight to hell because of what I am."

He lets out a long, agonized breath. "And sometimes I think I'd be better off dead, despite the certainty of hell. It would make life better for other people. Better for Brendan. My mother. My superiors. The Church."

He gets up again, leans against his desk and faces me. "Have you any idea what it's like living with the certainty of hell?" he asks, certain that I don't, certain that this state is reserved for the wretched few. I am reminded of Sister Rita's lesson on the Agony in the Garden. *Do you know how much pain it takes to sweat blood?* "Do you know what it's like to live without the hope of eternal life? Day and night to live without this hope?"

And like Sister Rita, he answers for me. "Of course you don't. Few people do. When I was in the seminary I heard about a priest who had sworn away the possibility of everlasting life. He lived in Germany during World War II, and he was escorting Jewish children to safety. The SS made him swear upon his soul that he wasn't lying when he said that the children were Christians and he was just taking them for an outing. For the sake of saving those Jewish children he swore away his own possibility of heaven. For the rest of his life he believed he would go to hell when he died because he had sworn away his soul."

"That's ridiculous," I say. "The end justified the means. Didn't anyone ever tell him that?"

"Plenty of people did. But it's what you believe in your heart that counts. I shuddered when I first heard that story; I thought, my God Almighty, what a hopeless life to live. I never thought I'd be living with that same hopelessness. But I do. Night and day. Day and night. I know God is all-forgiving, but to be forgiven I need to slaughter the Beast. Sorrow for sin is manifested in changed behaviour. And I can't do that. Maybe because I don't want to change badly enough. Sometimes I wonder if hell could be any worse than what I'm going through on earth."

He stops talking, takes off his glasses, and with both hands rubs away the perspiration that has collected in the soft flesh around his eyes. I notice how white and long and delicate his fingers are. He replaces his glasses and asks me, "Have you any idea what it's like living with the fear of being found out? Always wondering whether this is the day you'll be turned in? I've lived with that hell, too, for more years than I care to remember."

"Haven't you heard of psychiatrists?"

"When the anxiety attacks first began, I told my superiors about them. I was sent from one psychiatrist to another, but I couldn't bring myself to tell any of them about the Beast. The diagnosis came back that I was too scrupulous. I was trying to be too holy."

He laughs. "Too holy! Some holy! And don't ask me whether I prayed for help. I've done that too. *Ask and it shall be granted. Knock and it shall be opened*. Well, I asked and I knocked, and when nothing changed, I'd think I hadn't asked with enough sincerity, so I'd ask again. And again! And again! But the Beast still stayed. And the more I asked and the more I knocked, the worse the anxiety attacks got. Now I just suffer through them. I don't let on I have them. My superiors think they're cured. But they're far from cured. I get them at Mass. Right at the moment of transubstantiation, that's the worst time."

He raises both hands, thumb and index finger on each hand pressed together as if elevating the sacred host. He whispers, *"This is my Body!"* He turns to one side and reverently lays the make-believe host down on his desk. He picks up a can that holds his pens and pencils, and holding it aloft with both hands, he whispers, *"For this is the chalice of my blood of the new and eternal covenant, the mystery of faith, which shall be shed for you and for many unto the forgiveness of sins."*

This, too, he reverently places back on the desk as if it is actually a sacred vessel. Turning to face me, he asks, again not expecting an answer, "Do you know what's running through my mind when I hold the host up and say, *this is my body?*"

Stunned by his actions, I can't even shake my head. I simply stare at him, but he doesn't notice. He sits back down in his desk chair, spreads his hands, palms upward, on his knees, surveys them and then supplies his own answer. "What I am thinking is that these hands aren't fit to be touching this sacred host, this sacred vessel."

He tilts his head pensively and frowns. It crosses my mind that he would be good at confessions. I picture him in the confessional, ear to the grating, face averted. I am certain he would be a careful listener, a compassionate dispenser of penance.

"And I'm thinking these are no longer anointed hands. That's when the anxiety attacks happen. That's when I get dizzy. That's when the sweat pours off me. Everything goes black. I have to fumble on the altar for the pall and the corporal so I can put the sacred vessels down safely. And I'm terrified I'll tip over the chalice or the ciborium or I'll set the host down on the altar cloth instead of on the purificator and one of the servers will shout out that I'm doing it wrong — that I have now desecrated the host just like I desecrated the young boys."

He tells me that when he left the seminary, he had begged his superiors to send him somewhere to do missionary work — a leper colony, old age homes, palliative care hospices — anywhere where he wouldn't be near young boys. Of course, just as he had done later with the psychiatrists, he withheld from his superiors the real reason for wanting such assignments. So his request was denied.

"At one time," he says, "I was even thinking about feigning alcoholism, telling my superiors I was hitting the altar wine pretty heavily." He smiles thinly. "And that's one problem I don't have. At least not yet. But I thought it would get me sent away to a treatment centre, and once there I could find some way to rid myself of the Beast. Maybe I might be able to fess up confidentially to a counsellor." He suddenly throws out another question. "Do you know Luke's gospel about Zacchaeus?"

I shake my head, admitting my spotty knowledge of the gospels, Sister Rita's catechism lessons notwithstanding.

"It's the gospel that offers me my one glimmer of hope that I'm not as repugnant in God's eyes as I am in man's. You see, Zacchaeus was a rich publican, a sinner, and one time when Jesus was on His way through Jericho, He stayed at his house. Everyone was upset because Jesus lodged in the house of a sinner. But Jesus said, *'Today salvation has come to this house, since he, too, is a son of Abraham. For the Son of Man came to seek and to save what was lost.'*" He repeats, *"'Since he, too, is a son of Abraham.'"*

He fumbles amongst the rubble on his desk and picks up the discarded Roman collar and puts it back on, stuffing the ends through slits in the neck of his shirt. With the collar in place, he looks less vulnerable.

"I was sure that when I became ordained, the Beast would be conquered. I wanted so badly to be a priest." Once again, he runs his fingers along the edge of the collar, absently fondling it. "I thought the discipline, the studies, the celibacy requirement would help me. And I was so certain I would never do anything to scandalize the priesthood. Nor to scandalize my mother." He closes his eyes for a few seconds. "The disgrace is going to kill her. That haunts me. She's not well. She had a stroke a couple of years ago, and she never fully recovered. That's the only thing that makes me glad I'm not going to the penitentiary. Otherwise I couldn't care less what happens to me."

I think of Grandmother, who always said whenever she heard about some wayward young man whose crimes had disgraced him, "No matter the deeds he's done, he's still some poor mother's son." She would sigh heavily, probably thinking of Martin, dead long before his time, and repeat, "He's some poor mother's son. Somewhere some poor mother is crying for him tonight, wishing she could take on his pain."

"The laicizing isn't going to be made public," he says, breaking into my thoughts. "That should help her a little. She can say my health couldn't take the rigour of the priesthood." I notice a hint of mischief in his eyes. "Isn't that what they used to say when a priest or nun left their orders, or got kicked out?"

"That's right," I say. "That was the stock answer. The noble lie. Health gave out. Like a politician who anticipates defeat. 'I'm not going to re-offer because I want to spend more time with my family.'"

I bring the conversation back to ground. "What about your father?"

Knowing how Greg is reacting to Brendan's anguish, I can only imagine how Haley's father will react when he hears about the unpriesting of his son, much less the reason for it.

"Don't know much about him," he replies, shrugging his shoulders. "I was nine when he left us. And just as well. He wasn't much of a father or a husband. As far as I know he went out to Vancouver. Got mixed up in drugs. The sixties stuff. Tune in. Turn on. Drop out. The Timothy Leary scene. We heard he died from an overdose. That is, my father did. Maybe Timothy Leary did, too, for all I know."

Traces of compassion like those I had felt for the fossilized remains of Ed Strominski circle my insides. I want to comfort Tom Haley. I want to caress his shoulders, like I had caressed Brendan's the night before. I want to offer him platitudes, bake him brownies, tell him that this dark night will pass, that morning will come.

In the midst of this wave of compassion, a disturbing thought slices across my mind: had Greg been right when he accused me of confusing Tom Haley with Dennis Walsh? The same passion is evident. The same intensity. The same simplicity. Could these similarities have been the underpinnings of my desire for Brendan to join the Altar Servers' Association? Had I attempted to resurrect Dennis through Tom Haley? Had my selfish unmet need been instrumental in the ravaging of Brendan?

Guilt assails me, threatening to suffocate me. Rivulets of perspiration run down my cheeks and into my mouth. I search the pocket of my suit jacket for a tissue to sponge my face. I fan my damp hair with my hand. Cold drops of water trickle down my back and puddle at the clasps of my bra, and my spine itches in this spot. I want to rub my back against the spindles of my chair like a sheep scratching its haunches on a rock.

"You all right?" Tom Haley asks.

"It's a bit hot in here," I lie, pushing up the sleeves of my jacket.

He goes to the window and pulls it open. The evening air doesn't even begin to cool my flesh.

"I've got to go," I say, getting up from my seat and picking up my purse. "I've got to get back."

He gives me a puzzled look but says nothing. I practically run out of his office. I can feel him watching me from his window as I hurry down the rectory steps to my car.

When Greg asks me where I've been for the last hour, it is on the tip of my tongue to say I went to vanquish the enemy but found him already vanquished. Not wanting to spark an argument, though, I give him a half-lie. "Drove around. I needed to get away from the house. Went up to Signal Hill to air out my mind."

Chapter Nine

IN THE MORNING BRENDAN continues to pretend to be sick. Both Greg and I insist that he go to school. He steadfastly refuses. He threatens to vomit in the classroom. As a compromise, Greg promises to pick him up at noon and take him to lunch so he won't have to be around Willie Farrell during unsupervised times. He experiences a miraculous cure.

Although the House isn't having a fall session, I still go to the office every day. There is always some issue to tackle or someone dropping by in need of my help. As well, going to the office affords me time to read the newspapers to keep abreast of what is going on both at home and abroad. On this morning, however, it is not easy to concentrate, absorbed as my mind is with the chaos in the family.

The news in the local morning paper is neither new nor startling. The editor is still insisting that Ottawa extend Canada's fishery management authority beyond the two-hundred-mile limit to include the nose and tail of the Grand Bank. The federal fisheries minister claims he is doing all he can to stop European countries from ravaging the fishery just outside the two-hundred-mile limit, while the foreign captains try to bribe fishery observers to lie about their catches. Salmon and trout rivers which were closed on account of low water levels have now been reopened. The brewery strike is still on. In the letters to the editor section, a voter demands to know how many other Hibernia-type projects will be allowed in the waters surrounding Newfoundland, prophesying that our waters will become a sea of concrete. The Star of the Sea Association in the

Cove will be hosting a community breakfast on Saturday in honour of their parish priest, Father Wakeham, who is celebrating his sixty-fifth birthday.

I set the paper aside and make a note to remind myself either to go to the Cove for Father Wakeham's breakfast or, if I can't, to call him. Just as I am scribbling on my calendar, Greg telephones.

"All hell's broken loose," he says. "I had a phone call from George O'Connell. The story is all over the school."

"How? Who?" I shout, desperation making me forget that others can hear, and thinking that if I can get the how and the who there may still be some way I can keep Brendan's name out of the mess.

"Haven't got the ins and outs of it all," Greg says. "Apparently, Christopher left the school in the midst of the uproar there and went to where George was working to tell him. That's how George got the news, he called me, and I went and picked up Brendan. Willie Farrell went to Haley's after the morning Mass — he served the altar this morning — and he never went to school afterwards. I guess there was something going on in his class, a play or something, and Willie had a part. Anyway, the teacher phoned to see if he had gone home sick after Mass, and of course he hadn't, so John Farrell went looking for him and found him coming out of the rectory. And he hasn't any desire to keep things under wraps."

"No! No! No! It's not true." My voice is merely a moan.

"I'm afraid it's true. The way George heard it, John Farrell didn't get the story out of Willie at first. Willie made up some excuse why he was at the rectory. It wasn't until they were in the principal's office that he spilled his guts. He had missed a lot of school his father knew nothing about, forged his mother's signature on the absentee slips. It was the principal who wormed the reason for his absences out of him. John Farrell went nuts, screaming and shouting, saying he was going to kill Haley and sue the diocese and what all. He was so loud the class in the room next door, Willie's class, heard the commotion, and a lot of the boys there already knew what was going on with Haley, even if they weren't in on it themselves, so they got the gist of what was happening. They told the teacher the whole story. Maybe they thought they'd get blamed for being part of it if they didn't tell. Anyway, it's only a matter of time before the media gets wind of it."

"The media?"

"Yeah. George says John hasn't the slightest bit of interest in keeping it quiet. He's bloodthirsty for a financial settlement from the diocese. He thinks the bigger the stink he makes, the bigger the settlement."

"You've got to stop him. You've got to convince him not to go public. *We've* got to convince him." With my free hand I begin stuffing papers into my briefcase, and I fumble around on my desk for my car keys, making ready to go see John Farrell. With what little breath that is left in me, I keep up a steady stream of possibilities for Greg's scrutiny.

"We'll tell him it'll ruin Willie. We'll tell him just to threaten to go public. Threatening will be enough to get the diocese to come across with whatever money he wants. We'll tell him we'll pay him to keep quiet. We'll mortgage the house."

"Get hold of yourself, Tess! Do you hear what you're saying? You're advocating hush money! That's extortion! What you're suggesting is way outside the law!"

But I am beyond legalities. "Who cares?" I snap, " We'll borrow the money. We'll use Brendan's college fund."

"Tess, he'll want millions," he says. "You'll have to mortgage a lot of houses like ours to get that much money. People like John Farrell are not up to being reasonable."

I force my mind to settle down so I can think of some solution.

"I've got the answer," I say. "I'll go to Mrs. Farrell. I'll explain to her that it'll be bad for Willie if it gets spread about in the media. She's a nice woman. I've met her. She'll find a way to stop that no-good drunk of a husband from hurting her son more than he's already been hurt. I'm willing to bet on that."

The only sound on the line is the hiss of silence.

"Greg? Are you there?"

"I'm here." He heaves a sigh so deep it could have come from the bottom of his feet. "It's too late, Tess. Too late to do a damn thing. He's already contacted the media. Your assistant told me the paper had just called you — they know that's your church, though I don't think they know Brendan is an altar boy. She said she screened the call and didn't put it through. She didn't want you ambushed, and she's probably waiting to tell you about it right now. The reporter left messages on the machine while I was getting Brendan, and he called again just as we came in. Wanted to know how you felt about the scandal involving your church. I said I wasn't interested in discussing scandal and hung up."

In the morning the news breaks. It is in the newspapers. On the early morning radio news. On the television news.

A priest connected with St. Sebastian Church is alleged to have participated in wild sexual parties with a number of altar boys. It is purported that these orgies have been going on for some time. The situation only came to light when one of the boys, absent from school without an excuse, was found in the company of the priest.

With the breaking of this news, an ordinary Wednesday in late October suddenly becomes apocalyptic. In all of the televised street interviews, in all of the telephone calls we receive from supporters, in all of the rallying notes that are left on my desk and on Greg's, in all of the workaday encounters, no one simply says they heard about the scandal on the radio, saw it on television or read about it in the newspapers. Each person has to set the tragedy against a backdrop of his or her ordinary life, as if this is the only way they can absorb the enormity of it. And each person recalls in minute detail what they were doing and where they were standing or sitting when they first heard the news, as if it were John F. Kennedy's assassination or the end of World War II.

Rose Clarke telephones from the Cove to tell me that she and Frank were just puttering around in the kitchen getting their breakfast, taking their good old time because they had nothing special to do in the morning, when the news came on the radio. Frank kept saying over and over, "My God. I can't believe what I just heard. I can't believe it. That's Tess's church!" She had been filling the kettle with water, and she nearly froze to the sink. Bridey Flynn calls to say she was just taking a pan of cookies out of the oven, "the icebox kind," she explains, as if there is some significance to this. "The kind you keep in the refrigerator." So she said to Paddy, "That's the church where Brendan serves the altar." The news took the good out of her for the rest of the morning.

Brendan refuses to leave his bedroom. In between angry outbursts and tears he blames us for the situation he is in. If Greg hadn't gone to the palace, there would be nothing for Christopher to tell Willie, and Willie wouldn't have cut school to go to Father Tom's to talk over what was happening. That Willie had cut school to go to Father Tom's on many other occasions is not a point he is interested in considering. If I hadn't encouraged him to join the Altar Servers' Association, he never would have joined of his own accord.

Although we worry most about Brendan, we also have to think about Philomena. I have to get out to the Cove right away, before she gets around to listening to the mid-morning news or before outsiders bring the news to her. Even if she never considers that Brendan was involved in the orgies, just the fact that he was associated with those who were will be enough to worry her to death. Because Brendan absolutely refuses to come with us, Greg decides to take him fishing out in Big Pond. This will keep him out of reach of the media, and I will go to the Cove alone.

"Blessed God! Blessed God! Oh Holy Virgin Mother! Holy Mother of God!" Philomena cries when I tell her what she will be hearing on the news. Since it doesn't occur to her at first that Brendan may be involved in any way, her immediate concern is for the Church. She asks, "Are you certain about it all? Are you really sure it happened? What did Brendan say? He'd know what's going on. You don't want to spread scandal about the Church unless you're really certain."

"Brendan's one of the boys, Mrs. Phil. He told us himself. And his friend Christopher also told us it's true. He's involved, too. Every bit of it is true."

"Oh Glory be to the Almighty. Oh no!" She clasps her hands across her breast as she rocks her anguished body back and forth. "'Tis not true! 'Tis not true! 'Tis not true!"

After she accepts that there might be at least a kernel of truth in what I have told her, she says, "If it's all true like ye sez it is, then what that priest did to those boys is enough to make God rear up on His hind legs. 'Tis enough to singe the soul of a saint."

When she is more fully collected, she wonders whether Brendan's name will be spread all over the papers, all over the television, all over the radio. No, I tell her, on account of his age, but the media have already connected me to the parish, and because of my position, they'll hound us. In fact, the hounding has already begun. She prepares a snack for us, and as she pulls a slice of toast from the toaster and butters it with Good Luck margarine, she chastises herself for not having known there was something not right about Father Haley.

"Never took a fancy to him, that's what I didn't. Mind you, I only met him a couple of times at your place when I was in visiting. I thought he was too good looking, for one thing. A pretty boy. And for another thing he kept clearing his throat. Kept hacking away as if he had a pit-prop stuck in his craw." She slathers the toast as if she is angry with it, first one side of the knife and then the other, the way Martin used to sharpen his razor on a strop. "How could I let something like that pass right underneath my nose? I should have known that clearing his throat was a sign he had something to hide. A fellow down home when I was a young girl cleared his throat like that. It turned out that at night he was stealing gravel from a government gravel pit, pretended he was getting it from his own pit, and the next day he was selling it back to the government for a wharf they were building. A real schemer he was."

In the next breath, she turns her pain on me. "And where were you all this time? Surely a mother would know her son was in the hands of a blackguard?"

I offer little in my own defence. I say much the same as Brendan had said — that Tom Haley had always done good works. She waves this information away. "A cover, that's what. Just a cover. And you couldn't see through it."

I meet Frank Clarke on my way from Philomena's. He had seen me going in to her place and watched for me to leave. He leans in through the car window to commiserate. "That two-faced bastard. Suckin' up to God on Sundays and ravaging young boys on Mondays," he says without even mentioning Tom Haley's name. "He deserves to be strung up by the you–know-whats. And ruining those boys. Just children. Scandalous, that's what it is."

I make no response because I can't think of anything to say, and then Frank asks, already knowing the answer, "Brendan is an altar boy, isn't he? In that parish?"

"Yes, he is . . . was . . . an altar boy." I am unable to say that he was also one of "those boys." But Frank doesn't need my confirmation on that. Why else would I be out to see Philomena in the middle of the week?

He rants some more about Tom Haley and about the punishment that should be meted out to him, and then, the inveterate politician, he adds, "So girl, let's hope that leadership campaign doesn't get underway too soon. Things need to blow over. Lots of Catholics in the party. And when the Tories sniff out that Brendan is an altar boy . . . well, you know how it goes . . . even if they can't name names, they'll be hinting that Brendan was the one who squealed. And scandalizing the Church will be laid on your shoulders. Even here in the Cove you're going to find a backlash. No mistakin' that."

"You're probably right," I say, not caring whether he is or isn't.

"Anyway, I have too much on my plate at the moment to worry about that."

"Sure you have, girl. Sure you have. Clear this out of the way first." He invites me to his house, but I decline the invitation. I have to get back to St. John's in case Brendan needs me.

By the time I arrive home, Brendan and Greg have already returned from their fishing trip to Big Pond. I find Brendan in his bedroom, curled into a ball like a defenceless little animal, his arms and legs cuddling the tender parts of himself close against the day's onslaught. When I come in he reluctantly unrolls himself and sits up on the edge of the bed. I ask him if he enjoyed the fishing trip, he mumbles yes, but the apathy in his voice and the droop of his mouth tell me otherwise. I go over to the bed and sit down beside him.

"Grandma was disappointed you weren't with me," I say, feigning lightness. "She said you've got to come for certain on the weekend for her birthday. She's going to make the kind of chocolate cake you like — chocolate icing and . . ."

"Did you tell her?" he breaks in, apprehension putting a hitch in his voice. "What did she say? She hates me, I bet."

"Of course she doesn't hate you. You were taken in. She knows that."

"Did you explain that Father Tom isn't all bad?"

"I tried to. She didn't want to hear about him. Just about you."

"I thought she'd be mad at me. Like Christopher's grand-mother. She said Christopher brought shame on the Church. And on his dead mother. And on her, too. She said she'll never be able to show her face at bingo again."

"Poor Christopher," I say and let it go at that.

"Will you tell Uncle Danny?" For an instant I consider lying, but I decide there's been too much deceit in his life already.

"Yes, we'll tell him. It wouldn't be right to keep it from him." I'm careful not to say he will probably read about it in the Vancouver *Sun* or hear it on the CBC *National News*. Ashamed, he drops his head. "Uncle Danny will be on your side," I say, knowing this is the truth. "He loves you as much as we do."

"Not Dad," he says, not raising his head. "He hates me. He's ashamed of me."

"You know that's not true," I say, wondering what has transpired while I was in the Cove. "He just loves you so much he's furious that anyone would hurt you."

"He hollered at me today. I slipped off a rock and filled my waders, and I said I wanted to go home because my feet were cold, and he said to take off my waders and turn them upside down to empty them out. And when I said I still wanted to go home because my feet were still cold, he said I was being a namby pamby, and it was about time I grew up to be a man because I'm almost thirteen years old."

Fury at Greg almost chokes me, but I say, not sure whether I'm trumping up excuses or not, "Dad just wants to toughen you up to be a hardy fisherman like himself. He used to be out in a dory jigging cod when he was your age."

"I know. He told me that lots of times. He said some day he's going to take me out in a dory. And he's going to show me how to use Grandpa's gun — the one that's in Grandma's spare bedroom — and we'll go to the beach and shoot wild birds like he used to do with Grandpa." He shivers. "Yuck! He told me I'll have to eat them when they're cooked because we can't shoot the birds just for the sport of it. We have to eat what we shoot."

"You'll manage to clean them," I say absently. "The first time will be the worst time." My mind is assembling fighting words to hurl at Greg, not only for yelling at Brendan but for promising to teach him how to use Hubert's gun to shoot ducks.

As I leave the room to go downstairs, Brendan asks, "Do you think I could practice shooting tin cans first? That way I wouldn't cripple anything. I'd hate to cripple something. I'd rather we didn't shoot ducks at all. Just tin cans. Dad and I could have a contest to see who could shoot the most tin cans."

"Talk to your Dad about it. I'm sure he'll see things your way," I say with imitation certainty. The truth is I'm no longer certain what to expect from Greg. In the last couple of days, some foreign creature seems to have crawled into his body and taken up residence there.

On the weekend we drive to the Cove for Philomena's birthday. Because Brendan has refused to go to school since the scandal broke, isolating himself in his room and claiming to be sick, we are both surprised and delighted that he is eager to come with us. In fact, we were so certain he wouldn't want to go to the Cove that Greg planned to go alone. Greg's delight at Brendan's change of mind is obvious in his buoyant walk as he makes trips from the house to the car, loading suitcases into the trunk and piling in groceries Philomena cannot get in the Cove — fresh whipping cream, Boston lettuce, lemon caraway biscuits.

On the drive to Philomena's, Brendan remains in high spirits. He even consents to play road games with us, ones he had scoffed at after he turned twelve. We spy horses in the fields and sight graveyards to bury our competitors' count in. We tally station wagons, giving extra points for white ones. When we arrive at the Cove, he receives his customary hero's welcome from Philomena, who plies him with cookies and freshly baked bread.

In the morning when we are getting dressed for church, Brendan announces he isn't going to come with us.

"Of course you are," I say firmly, brooking no nonsense. "You're not sick. And it's your grandmother's birthday. Of course you're coming with us."

"I'm not going," he repeats. "I'm staying right here." He taps the arm of his chair. "Right here."

"Come on, me son," Philomena entreats. "We'll have the cake when we gets home. Chicken sandwiches first and then the cake." Brendan is unmoved.

I look to Greg for support, but he disappoints me. "Let him stay," he says easily. "We'll only be gone an hour."

Philomena agrees with Greg. As she pokes a linen handkerchief into her patent-leather purse, she says, "Oh yes, girl, let him stay. The Lord will understand. He's been through a lot. Go easy on him. If he wants to be alone, let him be alone. Things will get back on track in their own time."

"He's been alone all week," I retort, partly out of concern for Brendan's welfare and partly out of pique because I've been out-manoeuvred by both Greg and Philomena. "He shouldn't be alone on Sunday as well. If he won't go, I won't go." I pull off my gloves and begin to unbutton my coat.

"For the love of God, Tess," Greg says, "he's almost grown up. You don't have to mollycoddle him. If he wants to stay home by himself this once, let him. He just won't be able to make a practice of it, that's all."

I give in reluctantly and without a hint of grace. In fact, I am so annoyed with both Greg and Philomena that when we get to church, I leave plenty of space between us in the pew. Although the space is not wide enough for anyone else to notice, Greg notices, and he never attempts to slide over and fill the gap.

After church we drive back to Philomena's in silence. Greg brings the car to a stop in the lane, which has become so rutted from wash-outs that he can only drive partway up to the house. In a final effort to pull the morning together, he says, "You two take your time. I'll run on ahead and put the kettle on to boil. I'll get Brendan to help me."

He hurries off, leaving me to help Philomena pick her way through the ruts. The walking is more treacherous than usual because the night's frost and the morning's melt have dampened the muddy ground, making it as slippery as ice.

The instant we come around to the back door, I see Greg staggering down the high porch steps as if he is too drunk to walk upright. He lurches from side to side, railing to railing. Part way down the steps, he falls against the outside handrail and vomits over it, covering a clump of wild caraway bushes with the remains of his breakfast. His hands are bloody and his face is as white as the clapboards on the house.

I drop my hold on Philomena and rush to him, although the sight of him is so mind-numbing it seems I am walking towards him in slow motion.

"Oh my God! Oh my God!" I shout as I wrap my arms around his shoulders and lower him down to the steps. He looks at me but doesn't speak. His eyes seem crazed. His mouth is covered in vomit.

"What's wrong? What's wrong?" I keep shouting. My mind says *heart attack* — only a few days earlier one of our neighbours had suffered a heart attack, and it had been preceded by violent vomiting that had brought up blood. My voice is banshee wild, my eyes search his face. "What's wrong, Greg? What's wrong?" Philomena comes hurrying around the corner of the house. Wordlessly, she gapes down at us, eyes wide, purse sliding down her arm. "Quick!" I shout to her. "Call the doctor! A heart attack! No! No! Go get Paddy to take him to the hospital! It'll be quicker." I continue to cradle Greg's shoulders.

Philomena pays no heed to my shouting. She breaks out of her stupor and pushes past us up the steps. Greg lunges out of my grasp, grabs the tail of her coat and pulls her backwards on top of us. She breaks away and starts up the steps again, screaming, "Brendan! Brendan! Brendan!"

"Come back, Mom!" Greg shouts, hoarse and desperate. "For the love of God, come back! He found Dad's gun."

I let go of Greg and rush up the steps, overtaking Philomena. I sideswipe her against the railing.

"Merciful Jesus! "Merciful Jesus! I knew it! I knew it!" she screams, righting herself and hurrying back down the steps. "We've got to get him to the hospital." She flies off in search of Paddy.

Greg races up the steps after me, grips my arm just as I am about to open the porch door. I wrench free of his grip with a savage yank, certain that I can mend Brendan if only I can get to him. I can bind up any wound. I had saved him before. When he almost choked on a piece of apple. When he darted in front of a car in the middle of Water Street. When he drank the air freshener.

"Don't go in there, Tess! For the love of God, don't go in there!"

Greg snatches at my arm once more and jerks me back against him. The sudden weight of my body against his own throws him off balance, and both of us pitch to the ground, our fall broken by our careening from railing to railing and by Paddy, who is standing at the bottom of the steps. He had driven home from church behind us, and Philomena's shrieking had brought him on the run.

"Shot himself," Greg gasps even as Paddy is helping us to our feet.

Paddy drops his hold on us and tears up the steps. Greg and I reel into one another as Paddy pushes open the porch door and then bangs it shut. "Oh Christ, help us!" He staggers back, grabbing the railing for support. Slowly he comes back down the steps.

I try to loosen Greg's grip on my arm. "Let me go! Let me go!" I shout, struggling and flailing.

Paddy places one of his big carpenter hands gently on my arm. "Stay there, my dear. There's nothing you can do. You don't want to see him like he is. You really don't."

My body believes him even if my heart doesn't, and I collapse in Greg's arms like a kite suddenly hitting a downdraft. Greg pulls me back upright and tightens his hold on me.

The news spreads quickly from one neighbour to another, and a crowd gathers. Frank Clarke arrives and releases me from Greg's grip. "Greg, you go meet the priest and the doctor," he directs. "They should be coming any minute. Bridey called them. I'll look after Tess."

Frank helps me to a pile of rocks a few yards from the porch — rocks Hubert had dug out of the ground with a pickaxe when he was building his house, rocks that are now covered with the withering October remains of goldenrod and bachelor buttons and the brown-tinged white flowers of wild caraway.

Philomena is already at the rock pile, huddled as if she is very cold. She isn't crying, just staring off into the distance. Sounds come from her lips, whispering sounds, like wind funnelling through a keyhole. She doesn't acknowledge my presence, just continues to stare across the meadows. Every now and again I recognize a word here and there from the scatter of sounds leaking out of her mouth, enough to know she is whispering Psalm 129 from the Mass for the Dead.

Out of the depths I have cried to you. Lord! Lord! hear my voice. Let thine ears be attentive to the voice of mine supplication. In You, O Lord, I place my trust. My hope is in Your mercy. If You, O Lord, should mark our sins, Lord, who would know salvation? But with You is forgiveness.

The minute she finishes the *De Profundis,* she starts in on the *Memorare – a* prayer I know backwards and forwards, a prayer Grandmother had me say every night whenever Martin had a recurrence of tuberculosis. The prayer is so familiar that, even from Philomena's whispers, I can make out whole words, whole sentences. I join in and keep pace with her even though I see no reason to say it. Brendan is already dead. He is beyond my supplications. Beyond my petitions. For that matter, I am certain I am dead as well. Still, I pray the prayer from force of habit:

Remember, O most gracious Virgin Mary, that never was it known that any one who fled to your protection, implored your help or sought your intercession was left unaided. Inspired with this confidence, I fly to you, O Virgin of virgins, my Mother! To you

I come; before you I stand, sinful and sorrowful. O Mother of the Word Incarnate, despise not my petition, but in your mercy hear and answer me. Amen."

As soon as I finish the *Memorare*, I begin saying my own words, saying them out loud, words that make no sense to anyone but myself. I wonder if Brendan is wearing his new Levis. I say, no, he isn't. He would never mess up those new pants, never splotch them with blood. He had waited too long for them to come in at the Avalon Mall. He could have gotten the brown-tab Levis, but he wanted the red-tab ones.

Greg paces between the porch and the rock wall, stricken. From time to time he comes and asks me how I am holding up. When he leaves I can't remember whether or not I answered him because I am so mesmerized by his bloody footprints on the frost-tipped grass. After me, he goes to Philomena. She doesn't answer him either. From my perch I see a doctor and a priest come and go, bumping into each other in the narrow porch doorway. They come over to speak to me, but because I can't comprehend what they are saying they give my shoulder a compassionate touch and leave. I hear someone shout to make room in the lane for the Mountie's car. I watch Philomena, too shell-shocked to protest, being led away by Frank Clarke. She is still making the whispering sounds as she climbs down off the wall.

And I watch as two men from the funeral home take an empty stretcher into the house and leave with it loaded. On the way out a sheet covers the stretcher, Philomena's sheet. I recognize the yellow daisy pattern. Someone near me, probably Bridey or Rose, says the sight of the sheet is better than the sight of a body bag. I see Paddy put the narrow porch door back on its hinges after the stretcher leaves. And I see Greg once more walking over to squat down beside me. The cuffs of his white shirt are stained red. He places his hand over mine. I feel one cold slab of flesh overlapping another.

Other people come and go. Neighbours. They carry buckets

and mops and brooms and cloths to clean things up so we won't have to trample over bits and pieces of Brendan's skull. From time to time some of these same people come over to me and in muted voices ask whether I want to go their house, or sit in their heated car, or even move to the front of Philomena's house where the sun is shining so I won't freeze my kidneys on the cold rocks. "Let the tail follow the hide," Grandmother always said whenever she threw out the cover of a pot that she had scorched beyond salvage. I refuse to budge. With my heart already dead, I see no point in saving my kidneys.

Danny comes home for the funeral. We sit together in the visitors' room in the funeral parlour while we take a break from our silent staring at Brendan's closed casket. Danny's eyes flash fury as he enumerates the punishments that should be in store for Father Tom Haley. "It's all his fault. That slime-eating, puke-faced bastard should be made away with. It's totally that putty-faced shit's fault. Brendan took his own life. He couldn't stand the shame. You'll never make me believe he was trying to get Dad's gun to work so he could practice shooting cans." He says this as if I have been beleaguering him to accept Brendan's death as an unfortunate accident. "No siree," he repeats, "you won't get me to believe that. It's what that chiselling bastard did to him that made him do what he did."

Philomena sits beside him, but she doesn't nudge him to keep his voice down, nor does she order him to keep a civil tongue in his mouth in the presence of the dead, as she ordinarily would do. She merely pulls her black wool sweater closer around her bony shoulders. Over the last couple of days she has shrivelled into a frail old woman, the marrow squeezed from her bones, the juices drained from her body. Hers is the most terrible of griefs. Without words, without tears, she just sits and stares. Her lips never utter a regret. Her eyes stay as dry as the air in the windowless funeral parlour viewing room.

We bury Brendan on a leaden November day — November fourth, a Tuesday, a day so choked with fog that the foghorn on the downs at the far end of the Cove blats non-stop. The sky is a dirty grey. It keeps raining on and off. Philomena says that what is falling from the sky is not rain but heaven's shamefaced tears. What happened to Brendan is enough to scald the heart of the Almighty. To blister the souls of the saints.

Danny drives with us to the church service, but once it is over he sidles up to me and says that he and Paddy are going to renege on the cemetery part of the service. They are going to go back home to make sure the fires will be kept stoked so the house will be warm when his mother gets back.

It is a lame excuse; neighbours have stayed behind to look after things. I surmise that they're going to a tavern, not a decent thing to do at a time like this, but I lack the will to call him on it. Besides, I don't want to bring his defection to Philomena's attention, so I merely raise my eyebrows to acknowledge hearing him.

When we return from the cemetery, Greg, as usual, on account of the ruts in the lane, stops the car halfway up to the house. When we open the doors and step outside, we smell smoke. The three of us sniff the air and look around to see where it is coming from. Between the wind and the fog, we can't detect its direction, but when we get nearer to the house we hear the splintering of wood and the squeak of nails being pried loose.

"What the hell is going on?" Greg breaks into a run, and I race after him, leaving Philomena to fend for herself. When we come around to the back of the house, we see Danny up on a ladder wielding a wrecking bar, prying the clapboards from the porch. Most of the studs are already exposed. The air is filled with smoke from the fire Paddy has underway in the landwash.

"What the. . .what're you doing? What's going on?" Greg stammers.

Danny drops a clapboard to the ground. "Well, Paddy wanted to start a bonfire, and we didn't have enough wood." He drops down another clapboard.

Greg is in no mood for Danny's humour. "What stupidity are you two up to now? Mom'll freeze to death! What . . . oh, I . . ." Understanding dawns on him and, in the same instant, on me. "I'm sorry, b'y. I see what you're doing. It's the right thing. I should have thought of it myself. But couldn't it have waited? There's people dropping by."

"It's coming off, and it's coming off now," Danny replies, ripping out nails. "Let whoever is coming come in the front." He looks down at Paddy who is on his way back for more boards to put on the fire. "Ent that right Paddy? It's coming off now."

"That's right, b'y." Paddy stoops to gather up an armful of clapboards. "And like ye said, 'tis goin' back up. But not tonight. And we're goin' to put the door in a different place. Change the whole face of everything. It won't look like the same place at all."

Danny stops wielding the wrecking bar long enough to ask, "Where's Mom?"

The last time I saw Philomena she was walking behind us up the lane, but when I look over my shoulder, I catch a glimpse of her going in the front door. Greg also sees her. He says to Danny, "She's gone in the front door. She knows what's going on. She can't bear to see it being torn down. Maybe you should have warned her. Warned us."

"No time for that. It just came to us at the church. Paddy mentioned how terrible it was going to be for her to have to walk in and out through that porch a dozen times a day, so I said let's go back and rip 'er down and build 'er bigger."

Greg surveys the amount of work just to tear it down, let alone put it up. Perplexed, he asks Danny, "Is Paddy going to finish the job? You won't get much done by tomorrow afternoon."

"No, b'y. You got it wrong. I'm not going back," Danny drops another clapboard into the pile.

"Did you change your flight?"

"Nope. Cancelled it. No more lumber woods for old Danny boy."

"But you can't give up your job! What're you going to do? Your work is out there!"

Danny points to the landwash where Paddy is stoking the fire. "See that fellow down there? He's my new boss. Yes siree, Bossman Paddy. He found out yesterday he got a government contract to build houses on that stretch of land just up from the church. Senior citizens' housing. He's hiring me to help him. Carpenter's helper. That's what I'll be."

He screeches off another clapboard and throws it down for Paddy to cart away. "Imagine that! Old Danny boy a carpenter's helper. Still working with lumber, mind you. Can't seem to get too far away from the woods."

I hear the kitchen filling up with people, and I know I should go in to help Bridey and Rose with the hostessing, but all I want to do is stay outside and listen to the splintering of wood that I know is taking away the last remnants of Brendan.

I'm no sooner in the kitchen when someone, jumping like Danny to the conclusion that Brendan's death was not accidental, asks, "Wasn't there any sign?"

The question, asked kindly enough, drives a spike through my heart. "No. No sign at all," I answer, and because I still want to deny the actuality of what has happened, I tack on, "The storm door might have slammed up against him and knocked him off his legs. The wind in that door is something fierce. And he wanted to get some practice in to surprise Greg because he had told him he would take him target practicing one day."

I can taste my lies as they slip over my lips. I abruptly leave the kitchen and go into the den. Philomena is sitting in Hubert's chair, idling her finger over the groove in its arm. I see blame forming and reforming in her dry eyes. I am certain she is thinking that any mother worth her salt would have seen a dark cloud gathering, would have noticed a shadow cutting across the sun — unless, of course, she was the sort of mother who was preoccupied with worms in codfish, with the overpopulation of seals, with whether she would be nominated for the leadership of her party.

Without reference to the surrounding conversation, without taking notice of Rose, who is passing out crustless sandwiches, without any prompting, Philomena begins to tell about the time she and a couple of her young friends took her father's dory out for a joyride. When they returned to shore, they neglected to haul the dory high enough on the beach so it would be out of reach of the rising tide. Sometime during the night the dory was swept out to sea, never to be glimpsed again. Ever afterwards, her mind's eye saw the dry spot high on the beach where her father had always secured the dory, where she should have secured it if she hadn't been so careless.

I wonder if her off-the-mark story is her way of telling me I was careless with Brendan. Will my mind's eye always have a dry spot to remind me of this carelessness, and will that dry spot be Brendan's empty room? Philomena's drier-than-beach-rocks eyes? Greg's cool civility?

Shortly after Philomena's allegory, I make my excuses and go upstairs to bed. But not to sleep. Even when daylight disappears and night comes, I still don't sleep. I get up several times. Sometimes I go to the kitchen to make a cup of tea, and sometimes I sit by the bedroom window and stare out in the direction of the cemetery.

Although I cannot see Dickson's Hill from my window, I can see it crystal clear in my mind. I see the mound of fresh earth, just a whisper away from the gathering of Corrigans. I wonder if Brendan is cold and if he can see the November-grey sky, empty except for one pale, washed-out star. And I wonder if he is already feeling the vastness of eternity and the finality of forever. And if he misses his family, all gathered in the house where he had spent the happy times of his life. And I wonder, too, whether, if it were possible for him to relive Sunday morning, he would do things differently.

I get up at daybreak far more exhausted than I had been before I went to bed. Philomena and Greg never even pretended to try to sleep. Greg spent the night wandering from the den to the kitchen under the pretext of keeping the fires going. Philomena sat at the kitchen table and looked over snapshots that she has kept stored away in a shoebox, tied in bundles. While I begin to set the table for breakfast, she continues to look at the worn snapshots, picking out paragraphs in each cracked and brown-faced life to relate to Greg whenever he comes into the kitchen to stoke the fire. From the way she stares at each picture, I can tell that it comforts her to recall her many relatives already on the other side who could meet her grandson, a soul in special need of being met because his sudden death did not allow him to make any preparation for the journey.

"They were all on hand to meet him," she says, naming names. "And they made him feel welcome. I have no worries on that score."

Philomena's pictures are her treasured possessions. After Hubert died she began mislaying things — glasses, purse, keys — as if, now that he was gone, she was willing to let old age have its way with her. But she never mislaid her photographs. These she kept tidily arranged in their box, although they were stacked away helter skelter in her brain.

When I come to the table to set down the plates, she holds up a picture for my inspection. Greg's First Communion. He is dressed in a Sunday suit and has a white ribbon in his lapel. He is looking straight into the camera, sober and serious, the seeds of the lawyer already germinating within him. Danny is standing a little behind Greg. He is dressed in short pants, obviously his play clothes. From Danny's grin and his unkempt appearance, it is clear that he jumped into the picture uninvited, mischievously barging in on Greg's special day.

"That scamp," Philomena says, and I know she is referring to Danny.

I offer to refill her cup from the pot of tea she has kept brewing all night on the back of the stove. She merely shakes her head. When I continue to set the breakfast table around her, she gathers the loose pictures together so she can tuck them into their separate bundles before placing them back in the box. When she comes to the last picture, she runs her roughened hand over it. It is a photo of herself and Hubert on their wedding day. It shows them young and in love, not yet ripped and torn by the many heartaches yet to come.

"Oh my! Oh my!" she says, barely above her breath as she lays the box aside. "The twists and turns life takes."

Danny comes downstairs and takes his place at the table. For once the sadness in his eyes is not at odds with the rest of his features. He makes no cracks about Philomena's unkempt hair, her treasured box of pictures or her strong tea. For her part, she refrains from telling him that his torn T-shirt and rumpled hair remind her of an unmade bed. Greg comes in from the den and offers to butter the toast, which he does with his usual precision. I refrain from asking him to please hurry up because our tea is getting cold. No one remarks that, out of habit, I have set a place for Brendan.

After breakfast, Greg and I get ready to go back to St. John's. It seems as though we have been away a lifetime instead of less than a week. Because we had come to the Cove expecting to return on Sunday afternoon, we are not prepared for a longer stay, although to be sure Greg had to make a hurried trip back to our house to pick up suitable funeral clothes for ourselves and burial clothes for Brendan.

On the drive home, Greg and I come out of our stupor in order to volley blame back and forth at each other across the front seat. And there is plenty of blame to volley. Brendan's joining the Altar Servers' Association is no longer the main point of contention. Neither is his sexual abuse. Now it is his death by gunshot.

"Surely you must realize, Tess, that mere mortals like my mother and me can't possess your psychic attributes," Greg snaps in response to my accusation that, if he had insisted that Brendan come to church with us, he would still be alive. "Besides, if you knew so much, why didn't *you* stay home with him? But I suppose it wouldn't look very good if the MHA wasn't in church." He waits for this arrow to meet its target, then adds, "I knew you were just bluffing when you said you were going to stay home with Brendan. That's why I got so mad about your mollycoddling him. I knew you were just trying to force him to go with you for the sake of show."

Every insult, every charge, every accusation is close enough to the truth to cut to the quick, yet far enough from the truth to force us into a fighting defence. By the time we arrive in St. John's we are barely civil to one another.

Once we get inside the house, however, we pretend that nothing has changed, that the house isn't filled to the rafters with Brendan's absence. We get on with ordinary things. I sort the mail. Greg checks in with his office, then walks to the corner store to pick up milk. When it comes time to go to bed, we both stall, each of us aware that the accusations we had flung at one another in the car have made the queen-size bed far too small to accommodate the two of us.

"I'm going to the office," Greg says, placing the decision about who will sleep where in my hands. "Work's piled up."

I offer no protest, even though the very thought of being alone in the house with so much emptiness is enough to make my breath snag in panic. After he leaves, not saying when he will be back, I go upstairs to go to bed. Because Brendan's room is at the top of the stairs, I shut his door as I pass by, closing my eyes tight as I do so. But even with the door shut and my eyes closed, I can still see the yellow Grand Prix racing car models laid out on the table that had been put in his room just to hold them. And I can still see the checkered bedspread hanging unevenly, jibbing out at the bottom like the sail of a ship despite my ritual exhortations for him to straighten it properly. And I can still see the schoolbag with books spilling out of its mouth and the enlarged picture of a speckled trout over the head of his bed, the very first trout he had caught on one of his overnight fishing excursions with Greg.

I walk down the hall to the bathroom, where I shower for a very long time, letting the water gush over me, prolonging the moment when I will have to climb alone into bed. By the time I leave the bathroom, I have decided to forego the marital bedroom in favour of the room we always keep in readiness for Philomena's visits. Without removing my damp terrycloth bathrobe, I fall, physically exhausted and emotionally spent, on top of the green polyester bedspread.

I sleep fitfully throughout the night, several times waking to the sounds of crying, which after only a few dazed moments I realize are coming from my own lips. When day breaks I get up, no longer willing to coax and wheedle myself back to sleep. On the way downstairs, I notice that Brendan's door is open a crack. I go to shut it tight, thinking a draft has blown it open. Greg is sprawled on Brendan's bed, still dressed in suit and tie, the tie hanging slack, the jacket unbuttoned. Even in sleep, it is evident that he, too, spent the night crying.

I ease the door shut and tiptoe downstairs, where I make a breakfast I do not eat, and afterwards I go to my office, where I do not work. In fact, all I do is shut my door, turn off my phone and scour the hours and the minutes for clues I might have missed, clues that, if picked up, might have made a difference: a word said, a look missed, a behaviour gone unnoticed — anything that could have signalled imminent tragedy. But search as I may, I find no portents of impending death, no harbingers of a life about to snuff out. No single crow had flown overhead. No black cat had crossed my path. No picture had fallen off the wall. No sparks in a row had appeared on the underside of the dampers on Philomena's stove to signify a funeral procession. No pot had boiled dry. In short, there had been no warning signs at all.

The days pass, even though neither Greg nor I lift a finger to make them pass. We speak to each other only when it is essential to do so and, even then, only in the briefest of sentences. On Friday morning Greg informs me he is going to the Cove after work, and, on account of the promised snowstorm, he will be staying overnight.

He wants to ensure that his mother's porch is being put back on, and he also wants to give Danny money towards the cost of the lumber and supplies, something he had forgotten to do before he left.

He doesn't ask me to go with him, he acts as if he doesn't expect me to go with him, and I interpret this to mean he doesn't want me to go with him. Although I know that staying alone in the house for the weekend will be an agony beyond parallel, I refuse to admit this to him, and when he asks me if I will be okay on my own, I reply, "Fine! Just fine!" His suitcase is splayed open on Brendan's bed, and he is about to toss in a couple of pairs of socks when I add, "Like you said about me closing Brendan's door, it's time I faced reality." His hand holding the socks falters and hovers over the open suit-case for a moment, but he makes no response.

Over the past week, no matter how many times I have closed Brendan's door, Greg has always opened it wide, and he has never failed to admonish me that I have to face reality, that I must not turn Brendan's room into a crypt. In fact, to make sure this will not happen, he has moved most of his clothes into that room, and he sleeps there every night. He has even moved in a small chest of drawers, which is an inch too long for the wall it stands against. It juts out into the doorway, preventing the door from fully closing.

On Saturday morning when I pass Brendan's bedroom to go downstairs, my eyes fix on the slightly ajar door and then move beyond the door to the corner of the table that holds his model cars. Even this restricted glimpse of his belongings shoots breath-hitching pain through my body, and over breakfast I ponder about which situation would be the least painful: getting glimpses of his room through the partly open door every time I go up or down the hall or, as Greg believes, leaving the door wide open and getting used to seeing it as it is. Neither option, I decide, is bearable. A room emptied of Brendan's belongings appears to be the only answer.

I begin the purge of his bedroom immediately after breakfast. I drive to the grocery store and get cardboard boxes to pack up the stuff in his closets and drawers. I put these packed-to-overflowing boxes in the trunk of my car to take to some charitable organization on Monday morning.

As soon as his personal belongings are out of the way, I start in on the bedroom itself, taking down the curtains, pulling off the bedspread, even steaming off the layers of wallpaper right down to the bare plaster wall. I then drive to the K-Mart and throw things indiscriminately into my cart: a bedspread, window curtains and floor mat, none of which match or blend. When the bedroom is finished, I go to the basement and I strip-search it and then move on to the garage, grabbing up anything even remotely reminiscent of Brendan.

By Sunday afternoon the purge is complete, and when I open Brendan's bedroom door wide, I see a room that is as foreign to me and as uninviting as if it were a display room in a second-hand furniture store.

When Greg returns from the Cove, he comes into the kitchen where I have started to prepare supper. He stands in the doorway, suitcase in one hand, a brown paper bag in the other. He looks awkward, as if he has wandered by mistake into someone else's house and wants to make a quick retreat. When I turn towards him, he hurriedly hands me the paper bag.

"Mom said you might be able to use these. You like jam-jams. She had them frozen, ready for Christmas, but she wants you to enjoy them now."

Stranded as we both are in this new state of limbo — not lovers, not friends, just two people related by marriage and connected in misery through the memory of a dead son — I feel as awkward and as ill at ease as he does.

"How is she?" I inquire, fiddling with the pot roast I just removed from the oven and relieved to have the subject of Philomena to fall back upon.

"Looks so woebegone," he says, sounding just as woebegone. "Danny says she doesn't eat enough to keep a sick nun alive. She's just a shell of herself. But she refuses to see a doctor."

"And the porch?"

"Back on. A beautiful job. Changed the door opening. Switched around the steps. Gives it an entirely different look."

Once he has exhausted the surface conversation about his trip, Greg begins unloading his overnight case. He leaves the kitchen to take the handful of soiled clothing up to the laundry basket in the bathroom, necessitating passing by Brendan's room. In less than a minute he is back downstairs, hurrying past the kitchen, heading for the basement, the bundle of dirty laundry still clutched in his hand. I hear him rummaging in the closets underneath the stairs where Brendan's sports equipment has always been stored. He returns to the kitchen and stares at me wordlessly from the doorway, condemnation heavy in his eyes.

"It had to be done," I say self-righteously. "*Someone* had to do it!" That he should have been on hand to help me do it is left dangling in the air.

"You cleaned out *everything*? *Everything*?"

"Like you said, no point in making a crypt out of this house."

"I said there's no point in making a crypt out of his *room*. He was my son, too. Or did you forget that part, being so caught up in your own self-pity? Anyway, who gave you the right to wipe all traces of him out of my life?"

Despite the heat in the kitchen from the cooking food, I feel chilled to the bone. I force a detached indifference, a cool composure. "It's all in the car," I say. "Help yourself. Keep what you want to keep. I did what I had to do. You do what you have to do."

He turns away. "Don't keep supper for me," he says over his shoulder. "I'm going to the office."

The door slams shut behind him.

Chapter Ten

BY UNSPOKEN AGREEMENT, we take turns going out to the Cove on weekends — Greg goes one weekend, I go the next. When I see Philomena after a two-week absence, I am startled at how much ground she has lost. Out of her hearing, Danny tells me she doesn't sleep very much, just catnaps in Hubert's chair during the day and prowls the house at night.

"Why didn't Greg come with you?" she asks as I settle down in the den.

"Too much work to do," I lie.

"Losing a child can be hard on a marriage. Or it can make it stronger. I ought to know," she says, not calling me on my lie.

"He blames me for Brendan's death," I say, deciding to halt the charade, although I do not go so far as to tell her that I have taken up permanent residence in the room we had designated as hers. And I do not tell her that Greg comes home only to sleep and does that in the bedroom that has been thoroughly cleansed of Brendan. For that matter, I do not tell her that each morning the unused master bedroom with its celibate tidiness mocks the well-mannered facade that now passes for our marriage.

"Nonsense, girl!" She pulls her afghan around her legs, her tone reminiscent of an earlier Philomena. "He doesn't blame you. If anything, he blames himself. Or more likely, he thinks *you* blame *him*. Men are so full of themselves they think that we think everything is in their power. If something doesn't turn out right, it's because they neglected this or that. Like Hubert when little Bridget died. Thought it was his fault. Thought if he could have afforded a doctor instead of a midwife, the child would have been stronger. But that was nonsense. The child was born too early, and we didn't have them fancy little huts they put them in now. You know what I mean. I can't think of the name."

"Incubators."

"Right! That's the name. Incubators. Her death had nothing at all to do with Hube. Or, for that matter, his lack of money, unless perhaps if he had been a millionaire, then we could have flown her to a hospital in Montreal, which might have helped. But how many people are millionaires? He thought I was blaming him for her death when in truth I was just filled up with my own sadness. So instead of having patience with me, he got cranky. If it were now times when couples aren't so steadfast, he probably would have left me."

She halts her conversation long enough to pull wisps of her untended hair behind her ears and to heel in the footstool. "I 'members this woman from down home. In fact I was thinking about her the other day. Her husband left her after their only child was drowned. Left her for another woman. And the replacement was no oil painting, I can tell you that much. Had a face on her as plain as a Quaker's quilt. And I've seen better bottoms on a dory. But she was Johnnie-on-the-spot with the sympathy and the coddling. That's what he wasn't getting at home."

She reaches over and presses my arm. "Ferget about who's to blame, girl. There's enough for all of us. As for meself, I wish I had sided with you that Sunday and forced him to come to Mass with us. I'll never live long enough to put that regret behind me." She pulls more stray strands of hair behind her ears. "Not that I wants to live that long. I've dragged through enough of life as it is." She hoists herself out of her chair. "Now I'm going upstairs to try and get a wink of sleep. I can't seem to do much of that lately. But you go to bed whenever you wants to."

"But what about *Dallas?*" I ask. "You always look at *Dallas*. It's coming on in a few minutes."

Danny, who is sitting in the kitchen, overhears me. Eager for Philomena to show an interest in something, he calls out, "But Mom, you love *Dallas*. You love Bobby Ewing. Why don't you stay up and look at the program with Tess?"

"Because boy, I'm too bloody tired. And besides, I purely hates that J.R. Now Bobby is a different matter. But why would I waste a wink of sleep looking at that scoundrel J.R.?"

There is nothing in this exchange to tell me that this is the last Friday night I will spend in the Cove with Philomena. There are no harbingers. No portents. Greg goes to see her on the weekend of December thirteenth, and on the morning of the sixteenth, Danny calls me at my office to say Philomena died in Hubert's chair in front of the television set, her legs swathed in the afghan. He had tried to get in touch with Greg through his office, but Greg was already in court. He leaves it to me to find him there.

"I feel something terrible about how things came about," Danny confesses. "She died watching me put up a bloody Christmas tree she didn't want in the house. Overrode her all the way, I did. She said a house of mourning was no place for a sparkly Christmas tree. But I thought the tree would cheer her up, and that's why I put it up early." He does not wait for praise or blame but rushes on. "And I thought it would do you and Greg good, too, when you came out for Christmas. And Paddy thought the same thing, and he said the earlier we got it up the better, so me and him went up on the back of the Cove and cut down a couple of fir trees yesterday afternoon and dragged them home. One for Paddy. Put ours in the porch overnight to let the limbs thaw out and the snow to melt off. So this morning, somewhere around ten o'clock, right after her breakfast, I started trimming the thing.

"She wasn't mad at me or anything for putting the tree up, even though I had gone against her. In fact, she brought her cup of tea into the den to finish it off while she watched me. She wasn't talking much, but then she hasn't been talking much since" — he hesitates before bringing up another grief — "Well, you know how she pulled into herself after Brendan. But as soon as she sat down she said, right out of nowhere, 'Poor Rudy died in July. July just past. He was eighty-five.' Then she began to sing 'Springtime in the Rockies.' So I s'pose it was Rudy Vallee she was talking about. Earlier she had the radio on in the kitchen, so they were probably singing that song and it reminded her. Anyway, she sang the song all the way through. So then I started putting on the silver tinsel, and she said it reminded her of a glitter storm she remembered from when she was young. It had come the last of May. It had rained pure ice and killed the sprouting rose bushes. Then she said 'Oh my! Oh my! There's nothing as bad as a winter rain on summer bushes.' And that's it. She gives this big sigh and her cup and saucer fall on the floor."

After I hang up the phone, I call Greg's office, but his secretary informs me, as she already had informed Danny, that he is in court. She lets me speak with Mr. Cadagan and when I explain the reason for my call, he tells me to tell Greg to go on home, not to worry about the office, everything will be looked after.

Although it is snowing heavily and the streets are slippery, I go to the courthouse to waylay Greg on his way back to his office. I catch up with him just as he is coming out the back door on his way to the parking lot. He is loaded down with a briefcase in one hand, file folders in the other and his court robe over his arm.

"What's up?" he asks, in the frightened way a person asks when he senses bad news. "What's wrong?"

"Danny called," I say as gently as I can. "It's Mrs. Phil."

He blanches, but his mind grasps at straws. "Oh my God! How bad?"

"She's gone." To soften the blow, I hurriedly add, "She had a real easy death. Danny said she just slipped away sitting in your dad's chair."

He sets down his briefcase on the snow-covered step, rearranges his handful of file folders and straightens the robe on his arm. I recognize these actions as his way of staving off tears. But they show up in his voice anyway. "I've got to get back to the office," he says huskily. "Then I'll head out."

I tell him about my conversation with Mr. Cadagan. "Everything is looked after. And I packed your suitcase. It's in my car."

"What about you? Are you coming out now or later?"

"Danny wants us both right away," I reply. "He sounded frantic. I called the Mounties. The roads are too bad for my little car. It's been snowing out that way all day. I'll have to drive with you. If that's okay. I'll take my car back home."

"Fine," he says. "It's fine with me." I can't read anything in his voice. "No problem. Where's your car?"

"I'm right beside you." I point to the spot in the partially ploughed parking lot where my Honda is parked beside his green Chevrolet. We'll transfer the suitcases to your car and then I'll take the Honda home and drop it off. You meet me there."

We make the luggage transfer, and we get into our separate cars. "Be careful on Long's Hill," he warns as he pulls out, leading the way. "Once you start up it, just keep on going, smooth and steady, or you'll never make it."

Although the highway to the Cove was given a once-over ploughing earlier in the day, snow has drifted in windrows across the road, making the driving treacherous. Greg hunches over the wheel, never taking his eyes from the road. Because as usual the snow is damp, every so often he has to pull over to the side of the highway to remove the buildup of slush from the windshield wipers.

Our conversation is limited to the logistics of burying Philomena. I repeat things that Danny told me when he called, things she had told him a few weeks earlier, things which at the time he had thought were ridiculous and he had told her so, now much to his regret. She told him she wanted to be waked at home, that until she got used to being dead she didn't want to be surrounded by dead strangers. She had come to this conclusion after waking Hubert and Brendan at the funeral parlour and having to leave them alone all night. And she wanted to be buried with a Requiem Mass. She didn't have the frills when she got married, so she wanted the full quintal of fish when she got buried.

I also tell Greg that Paddy Flynn and Frank Clarke are making the arrangements for having the grave dug. They are going to rent a piece of equipment from the town council that can dig into even solidly frozen ground, though the ground on Dickson's Hill isn't solid yet because there has been more snow than frost. Paddy has drawn up a list of pallbearers, men who will be available on Wednesday without having to ask people to take the day off from work, but they are leaving the final say up to him. And I tell him that Philomena even has her waking dress picked out — her wine-coloured wool with the accordion pleats, although the belt is to be left off because, she said, she would feel smothered to death with it, the way it cinches her waist.

Neither Greg nor I mention Brendan or the excruciating pain we know we will feel when we lay Philomena down beside him, his own grave still a fresh hump in the snow, not even having had time to settle. And I do not pass along Danny's joke that we should ask the funeral parlour for a frequent burial discount because of having three funerals in such a short time.

"December's not a fit month for dying," Greg pronounces after we are back on the road, having pulled off for what must be the tenth time to bang the wipers against the windshield and clear the headlights of caked slush. "At least it's not a fit month for dying in these parts."

"But what month is?" I ask, recalling other burials, other months. "They've all got their shortcomings, especially in the winter." After a moment's considering, I allow, however, December has to be the worst month. "With Christmas and all," I say. And I tell him that if

Philomena had been given any say in the matter, she would not have chosen to die in December.

His mouth forms a small, wry smile, the first smile I have seen on his face in many weeks. "I can't imagine Mom not having a say in something that important to her. She always had her say about everything else."

"That's for sure." The picture of Philomena arguing with God about a fit month for her to go home forms a smile even on my lips. "If she had any say in the matter, she would have chosen August. The last half of August. She once told me that she loved the last two weeks of August the best of all. Everything has calmed down by then, the temper and frenzy have gone out of the summer, and, she said, you can be lazy without feeling guilty — too late to sow, too soon to reap. And there's less likelihood of rain.

I tell Greg her story about her hoity toity sister, Loretta, who came from Toronto for their mother's funeral. It was in the early sixties, just before resettlement got underway. Mid-June. Raining a continuous pelting rain, and of course it was bitter cold because the icebergs were still in the harbour. Worst of all, as soon as they got to the grave site there was an extra heavy downpour, and Loretta's wool-crepe dress, which according to Philomena was already too short to meet the decency standards of the village, began to shrink even shorter. In fact, by the end of the service you could see the hitching and britching that held up her stockings.

"Hitching and britching?" Greg asks.

"Women wore garter belts at that time," I explain. "With suspenders to hold up the stockings. And short dresses had just come in style. Philomena said that when Loretta bent over to put a handful of clay into the grave, a highfalutin custom she picked up in Toronto, you could see all the way to New York."

Greg glances my way and laughs. "Now I remember her telling that story. I had forgotten all about it. What a woman she was for stories."

We arrive at Philomena's house just as the people from the funeral parlour are lugging a mahogany-coloured casket through the front door and angling it this way and that way so it won't get wedged in the narrow frame.

Not wanting to interfere with this operation, we go around to the back door, where we bump into Paddy and Frank. They are dragging out the Christmas tree, ornaments and all. Frank holds the storm door wide open so the tree can be pulled through. In the gale force winds, the silver tinsel icicles go streaking across the frozen meadow like shooting stars on a clear night.

"Hoooly Lord dyin'," he shouts as he stands wide-legged on the new porch steps, bracing himself against the wind. "Grab hold of the railing, Paddy me son, or the divil ever ye'll be seen again. Ye'll be going around and around in space like that Russian satellite that got lost — Spudnuk, or whatever in the hell 'twas called."

There is more commotion inside the house. Neighbours are coming and going. The kitchen table is already laden with donated food. Danny is rearranging the parlour, bringing in chairs from the kitchen to support the casket. Rose is rearranging the refrigerator to accommodate the perishable foods, and Bridey is rearranging the pictures and knick-knacks on the parlour tables to make room for the flowers and candles. Clearly, everything is well in hand.

It is after midnight before the crowd withers down to only Paddy Flynn, Danny, Greg and me. Greg announces he is going to bed. He says he will douse the candles in the wake room on his way upstairs and close the parlour door until morning. Danny announces that the Black Horse is making him wish for a feed of capelin. "You wouldn't happen to have any at your place, would you Paddy?"

"Yes, b'y. Tons of them, b'y," Paddy says. "Youngsters won't touch the things. Just me and Bridey. I'll go over and bring back a few handfuls to roast."

He starts to get up out of his chair to go get the capelin when I veto the plan. "Maybe we shouldn't roast them here. The smell." I'm thinking that the windows are frozen shut, so the smell of roasted capelin will still be in the house in the morning.

"Yer right, girl," Paddy agrees. "I forgot about that. People'll think the stench is coming from the corpse." He turns to Danny. "Tell you what. I'll roast them at my place. I'll phone when they're ready. Come on over."

As soon as we have the kitchen to ourselves, Danny and I settle back, side by side in the wing-backed velour chairs that had to be moved out of the parlour in order to make room in there for the straight-backed kitchen chairs. I make a cup of tea and Danny opens another Black Horse. We talk quietly, mostly about Philomena — the goodness of her, the orneriness of her, and the ways in which her life touched ours.

"She blamed me for Brendan's death," I say, surprised at myself for admitting what I had never voiced before. "It put a wedge between us. She never came right out and said so, but I knew she felt that any caring mother would have known her son was being molested."

"Nonsense! Bloody nonsense!" Danny says, with more indignation than the moment calls for. "There is no way you could have known that! No way in God's earthly world. And she should have been the last one to lay that on your shoulders."

"Well, you know how much she loved Brendan," I say. "And if it had been one of her sons, she would have known. Every time she looked at me, I saw that message in her eyes."

Danny leans back in his chair, closes his eyes. He is silent for so long I think he is napping. He then straightens up and sits the bottle of beer he has been clasping in his hands on the counter beside him. He sits it down as if it weighs a ton. He carefully wipes his mouth with the heel of his hand and then wipes his hands clean, brushing one over the other. He looks at me as if he is going to say something, then changes his mind. He looks away. He picks up the beer bottle and then puts it back down without drinking from it.

"She . . . I'm not sure . . .," he begins, weighing the pros and cons of going further. He doesn't turn my way but keeps staring across the kitchen and out through the window at the snowbanks that, under the night sky, are more blue than white. He says in a tone edged with anger, "She was bloody well wrong. She wouldn't have known. She would've had no more idea that something was going on than you did. Not a whit more notion." He stares into my eyes, daring me to contradict him.

On Philomena's behalf I do just that. "You know what a mother hen she was, much more ferocious than most mothers."

He reaches for the bottle of beer again and picks it up. Once more he does not drink from it. "Take it from me, Tess," he says, wagging the bottle in my direction, "she would've had no more idea what was going on than the man in the moon. And if she was standing before me right this minute instead of in there, I'd blow her out of the water by telling her how wrong she was on this one. I'd set her back on her heels."

An uneasy feeling passes over me, an anxiety I can do without. "I'm going to make another pot of tea." I push back my heavy chair in the hope that, by going to the stove, I can move the conversation away from Philomena "I feel like a fresh cup. How about you? Ready to give up the beer?"

Danny reaches across his chair and lays a restraining hand on my arm. "Don't move!" he commands. "Sit back down. I've got to say this right now. Maybe it's not the right time. But I don't give a shit anymore." He thumps the bottle of beer on the table as if he is calling a meeting to order. "Same thing happened to me," he says. "Like Brendan. When I was his age."

"You took Hubert's gun?"

"Hell no! I was sexually abused."

I slump back into my chair and begin drowning in the same sick sensations that had flooded my body the evening George O'Connell told us about Brendan's molestation. I want to scold Danny. I want to say, Don't joke about this. It's no time to joke. But I don't have the breath for scolding. Besides, I know Danny isn't joking. "Who? When? A priest?" I finally manage to ask.

He reaches over the table and picks up the package of cigarettes he had tossed there earlier. He plucks one out and jabs it between his lips. He tries to light it, but his hands are shaking so much he can't strike the match. He fumbles the cigarette back into the package and throws it on the counter.

"Hell, no, girl. Not a priest. A blood of a bitch bastard in Dad's church. That's who did it to me. A custodian for the church. Looked after the furnace and the grounds. Whitney, his name was."

"Oh my God!" I say, not knowing what else to say. I remain sitting in my chair, unable to make my body reach out to touch Danny, although the moment calls for some sign of compassion other than words. With his eyes averted, focusing on the window, he lays bare the secret he has kept for almost a quarter of a century.

"You're the first person to be hearing this. No, the second, I s'pose. If you count Dad. Told him in a half-assed sort of way. I said I had heard Whitney was friggin' with some boys. He said I shouldn't believe everything I was told and not to say anything about it to Mom because it would stick in her craw forever and she'd never let him hear the end of it. She'd never let me come to church with him again." He reaches for his cigarettes once more, and this time he can steady his hands enough to light one. He exhales a mouthful of smoke. "Blood of a bitch," he says, more to himself than to me. "After all these years I'd still like to kill that bastard."

"What happened to him? I hope he was caught. I hope he's still in jail. And I hope . . ." I say all of these hopes, although I truly don't know what I am hoping has happened to him. I just want it to be something terrible enough to rival the torture in Danny's eyes.

"Jail! Hell no! Not on your life! I was too shitless to tell. So were all the others." He shrugs. "I s'pose there were others. I always hoped there were. Well, not hoped, exactly. You know what I mean. Just never wanted to think I was the only one. Dad used to send me over to the church to help out on Saturdays. Put out the new bulletins. I was supposed to help Whitney move the pews so he could clean under them. That kind of shit. Dad said Greg was always helping out at Mom's church so I should help out at his."

"And Mr. Hube didn't think you were telling the truth?" I ask, confounded that Hubert would have let something so terrible go unstopped.

"No. Imagine that! He didn't believe his own son." He gives me one of his Danny-style grins.

"Well, you know, in fairness to Dad, I was always a bit of a codder, always quick with the joke. Always quick to exaggerate things for a bit of fun. So this day I said to him, I said, 'Dad, that fellow Whitney likes to paw young boys, and I don't want to be around him.' Dad gave me a little skite up the side of my head with the flat of his hand. 'Get along with ye, b'y,' he said, 'yer only tryin' to get out of work. And don't go coddin' about something as serious as that. You could steal the man's good name. And fer the love of God, don't go talking like that to yer mother. She'll believe you when she should know better.'"

Once he starts the telling, he doesn't seem to want to stop it. He wants to rid himself of all of the details. "I was twelve that first time I told Dad. We had it out again when I was seventeen. We had been arguing about something else — can't remember what it was, nothing serious — and I threw it up to him that he didn't do anything to help me when Whitney was buggering me."

He pauses, shakes his head, recalling the shocked look on his father's face at the use of the vulgar term. "My sonny b'y, he almost had a kitten when I said that. Especially when I used that word. And he tried to defend himself, saying he had no idea. But I wouldn't let him off the hook. I said he knew all right. He just didn't want the

Catholics to know — especially Mom — that a puking blood of a bitch like Buggering Whitney was as twisted as a corkscrew, and he was sitting up in a front pew on Sundays."

He stops talking long enough to take a deep drag on his cigarette. He lets the smoke out slowly, watches it as it travels across the room towards the window. By now all signs of the come day, go day, happy-go-lucky Danny have vanished. "Nothing could ever be the same after that. I left home the next day. I was always talking about leaving, so that part didn't come as any surprise, I s'pose. We never brought it up again. Never mentioned it, no matter how many times I came home."

"How long did it go on?" My mind rushes to calculate the years of torture. "From the time you were twelve until you were seventeen?"

"How long?" He skirts the question, as if to add up the years would be too painful. "I finally outfoxed the blood of a bitch. I took a chance he was doing the same thing to the other boys, bribing them to go into the furnace room with him, so I told him that the bunch of us had gotten together and swapped stories and the jig was up. He would never bugger another one of us. There was strength in numbers.

"My sonny boy, he turned as white as the driven snow when I said that, so I knew I was on the right track. So then I really let him have it. I told him that if he touched any one of us again, we were going to gang up on him and ram a mop handle up his arse so far he would be able to mop the floors and paint the walls at the same time. Or we might even skewer him through the arse on a picket fence."

He pauses, takes another long drag on his cigarette and sends the smoke out of his mouth in rings. These, too, he watches as they trail away. When he speaks again, it is as if he is talking to himself. "Left me alone after that. I hope he left the others alone, too. But that's what haunts me. Maybe he didn't."

He savagely crushes his cigarette in the over-filled ashtray, taking a long time to mangle the butt. His shoulders are slumped. "I should have done more. I should have told Dad in such a way that he would have had no doubt about what was going on. Just hinting about what was happening to me wasn't good enough. If I had told him outright he wouldn't have been able to toss away the barefaced truth, even if it did give Mom more ammunition for trying to get me to go to her church.

"But he should have believed me anyway, shouldn't he?" He doesn't need my answer, and he doesn't wait for it. "I shouldn't have had to carry this bloody beach rock around my neck for all these years. It weighted down my whole life. Every time I'd meet a woman I'd say to myself, Do you really want to tell this woman what happened to you? And the answer would always be no, because I would be afraid she'd think I was — you know — that maybe I had asked for it. So I'd make up some excuse to break up with her. And all because of that sanctimonious blood of a bitch."

By the time he is finished with the telling, my fury is so thick and so intense that when I speak, I stutter. "Damn him . . . I'd like to . . . we've got to . . ." I raise myself from my chair, ready to fight then and there. Like Greg on the night George O'Connell came to our house, I want to pummel Whitney to within an inch of his life. I recall that Philomena said God would rear up on His hind legs over Brendan's abuse. If I were God, I would now be rearing up on my hind legs.

"Greg was right all along," I say, "but I never believed him. He said love and brownies wouldn't be enough to cure Brendan. This thing has stayed with you all this time. It has hounded you ever since."

I begin to pace the kitchen floor, uttering threats. "We've got to do something! Someone has to put a stop to this! We've got to expose him!"

"What do you mean? Expose him?" Danny says. "I don't want that stuff dredged up now. I only told you because I didn't want you to carry around the blame for Brendan's abuse."

"Is Whitney still alive?"

"As far as I know. I kept tabs on him as best I could. Don't know why, but I did. I know where he moved when our village was resettled."

"Then we're going to do something about him," I say, wishing I had said the same words to Greg two months earlier. "It's the only way to make things right. It's the only way to give you some peace. And you won't have to do it alone. I'll be behind you all the way. I promise you that."

Danny remains quiet, lights up another cigarette, opens another bottle of Black Horse. I can feel the time passing as if someone is counting down the minutes to midnight. By the time he does speak, there has been so much silence in the kitchen that the sound of his voice startles me.

"By God, girl, you're right," he says, standing up, rejuvenated, ready to fight. "That's just what I need. Him exposed for what he is. That's what always stuck in my craw. That bastard got off scot-free. And if there were other youngsters – not just me — it might help them to know he got his comeuppance. And with Mom gone I don't have to worry about shaming her." He stops short. "But what about Greg? He's had enough shame."

At that moment the telephone rings, and although we have been expecting Paddy's call, it still jolts us. Danny picks up the receiver on the second ring and speaks into it very quietly so as not to wake Greg.

"Now I wish I hadn't promised Paddy to go over there," he laments when he hangs up. "The craving's gone. I'd rather sit here and talk. Imagine that! I'd rather talk than eat roasted capelin. Maybe I should've told him I don't want to leave you here alone. Besides, it's heading for two o'clock."

"Nonsense. You go on. Have your feed. You've been tied to the house all day. We can talk later. You waited this long, another few hours won't matter."

He reaches underneath the table, pulls a couple of bottles of

Black Horse out of the carton stashed there, and stuffs them in his jacket pocket. Then he goes to the porch to get his winter coat.

After Danny leaves, I sit alone in the kitchen trying to absorb what has just unfolded. One of the first chores I did in the morning when I arrived at Philomena's was to clean up her bedroom, change the sheets and lay out extra blankets, making her room ready for myself for the night. But now I have no use for the bed. The rapid switch from shock at Danny's disclosure to invigoration at the prospect of helping him bring his abuser to justice has banished sleep. When my thoughts factor in the possibility of helping those others who in all likelihood Whitney had victimized, as well as those who as yet hadn't had the misfortune of crossing his path, my brimming guilt makes room for the tiniest speck of peace, perhaps a token of a bearable future, maybe even a joyful one.

I get Philomena's afghan from the den, wrap it around me, curl up in the parlour chair and think of how to begin and where to begin. When my grandmother died, she left her house to my mother, who in turn left it to me. I have kept it rented all these years. Perhaps I could sell it to raise funds, perhaps I could turn it into a safe haven for the sexually abused. And then, too, there is the matter of the Liberal leadership campaign. If I do win the nomination, and if our party does form the government, I may be in a better position to supply help to those who have been sexually abused, particularly to young people who have been abused by people in positions of trust.

There are a lot of ifs and maybes in my plan to help Danny and those others. There is, however, one certainty. I want Greg to share in my peace. Since Brendan's death he has become lukewarm towards the social code of his prestigious law firm, and he has also become less than enthusiastic about being made a partner. In the early days of our marriage, he had talked about someday owning his own law firm. Perhaps now is that someday. If he does get his own practice underway, it will allow him the opportunity to give his expertise to Danny and the others without fear of reproach.

Swathed in the afghan, I squirm in the chair, anxious for morning to come. I want to tell Greg he had been right when he said a brownie and a hug would not be enough. And I want to tell him he is not responsible for Brendan finding the shells to the gun. No one could have imagined that the minute he was left alone he would go searching for them, nor that he would find them, buried as they were underneath old hats, empty shoe boxes, Christmas tree ornaments and other odds and ends accumulated over more than fifty years of marriage. I want to admit to him that it was selfish of me to discard Brendan's belongings the way I did.

Above all, I want to tell him that I had never loved him more than when I watched him, face stricken, shirt blood-spattered, walking across the frozen grass, walking towards the rock wall, coming to inquire about his mother, coming to comfort me.

I tug the afghan closer around me. I look across the kitchen and out through the window. Dawn is just beginning to push away the night. High in the spruce trees, two upstart crows are trying to hurry morning along.

Ackowledgements

I wish to thank Mike Judge, Roger Judge, Dr. Joanne MacDonald, and the staff at the Research Department of the Harriet Irving Library at the University of New Brunswick for their help with research; my editor, Laurel Boone, for her sharp and incisive editing; my agent, Victoria Ridout, for her non-tiring and dedicated help in getting my contract brought to completion; the Silverwood Breakfast Group, for their gentle but thorough criticism; and Dale Estey, Lillian Bouzane, and Fran Innes for being just a phone call away.